MW00794920

LOTTERY IN PARADISE

PARADISE SERIES

BOOK 11

DEBORAH BROWN

LOTTERY IN PARADISE
All Rights Reserved
Copyright © 2017 Deborah Brown

ISBN-13: 978-0-9984404-1-5

Cover: Future Impressions

PRINTED IN THE UNITED STATES OF AMERICA

LOTTERY IN PARADISE

DEBORAH BROWN

Chapter One

Another warm, sunny day dawned in the Florida Keys. Skyrocketing north on the Overseas Highway would eventually get one to Miami and beyond, and to the south, it ended in Key West. Today's drive was marred by the woman behind the wheel hanging a sudden u-turn and slowing slightly before careening around the corner, using a little-known shortcut, then jamming on the gas again in pursuit of the flatbed that had taken her beloved Porsche into custody.

"Fabiana Merceau, slow the heck down," I yelled over the sound of the traffic. For once, the irate Frenchwoman, her long brown hair blowing in the wind, had her window rolled down. She'd apparently forgotten her own rule, one she'd nagged me incessantly about when I hung my head out the window, which reminded her of a dog. "Pull up alongside the truck, and I'll get the name off the door. You can call and find out what's going on. It's not like you've missed a payment."

Part of the bargain Fab had struck with her best and currently former client, Brick Famosa, was that, as his private investigator, one of her perks was the latest shiny sports car. The woman changed autos like she changed her stiletto heels, but this model had lasted longer than the rest. Brick and Fab's relationship had recently exploded over his complete lack of support. After her established track record of doing whatever it took to get a job done, even skirting the law, he'd grown complacent in the knowledge that it wasn't his butt on the line. In the heat of the moment, she'd lied and told him she was Europe-bound for several months with her boyfriend. I suspected that Brick and she would sweep the hard feelings under the rug when the two figured out a way to say "I screwed up" without admitting fault.

Fab hit the steering wheel with a closed fist. "I'm going to run that jerk off the road."

"No. You. Are. Not. And you're not going to shoot out his tires either." Though there was a zero chance of that happening. As talented as the hot, sexy woman was, she couldn't steer and shoot at the same time. "We'll act like normal people and call the police." *Normal*, I laughed to myself. I hadn't heard myself described that way in a long time. Mostly, I heard "weird" bandied about. An over-exaggeration – I'm familiar with weird, and that's not me.

"You better come up with something better than that." Fab pulled up alongside the truck on the driver's side.

I powered the window down and hung my head out, my hand in mid-air, ready to flag the man down, even though I knew that chances were slim that he'd pull over. Pulling my head back in the window, I said, "Change of plans." I pushed my red hair back into place, smoothing it down, certain it was a wind-whipped mess. "The fancy tow truck is one of Brick's."

Brick and I had a tenuous relationship; it was hard to trust him when I knew he never put Fab's safety first, or mine either. He opposed our relationship, knowing that several times I had convinced my daring friend to calm down and rethink her plan. As backup to Super PI Fab, there were few jobs that didn't include flying bullets and running for our lives. I was happy for the respite. So were our boyfriends, who'd had a face-to-face with Brick, laying down the rules: no more withholding details, and if it came out after the fact that he knew there was a high chance of danger, it would be the last mistake he would make. My boyfriend followed that up with a right cross to Brick's eye.

Fab made an outraged sound. "I don't believe you."

I put my hands over my ears. "I'm sitting right here, and I'm not hard of hearing."

"Why would Brick tow my car?"

I fished my phone out of my pocket and held it up. "Ssh. I'm going to find out."

Brick answered on the second ring. "Madison

3

Westin! What do you want?"

I hit the speaker button. "Fab's car just got towed."

Total silence. I could hear him breathing, so I knew he hadn't hung up.

"It's not like she's driving it, cavorting around Europe with that pretty-face boyfriend she hooked up with," he grouched, loud enough that I pushed the phone farther away. "I didn't want *you* even sitting in it."

I should send him a copy of my latest physical, showing me to be cootie-free. "A heads-up would have been nice. When Fab calls, I'm going to tell her you had someone sneak onto my property and steal it. You'd never do your own dirty work. I'll leave off that you're a lowlife; she's probably already figured that out."

"Tell her whatever you want," he roared. "It's my damn 100K sports car. I'll do whatever the hell I please with it." The line went dead. I looked at my best friend and wanted to give her an awkward hug over the console of the Hummer.

The conversation was a good reminder of why I'd rejected the work/car trade deal and insisted on paying for my SUV. Instead, when Brick had come through with a good price on the Hummer, lowering it significantly below sticker, I'd snapped it up, not finding out until later that his family members fighting over it had sent the price plummeting for a fast sale.

"You could return from Europe tomorrow," I suggested.

"It's time for me to buy a car."

"You know my new step-daddy could get you a good deal. Just remind him you're loved like a sister."

She crunched her nose.

"Or..." I half-laughed, "You could talk to Mother first."

Mother had recently married her longtime badass boyfriend, Jimmy Spoon. The twosome were happy. The groom had taken his checkered past and turned himself into a pillar of the community that folks either respected or feared.

"I can't believe Brick would do that to me." Fab sighed, honking at the car next to her. He honked back and waved.

Fab powered her window up.

"We could steal it back. The only problem is you couldn't drive it anywhere because he would report it as stolen."

"It would be fun if I could see the look on his face."

I laughed along with her, picturing his outrage and frustration.

* * *

Fab drove back through Tarpon Cove to almost the end, turning down a side road, then another, and pulling into the driveway of my white, two-story Key West-style house with wraparound porch, which I had inherited from my Aunt Elizabeth. Growing up, my brother and I had spent the summer months each year playing on the beach. Aunt Elizabeth and I had scoured local nurseries with an eye out for new tropical plants. Since moving in, I'd added my own touch, filling the courtyard with brightly colored pots. The last hurricane that whirled through left broken pottery and plants in its wake that I hadn't yet replaced. The seashells I'd scored from the beach to use as mulch had disappeared into the fierce winds, which had left me with very few unscathed pots.

The driveway easily held two cars, and normally the Porsche would be sitting there. Fab parked, taking her half out of the middle. "I need a drink," she said, opening the door.

"The guys are here." I turned and pointed across the street to where the large testosterone truck and Mercedes were parked. The family who'd bought the house as a weekend residence encouraged us to use it for extra parking when they weren't around. They liked that the house appeared to be occupied. "You can take center stage for the car drama," I said to Fab's back as she headed into the house.

I followed her inside, banging the door closed, which I normally frowned at; today, it released some frustration. I turned left to find Fab's boyfriend, Didier, a big smile plastered on his face, holding up a pitcher of margaritas — my favorite. The one-time supermodel turned real estate investor had an impressive set of abs, revealed by his bathing trunks, his black hair damp from a swim. His blue eyes filled with concern as he set down the pitcher and crossed into the living room, holding out his arms to the woman he loved. I heard whispers in French and sighed, wishing I knew the language so I could eavesdrop.

"We'll be back," Didier said, scooping Fab into his arms and heading up the stairs.

I flung off my shoes and tossed them in the direction of the boot tray that sat inside the front door. I fist-pumped when they bounced off the wall and into the copper tray.

I'd barely got my fingers wrapped around the stem of a salted glass when strong arms encircled me from behind. Hands grasped my waist, and in one sudden, powerful movement, I ended up against a rock-hard chest.

"Ouch," Creole grumbled from behind me. He lifted the back of my shirt and removed the Glock from my waistband, setting it on the counter. He turned me in his arms and laid a thorough, crushing kiss on my lips. "Why the gun? A job you failed to inform me about?" He drew his eyes together in a frown.

His blue eyes, almost cobalt today, stared down into mine and waited for my answer. Over six feet and well-muscled himself, he was also dressed in swim trunks, his dark hair plastered back against his head. He and Didier were workout partners, often including my brother as well. When not working undercover chasing bad guys, Creole joined the guys for long runs on the beach and peddling a ridiculous number of miles on their bikes. His birth name was Luc Baptiste, but he never used it, favoring his moniker, Creole. Only a handful of people knew his real name, and no one called him anything other than Creole.

"You know…" I shook my finger at him, which he promptly nibbled on. "Fab hates it when I leave the house without my Glock or other suitable firearm." I leaned into him, wanting another kiss.

"And?" he said sternly, although his eyes twinkled.

"I owed her a shopping day without any complaining. We didn't get far." I went on to tell him about the shock of her repoed car whizzing past us and detailed what happened after.

"Bastard!" Creole growled. "Didier and I have our fingers crossed that neither of you will ever work for him again." He grabbed my hand and cut through the living room to the stairs. "Come on, let's get you dressed for a swim."

Chapter Two

It was a perfect warm night with a gentle breeze. The four of us sat around the pool in chaises, finishing off drinks after Didier's dinner of shrimp tacos. He'd cut up an impressive array of vegetables for grilling so we could assemble the tacos to our liking.

After moving in, I'd given the drab patio/pool area a major overhaul, making it an extension of the house. I'd also done away with the small dining room and removed one wall, opening up the living room and kitchen. The addition of the outdoor kitchen and eating area made it easy to accommodate my family and their significant others and turned it into the gathering place for most family functions. The fun part had been tracking down comfortable poolside furniture and colorful pillows.

The sun quickly sank low on the horizon, and the darkened sky started to blink with stars ready to make an appearance. The lights clicked on via the newly installed timer. I had a passion for outdoor lighting, and no one dared to say I overdid it. White Christmas lights draped the back fence, wrapped around the trunks of the palm trees, and twisted in the potted plants that lined the pool area. Here too, the last hurricane had left its calling card, sending more pots and plants airborne, quite a few landing in the pool, requiring it to be drained and cleaned. Now the blue water sparkled, lights floated on the surface.

My back to Creole's chest, he leaned into my ear and whispered, "Let's go to the beach house."

He owned a waterfront home in an isolated area a couple of exits out of town. As an added advantage, he shared the solitary road that dead-ended in each direction with only a handful of neighbors. He'd bought the "deal" from an investor eager to unload it and had taken his time renovating it. Open space and comfort were foremost in his mind, and he accomplished both goals. He and I were the only ones that knew its location. I had wrestled a promise out of Fab that she'd never follow me there. Creole didn't want unannounced visitors, and in his line of work, he didn't want to give trouble a chance to come knocking.

Before I could answer, a scream filled the air. The four of us bolted up, almost in unison.

"It's coming from the neighbor's." Fab jumped out of Didier's arms, landing on her feet, and pointed to the cedar fence that marked the property line before heading into the house.

"Bring my Berretta. It's in the junk drawer!" I yelled after her.

She snorted a not-so-subtle reminder that she

knew where everything was kept in the house better than I did. When she first moved in, she organized the garage to her liking and mine; now I could actually find what I was looking for, though she preferred to do it herself. I overlooked her annoying habit of rooting through the house's closets, cupboards, and drawers. I'd tried to interest her in organizing all of them, but she only laughed.

I'd never regretted the day I arrived home to find Fab lounging on the couch, suitcases in the foyer, boxes in the garage, announcing she'd moved in. To think the woman had initially rebuffed my invitation to be friends. It was a reminder to not give up, and I was happy I'd worn her down. Since Fab had never voiced any objections, I assumed it had worked out for her as well as it had for me.

Creole jumped up, taking me with him, and set me on my feet. "You and Fab will stay here. Besides, I'm going to need your Berretta."

Fab flew out the French doors, handguns in both hands; no room in her string bikini. Without a word, she handed mine to Creole.

I sent her a look that should've singed her eyebrows.

"You can thank me later; I just saved you from a fight with your boyfriend." Fab took a couple of steps toward the path that ran alongside the house. We used to call it the "secret path," but too many people knew about it now.

Didier reached out, grabbing her arm and bringing her to a halt. "You're not going either. Let Creole handle it. Then I don't have to worry about you getting hurt or ending up in jail."

Fab's face flushed with anger. She jerked her arm out of his hold and stomped away, catching up to Creole.

I grabbed up a wraparound skirt from a nearby chair, tying it around my waist. "Come on." I tugged on Didier's hand, dragging him into the house to get shoes and out through the front door. "We're not going to miss the good stuff." By the time we got to the curb, sirens could be heard in the distance.

Fab came running out of the driveway of the house next door. "The neighbor is dead," she said breathlessly. "He's lying in the doorway."

Flashing lights careened around the corner, and the siren shut off. The three of us stood in silence, heads turned toward the police car.

"You might want to do something with your gun besides hold it in your hand," I said, though I had no idea what. She certainly couldn't put it in her bikini. The two pieces of string holding a meager piece of material in place wouldn't take the extra weight. "It won't fit in your bathing suit."

"Put this in the house for me." She stuck out her Walther.

I shook my head. "You need to be responsible for your own firearm." I used the lecturing tone

I'd perfected after hearing it from Mother over the years.

"The only reason I don't pull your hair out is that you're my best friend and I'd probably never find another one."

I stuck out my lower lip.

Fab emitted an unrecognizable sound and raced past me into the house.

"I notice she didn't try to pass it off on me." Didier frowned, crossing his arms, unhappy with his girlfriend. The hot couple had been fraying around the edges lately, often exchanging unhappy glances and grouching in French.

"Did you really expect Fab to stick her feet in the pool and ignore the drama? Leave it to Creole? You knew exactly what you were getting into when you met her; you can't expect her to change now. If you succeeded in making her over into a milquetoast yes-woman, you'd be bored in a half-second." I didn't add that that plan had no chance of success. "Careful what you wish for."

Didier and I moved closer to the crime scene. Since the arrival of law enforcement, a few neighbors had come outside, vacating their doorsteps to get a closer view.

Scotch Thomas, the newly deceased, had bought the house six months prior from my previous neighbor, who went to live with his daughter and "let my grandkids drive me crazy." Scotch had so far been a good neighbor—no wild parties and no collection of odd friends. He'd kept to himself, working on an old junker in the garage located on the other side of the house. The weekly newspaper had recently run Scotch's picture, showing him under a banner proclaiming him the newest million-dollar scratch-off lottery winner.

Kevin stepped out of his police car, surveyed the street, and nodded in my direction.

"Let's hope this guy wasn't murdered, or Kevin will be over here arresting the lot of us." Didier nudged me. "You in particular. You're always his first choice as a suspect, even though you've never murdered anyone. Have you?"

I narrowed my eyes.

"Clean rap sheet?"

I felt bad that the elegant Frenchman had begun learning about the seedier side of life shortly after moving in and listening to careful edits of Fab's and my adventures. Not that he had any choice in the relocation, as Fab had moved his belongings and surprised him with it after the fact. It didn't take long before he was accepted as a family member.

"Not sure." I wanted to laugh at the surprise on his face. "I've had a couple of arrests, but once they found out they had the wrong girl, I was released. Don't know if that stays on my permanent record or not."

Fab joined us. She'd pulled on a pair of jeans and a top and brought Didier a t-shirt.

I glared at her for not bringing me a cover-up, and in return, she ignored me. I excused myself and ran into the house and up the stairs. It took less than a minute to jerk a sundress over my head and grab up a shirt for Creole and run back outside.

"Catch." I tossed the shirt to Creole, who had reappeared after rerouting people away from the crime scene until the cops showed up.

He caught it easily and winked, pulling it over his head. "The girlfriend, Ruby Dailey, found the body, the front door wide open. They had plans to cook dinner together and watch a movie. "

"We didn't hear any gunshots," Fab pointed out. "How long do you think he's been dead? I'm not good at guessing just by looking."

More police cars blew around the corner, followed by an ambulance and fire truck.

"That's the coroner's job," Creole said, his attention on the comings and goings. "He didn't shoot himself. There was no gun lying nearby. This is a murder case."

"Ruby have any clues?" I asked.

"It's hard to get details out of a hysterical woman, and in addition, it's not my case." Creole pulled me to his side. "I spotted an old beach chair and suggested she sit and pull herself together so she could be helpful to the cops. Told her if she needed a ride home to come over."

Kevin Cory walked up, his patented smirk firmly in place, twirling a pair of cuffs on his finger. "Anyone want to confess now?" His brown eyes bore into mine. "Make my job easier."

The man had a clear-cut case of split personality. There was the uptight sheriff's deputy, whose mantra was arrest first, then ask questions, and whose slicked-back hair was plastered to his head with a shiny goop that accentuated his snootiness. But in his off-duty persona, he was the life of the party, giving credence to the saying: work hard, party in the same fashion. In that persona, windblown and tanned, you'd mistake him for any other boy-next-door beach dude.

"None of us killed him." I flashed a brief smile.

"Any of you know anything?" Kevin asked and briefly turned away, apparently bored.

Creole took a step forward. "We were on the patio, heard the girlfriend scream. Scotch hadn't live here long and kept to himself, no disturbances."

"If you remember anything else, I'm sure you have me on speed dial." Clearly distracted, Kevin headed down the driveway.

"I'm surprised he didn't arrest us." Fab kept her voice low.

Didier nodded in agreement.

"Rumor has it…" I cast a glance toward the street, where Creole had just caught up with Kevin, and they stood off to the side talking.

"Kevin got reprimanded by Sheriff Tatum and was told not to bring any of us in without a warrant."

"Let's go inside." Didier put his arms around Fab and me and steered us in the direction of the front door. "There's nothing more to learn tonight."

Chapter Three

Coming out of my bedroom, I paused to give Fab's door a hard kick, a little trick I learned from her. Not hearing an angry tirade in French, I paused at the top of the stairs to make sure no one was in the living room, threw my leg over the banister, and rode it the short distance to the bottom. Smoothing down my skirt, then following the smell of coffee into the kitchen.

Fab sat at the island, scowling at me. "I heard you kicking the door."

I ignored her, scanning the counters for my can of coffee mix, which Fab referred to as 'canned ick.' "Did you make me coffee?"

"You're cheerful," Fab observed with suspicion.

I took one of my seashell mugs from the cupboard, filled it with water, and stuck it in the microwave.

"Earlier, a couple of young guys showed up, snooping around the house next door." Fab watched me closely for my reaction.

I closed my eyes, shaking my head. "Just great. Murder… now what?" I retrieved my mug, stirred in the mix, squirted a bit of whipped cream into my coffee, pretending it came from my favorite coffee place, and slid onto the stool across from her. "Didier leave early?" She nodded. "So you thought, well heck, I'll lurk around the neighborhood. I didn't hear gunshots; did you forget your gun?"

"Didier made me promise not to shoot anyone unless it's self-defense and there are witnesses."

I tried to bite back the laughter but failed.

Fab downed the rest of her latte and banged the mug on the countertop. "Do you want to hear the rest?"

I winced, breathing a sigh of relief that the mug hadn't broken into pieces.

"They weren't professional burglars. While one tried to kick open the front door," Fab said in disgust, "the other checked for an unlocked window, didn't find one, and didn't have the guts to smash one in. The side gate was apparently locked, and after a couple of failed attempts to scale it, they disappeared around the far side for less than a minute and were back. They hopped into a rundown pickup with out of state plates and took off."

I held out my hand. "Show me the picture."

Fab took pictures of everything, and that included dead people.

She flicked through her phone and handed it over. "Never seen the car before. Wonder what they wanted? We could have the tags run."

"I'll tell Creole and let him handle it. That will

make Didier happy."

Sadness flickered across her face. Translation: she'd seriously annoyed her boyfriend and he was mad once again. It was her own fault that she made promises and then didn't live up to them.

"I need the SUV." I stood and grabbed the keys out from under her hand. "Technically, it is my car."

"I'll drive," Fab grouched.

"First one in the driver's seat gets to drive." I headed out of the kitchen, opening the front door. Fab yanked me back by the back of my shirt and slipped past me.

* * *

Halfway to Mother's, I got a text from Crum: "You better get over here." I tried calling back, but the call went to voicemail. Fab hung a u-turn and muttered, "Hope it's not another dead body."

"The last one was at least natural causes."

I breathed a sigh of relief when Fab's heart-stopping drive came to an end as she rounded the corner to the property that I owned. Two police cars blocked the driveway. Fab circled the block and backed into the driveway of the building the neighbors called "the yellow house," a duplex now owned by my manager, Mac, and an ex-tenant, Shirl. It was directly across the street from The Cottages and offered a view of the property.

I'd inherited the ten units from my Aunt Elizabeth—individual cottages built around a U-shaped driveway and backed up to the beach with easy access. Out of view from where we were parked was the large pool and tiki bar area.

My first project had been to give the property a sprucing up: repainting each unit in different art deco colors and updating the landscaping, filling in bare spots with flowers and trees and plenty of lighting.

Fab and I had on our usual work attire, me in a short full skirt that was long enough to conceal my Glock when it was holstered on my thigh, with my top covering it if I wore it at the small of my back, Fab in skinny jeans and a sleeveless top that covered her Walther and accentuated her toned arms. Today, she had ditched the stilettos and opted for a pair of flats.

I retrieved my phone from my pocket and called Mac on speed dial. It had been another lucky day for me when she walked into the pool area, announcing she was ready to apply for the job before I'd even told anyone I needed a manager. Well, I'd told one person, and that was all it took. Mac possessed the right amount of crazy to relate to the tenants and keep them in line—for the most part.

When Mac answered, I barked, "Why is law enforcement parked in the driveway?"

"Oh hell! Why does the good stuff always happen when I'm gone?"

I heard the honking of horns.

"I'm three minutes away and will get you an answer." Mac hung up.

"She could've at least said good-bye," Fab grouched.

"My guess is, much like you, she needs two hands to cut through traffic and get here faster." I turned and smirked out the passenger window. I'd finally gotten used to Fab's driving and no longer gripped the sissy bar with my eyes squeezed shut.

"Quick, slide down in your seat before he sees us." Fab hunched in her seat, eyes level with the dashboard.

He who?

I looked out the windshield. Kevin was making his way down the driveway straight for us. "Do you think I could call the sheriff's department and ask that they assign another deputy to show up once in a while?"

Kevin and I pretended to get along. His sister, Julie, had dated my brother, so Kevin got invited to an occasional family dinner, which didn't need to be more awkward than they already were, just due to his presence. He was a tenant my brother had snuck in when his previous residence burst into flames. It had been suggested several times that he move out, but so far, he hadn't taken a single hint.

Now that Julie had moved to California, we kept up the pretense for her teenage son, Liam, who had stayed behind to finish his senior year in high school. She'd recently gotten a second part in a movie, and I suspected the move was now permanent. I wanted to question Brad about their relationship status but minded my own business, which was hard.

Mac whizzed around the corner in her pristine white pickup and squealed to a stop in front of her house. Kevin, who had started across the street, came to a halt halfway and backed up. He scowled when she hopped out of her truck, whipping off her ground-dragging floral skirt and throwing it on the seat, leaving her clad in running shorts and a top that she smoothed over her large assets and patted into place.

Kevin smirked, staring at her chest and not raising his eyes as he crossed the street. He knocked on the driver's side window of our car as Mac opened the back door and slid across the seat, reaching over and hitting the locks.

Fab cracked the window. "Yeah, what do you want?"

"Anyone die?" I yelled across the seats.

Kevin twirled his finger for Fab to roll down the window.

"This better be good," Fab grumbled.

"Look you two, I'm doing my best to be friendly; you could make the same effort. I don't mind going back to being a complete bastard."

Kevin smiled.

"Friendly? That's what you're doing?" I stopped myself from an eye roll. "We can do friendly, can't we?" I smacked Fab's arm.

I had no idea what look Fab sent Kevin's way, but his brown eyes went hard with annoyance. He turned and walked back across the street.

"You couldn't be reasonably agreeable for two minutes so we could find out what is going on?" I opened the door, burning Fab with a glare.

I crossed the street as Kevin's patrol car reached the end of the driveway and turned in the opposite direction, the other cop car following behind.

Annoyed, I headed straight for Professor Crum's cottage. He would know what was going on and would hopefully offer up a straight answer that made sense. He was the second tenant my brother had sneaked in behind my back. I'd finally threatened bodily harm if he did it again.

Before I could raise my hand to knock, the door opened. Crum filled the doorway with his thin, wiry, over-six-foot frame, white hair sticking up. I stayed focused on his face, but out of the corner of my eye, I caught that he had on his signature tighty-whities paired with purple clogs. Shocked didn't quite cover my reaction when I was informed that there were no laws to prevent him from prancing around mostly naked.

The retired professor's references were impeccable. The woman I spoke to at the prestigious California university where he'd tenured had nothing but good things to say. As for me, he'd made a poor first impression, and subsequent meetings hadn't improved on it.

He stood aside and swept out his arm, welcoming me inside. I peeked in before stepping over the threshold. The couch was covered in newspaper, and Harlot the cat was curled up next to a pillow, sound asleep.

I ignored his offer of a chair and stayed standing. "Tell me what's going on."

"Another dead body," he said and then burst out laughing.

Sensing this was going to be a long story, I sat next to Harlot and stroked her fur; she rewarded me with a purr. "Let me in on the joke. Kevin didn't say a word."

"Joseph was late getting back from his doctor's appointment, and some new lady friend stopped by. When he didn't answer, she went around peering in the windows. The blood-curdling scream that came out of her mouth made my chest hair stand on end." He patted the few white hairs. "She claimed to see a dead person. Before I could check it out, she had 911 on the phone. When I heard the sirens coming up the street, I went inside and locked the door."

"Why? Did you kill anybody?"

"Nooo. The woman overreacted. I don't want

to get too grisly, but what she saw was Svetlana lying over a chair at an odd angle, legs in the air. She made up different scenarios as to how Svet had died, and only Kevin's threat of arrest put a stop to the hysteria."

"Who dies with their legs in the air?" I tried not to laugh. "Is Svet okay?" The "woman" in question was actually a well-endowed rubber doll that Joseph had inherited, along with outfits and wigs. "Is Joseph treating her okay?" I liked Svet and sometimes forgot the hot Swedish woman was full of air. She'd turned out to be the ideal tenant—quiet, never talked back, never a problem; my other tenants could use her as a role model.

"Joseph actually smiles once in a while. It's odd to hear him talk about her; you'd have no idea she's not, uh… human."

"The rest of the story…" I said, impatient with the man.

"At the same time Kevin blew in the driveway, Joseph came strolling up. Kevin told the woman to get a grip, and she threw herself in his arms and started wailing. I thought old Kev would lose his lunch. He got her to sit down, where she soaked his handkerchief before finally pulling herself together and lamenting that she'd fallen in love with a pervert. To which Kevin snorted and inquired how long they'd been dating, as he hadn't seen her around. She answered once, but that Joseph had forgotten his wallet and she paid, which brought on more tears."

Cheap bastard!

"How's Joseph doing?" I asked.

"In pure frustration, Kevin barked 'jail' at him, and the blood drained from his face. I think Kevin felt bad because he told him to go inside and lie down."

"How did you hear all of this if you were inside your cottage?"

"I never close the bathroom window. I've got a bird's-eye view of the hotspots, the ones that provide the most entertainment, and the ideal place to eavesdrop. This time, they were close enough I could hear every word."

I wanted to warn him not to start peeing out the window like the man in the building next door. Instead, I made a mental note to tell Mac; she could have *that* talk with Crum.

"I'm sure Fab is stomping her dainty foot in frustration." I scratched Harlot around her neck and crossed to the door. "If Joseph is still looking pale, ask Shirl to check him over. She'll know if he needs to go to the hospital."

A childhood friend of Mac's, Shirl had been our resident RN. She'd moved in after a messy breakup for what was supposed to be several days, but turned into over a year, and now lived across the street. Everyone loved her, as she dealt patiently with their health complaints, some made up for attention, some not.

Crum opened the door, sticking his head out. "All clear."

Once I set foot on the driveway, Fab yelled from where she held court next to Mac, "Hey. Let's go."

"I'm surprised she wasn't over here listening in. So unlike her."

Crum grunted. "Spotted Fab talking to the most recent tourists from Canada. You know, the latest bunch fits right in. During the hubbub, they dragged out Joseph's stash of beach chairs, sat themselves down, and made no bones about listening in. They didn't flinch at the glares Kevin shot their way. A sturdy bunch; comes from surviving all that cold weather."

"Thanks for the info." I waved and cut across the driveway to meet up with Mac and Fab. "Miss January okay?" I asked Mac. "She missed out on the excitement."

Miss January and Joseph were both inherited tenants from my Aunt Elizabeth. Both had been labeled terminal by their doctors long before I took over, but they continued to defy the odds, neither giving a thought to cutting back on cigarettes and liquor.

"Miss January got drunk earlier than usual and fell asleep in her chair on the porch. I found her lying in a heap on the ground next to it. Had to hoist her up by the arms—barely got her standing—and helped her to bed. She got a little sniffly over Score. We need to find her a new boyfriend; then maybe she'll stay sober for an extra hour or two."

Score was the boyfriend she "found" on the beach and dragged back to her cottage, where he'd lived in a perpetual state of drunkenness until he passed on.

"Find someone closer to her own age," I suggested. Score had been in his nineties, close to one hundred. The problem was Miss January looked closer to Score's age than the forties her identification stated. And the boyfriend pool slimmed down after a certain age.

I watched as Fab crossed the street and got behind the wheel of the SUV. She'd barely got the door closed when she laid on the horn. I shook my head.

"You better hurry up, or she might leave you." Mac laughed. "If that happens, I'll give you a ride."

"If Fab did that, I'd kick her designer-clad butt." On the other hand, given how she exceled at martial arts… "Maybe not," I said in response to Mac's raised eyebrow. "I'd whine to her boyfriend and to Mother, and she knows that."

Fab laid on the horn again.

I waved to Mac. "Call me if any more dead bodies turn up."

Chapter Four

I did a double take when Fab turned off the Overseas onto the road that led to the house. "Why aren't we going to Mother and Spoon's? You need a car, or did you forget?"

"I'm in no hurry. I'll just drive your car."

"I'm telling you now, sharing my car isn't going to work. Why are you dragging your designer shoes?"

"I'm thinking Brick is going to come to his senses and send the Porsche back." Fab parked in the driveway.

We both got out, slamming the doors, and headed to the front door.

A lump on the ground caught my attention. "What the hell?" I pointed to the front door knob lying on the brick step.

Fab whipped out her Walther from the waistband of her jeans. "I hope you have your damn gun on you." She tossed her hair and headed for the back yard.

She wasn't quick enough to hide her slight smirk as I went for my Glock. "You be careful," I whispered hoarsely.

Now what? Damn, I forgot to ask. No one

would be going in or out the front door until the lock was changed. This wasn't a professional job. I snickered to myself. Since I hadn't been invited as backup, I decided to go back to the SUV and wait for shots to be fired. Normal people would call the police. But why annoy Fab and deprive her of the opportunity to shoot someone?

I had just slid into the passenger seat when Fab reappeared, opening the front door from inside, her handgun reholstered.

"There's no one here," she yelled. Lowering her voice as I met her halfway, she added, "The back was locked up, and there's no place to hide in the pool area. There's no sign anyone made it into the house. Bigger question: Did whoever it was want something specific, in which case they'll be back, or did someone decide on a whim that it would be fun to break into a house today?"

"We're lucky that whoever it was didn't have lock-picking skills. Who's going to tell the guys?" I asked.

"Let's just replace the door knob and keep it to ourselves. They don't have to know everything."

"They always find out. Besides, can you change a lock? I tried once and then called a professional." I chewed on my lower lip. "How do we explain new keys?"

"I've got this handled. You grab the old lock." Fab stomped across the kitchen to the garage and returned with a brand new lockset and screwdriver, the island becoming her workspace.

I was impressed but didn't ask where it came from and instead asked, "What's up with you and Didier?"

I saw the sadness that flitted across her face and disappeared. "He wants me to change professions," she said quietly, taking a pair of kitchen shears to cut away the plastic packaging on the lockset.

"And do what?"

"That's what I asked. I threw in his face that if he wanted a trophy girlfriend who always says and does the right thing, he should've figured it out a long time ago. Suggested he stop looking for reasons to break up and just walk out."

Fab sorted the parts on the counter. I watched as she removed the lock cylinder from the old knob and put it in the new one. Armed with the screwdriver, she crossed to the front door to dispatch the remains of the old knob and put the new one on.

Leaning against a stool, I said, "You need help, I'll get the number for a locksmith."

Fab shook her head and had the lock off in an impressively short amount of time. She motioned me over, handing me the old parts, which I dumped in the trash.

"What do *you* want?" I asked.

"For the first time in my life, I have no idea. I'd like to be able to figure out whatever the answer is without ultimatums."

Fab lined the pieces up on the floor and snapped her fingers, gesturing for me to be useful and hand her the parts.

"Think about what you might love doing and open another business," I suggested. "Or expand your one-woman operation and hire other people to dodge bullets. Let them worry about staying off the radar of local law enforcement and avoiding ugly orange jumpsuits."

"Since I'm not in the mood to interview a boyfriend replacement—" She lifted her head and rolled her eyes. "—I'm taking Didier to dinner and an overnight in Miami. Throw in some sex, and that should bring back his good mood."

"About the sex thing, don't make it look manipulative."

Fab laughed. "You're dispensing sex tips now?" She laughed again. "That felt good."

"Don't be mean. Does Creole look unhappy? No," I answered for her. "Pay attention. You're going to tell Didier before you leave on your romantic evening about this attempted break-in and not wait for it to ruin your evening." I took my phone out, ignoring her scowl, and texted Creole. "This isn't that big a deal. Not worth getting into a fight over."

The boyfriends had a hard and fast rule that they be the first to know when things went awry; if they weren't, an argument was ensured. I'd gotten better at reporting in. Fab just wanted to dig in and be contrary, even when she didn't have a good reason, which was most of the time.

"Clean up your mess and let's get to Jake's for tacos."

Chapter Five

On the main strip in the middle of town sat Jake's, a dive bar my Aunt Elizabeth once owned a half-interest in. Due to its namesake's inability to stop gambling, I'd bought out his half-interest and he skipped town. Rather shocked by my aunt's business dealings, I wished I could have asked her, "What were you thinking?" It didn't take long after her death for me to discover that she'd led a secret double life, which she'd left to me, giving me a life I loved. Making Tarpon Cove my home was the best decision I ever made.

I'd inherited the rest of the block with the caveat that I never turn it into high-rise condos. As for the other businesses on the block, I got the impression their owners didn't have the goal of making money. Junker's, an old gas station, had been converted into a garden antique store and finally started to eke out a profit when the missus advertised to out-of-town dealers wanting to drag junk back to their stores and jack up the prices.

A couple of years ago, Fab had accepted a lighthouse in payment for a job in lieu of cash. It had arrived in the middle of the night, off-loaded without anyone seeing anything. Her original idea was to use it for office space, but that didn't last a day. She'd hated the isolation and theoretically moved to a table on the back deck of Jake's for meeting clients, which hadn't actually happened yet. Most of her clients preferred the anonymity of the phone. Currently, the lighthouse drew tourists who wanted to stop and take pictures.

Twinkie Princesses, a lime-green and pink roach coach parked at the end of the driveway parallel to the road, boasted they'd "fry anything." If only either of the two women owners ever showed up to work. They were the perfect tenants—paid their rent on time, didn't invite trouble, and no police calls—so I said nothing.

Fab drove just under the speed limit; her incentive a cop on her tail that I suspected was Kevin, though I couldn't verify that through the tinted windows. The parking lot of the tropical-style tiki bar was about half full. One of the first things I did after taking control was spruce up the dilapidated building with fresh paint, plants, and lighting. Power washing and bug control raised the "F" health rating to an "A" one step ahead of being closed down. The old locals that Jake had run off had returned, along with new ones, and even tourists once we were written up in a couple of magazines: "Best Mexican food in the Keys."

Bypassing the kitchen entrance, Fab scored a parking place in the front, and we entered through the front door for a change, waving to the bartender. The jukebox blared over the customers' voices, the pool tables were taken, and there were two in line for the dartboard.

I sighed and tried not to dwell on the fact that any day now, my superstar bartender, Phil, aka Philipa Grey, would be handing in her resignation, now that she'd passed the bar on the first go-round. So far, she'd been mum about her future plans, and I didn't bring it up.

"Margarita, rocks," I ordered as I slipped onto a stool. A regular moved over one so that Fab and I could sit together.

"I'm driving," Fab said. "Something sparkling with a lime."

"How's tricks?" I eyed the leggy blond over the rim of my glass.

Before Phil could utter an answer, accusations, including a liberal use of the F-word, filled the room. Chairs were upended; bodies crashed to the floor. The men at the bar turned on their stools for a ringside view. The lone woman at the other end of the bar glanced up, briefly taking her eyes away from the video poker machine. The patrons seated at the tables stood, and a couple of women climbed up on the tabletops. As fists flew, cheers went up for one man or the other.

I sent a look of annoyance at Phil, reminding her that bar fights fell under her job description. She let out a loud sigh and reached for the Mossburg conveniently stored behind the bar for these "just in case" situations. The universally recognized clack of the pump shotgun brought a hush to the bar. The brawlers didn't react, and no one tipped them off. Phil waited calmly for about three seconds, then lodged a bullet in a beam crossing the ceiling. That brought the fight to a halt and sent a few customers running for the door.

I poked Fab. "Go chase those people down; they need to settle their tabs. No one stiffs Jake's."

Her deranged smile firmly in place, she hopped off her stool and sprinted toward the front door.

Phil called out to a couple of regulars, admonishing them to make sure the fight didn't resume. The two burly men climbed off their stools and strode over to the brawlers, shoving them apart with their feet, helping them to stand. Both immediately sank back down. Two drunk women pushed through the gawkers; shouting at one another over whose fault it was, they ran to the men, slobbering over them to get up.

Glancing at Phil, I motioned to the pair of bruisers. "Get the two on the floor out of here before law enforcement shows up." As the words came out of my mouth, sirens could be heard close by, and I hoped that didn't mean the cops were turning into the parking lot.

"Get your ass up." A short, squat man stood, what appeared to be vomit stuck to the lower legs of his jeans. The woman with him hooked her arm in his. "Bathroom?" she asked, eyes flitting around.

I pointed to the hallway leading to the kitchen, covering my nose as they passed. "I'd like to sneak out the back door, but we're parked in front," I whispered to Phil.

"Stay seated," Kevin shouted from the door. After the room went quiet, he continued, "My partner and I are going to want statements from all of you." He zeroed in on me. "Where's the body?"

I pointed to the middle of the room, where the remaining man sat on the floor, head in hand, his fingers smeared with blood. Out of the corner of my eye, I caught the other couple making a clean getaway, bypassing the bathroom and heading straight for the back door.

Fab did her trick of appearing out of nowhere and pushed a handful of cash across the bar to Phil. "The runners wanted me to apologize for their bad behavior. They estimated the tab. I thanked them and told them to hurry back."

I rolled my eyes. "What really happened?"

"What? That was a good story." She humphed at me when I said nothing. "Fine. I told them it was a felony to run out on a bar tab, punishable by a year in prison. Added that Jake's prosecutes and they wouldn't be the first we sent to the big house."

Phil made a sound much like a muffled laugh.

A stretcher cruised through the front door, and Kevin waved the two medics over to the man, whose head was now in his woman's lap. Kevin bent down to talk to him. After a cursory check, the man was strapped down and rolled out. The wife held his hand, walking by his side.

"If they sue, I'll be your first client."

"Your insurance has got you covered. Don't forget to call them." Phil held her hand up. "No more questions. When I accept an offer, I'll let you know. Don't worry. I won't dump you without notice, and we can still conduct our side business."

"What business?" Kevin stared her down, his eyes dark dots.

Phil never flinched. I waited for her middle finger to pop up, but to my disappointment, she maintained her cool.

We both ignored his question.

"No one's dead, so I guess your work here is done." I squinted at him. "That man under arrest?" I pointed to the door. "I'm not pressing charges, if that matters."

"What started the fight?" Phil pushed a bottle of water across the bar top at Kevin.

"A fart," he said with a straight face.

Fab burst out laughing. "Such a classy crowd."

I shook my head, certain I had lint in my ears and wasn't hearing correctly. "You're not funny." I didn't bother to point out that he didn't have a sense of humor – why start now?

"Bob and Wanda are the couple on the way to the hospital. Bob will need his nose straightened unless he prefers a crook in it. The woman who made a run for it out the back, dragging her man by the arm, passed gas on Wanda, or near enough, and that started a war of words." Kevin was enjoying the retelling of events.

"You're making that up." I frowned at him.

Kevin clasped his hands over his heart. "You want to hear the rest?"

"Show of hands," Phil intervened, raising hers slightly.

Fab raised her hand.

"Proceed, officer," Phil said. "The hell yeses have it."

"Another water?" He handed back the empty bottle. "Where was I?"

I glanced at him, shaking my head.

"Bob tried to intervene between the two women, telling them to 'shut it.' Most men don't need to be told that's a bad idea." He grabbed up the new water bottle, nodding at Phil. "The man who beat it out the back threw the first punch, tackled him to the ground, and the fight was on. The shotgun blast put an end to the fun." He glowered at Fab, who returned it, eyes narrowing.

"It's an effective way to end disagreements," she said.

"According to witnesses, no one could ID either couple. They're not regulars, which surprised me. Did get a partial plate. Told Bob and Wanda not to get behind the wheel of their car until they sober up. And when they do, the road out of town goes north. Until then, this town has cabs and they should use them."

"I'm trying to picture your farfetched scenario in my mind, but I'm coming up short. How did the woman actually… on her…" I trailed off, not sure how to phrase what I wanted to say. My mother would die if she heard that I used the other F-word in public. "How is that possible?"

Fab's face clearly communicated that I didn't need the answer.

Kevin coughed a laugh, screwed the top back on his water bottle, and slam-dunked it into the trash. "I'd guess, judging by the smell emanating from the victim, it was fart spray. Comes in a can, in case you didn't know."

I lowered my head, my shoulders shaking with laughter. Phil poked me in the side, laughing. Fab looked disgusted.

"You're lucky; the culprit must have been a first-time user," Kevin said to me, eyes full of amusement. "She only got off a short shot. If she'd sprayed the joint, your bar would be empty and you'd have to get the crime scene cleaner that you're so friendly with over here to fumigate the place. It ought to be illegal to shoot the stuff off. This isn't the first time it's started a fight."

"Cleaner Dude is Mac's connection. He has the hots for her, but she says it creeps her out to think about dating and… other stuff." My cheeks burned.

"I know him; he's a weird piece of work but does a good job."

I was supposed to call Creole when I had contact with law enforcement; dead bodies and a few other things were on the list, but this one I would save just to see his face when he realized it wasn't a made-up story.

Kevin's phone pinged. He snaked another bottle of water, nodded and grunted, which I took for "see you," then left. He met up with my brother at the front door.

My guess was they were talking about Kevin's sister, Julie, and her son, Liam, the only two subjects they had in common. The conversation didn't last long before my brother waved and headed my way.

"Who died?" I asked him.

Chapter Six

Brad had changed a lot in the last couple of months, after a girlfriend from the past showed up, wreaking havoc. Gone was the easygoing boy next door, replaced by a more serious version. He had been in good shape before, but now his workouts had taken on a different intensity; his abs were rock hard, and he carried himself like a man you didn't mess with. He had tossed aside the tropical shorts and shirt he'd often donned as a commercial fisherman, and they'd been replaced by tailor-made clothes. He'd hired a captain for his fishing business and partnered with Didier, the two making a name for themselves in commercial real estate. The black suit he wore was fitted and well made, showing off his lean physique. His sun-bleached hair had a slightly messy look.

"Nice." Phil whistled.

I agreed silently with Phil. He looked hot, even if he was my brother.

Brad ordered a bottle of Stella. Jake's now carried a selection of European beer that only our boyfriends and my brother requested. The locals liked their beer cheap and on tap.

"You've been calling; thought I'd return your call in person," Brad said to me, his brown eyes twinkling with amusement. He reached for the bottle, taking a long drink. "Put it on the boss's tab," he told Phil. He hooked his arm around my shoulders and turned toward the deck. "We need to talk. I'll take her home," he told Fab over his shoulder.

Fab growled at him, which made him smile. He knew she hated being left out of anything. If there was any way for her to circle out to the deck ahead of us to hide and eavesdrop, she'd do it.

"Fab won't go anywhere," I said.

"I know. I wonder how hard she worked to perfect that outraged look."

Brad headed to the table tucked in the corner of the deck, just outside the door. It had a perfect view of the inlet of water that ran below. He took off his jacket and laid it over a chair, tossing the "Do Not Sit Here" sign aside. Early on, I'd made the table private for family and friends. Despite the sign, people sat there anyway and only got the hint when no one came around to take their order. There was no cheating and ordering drinks at the bar. The bartenders told them to change tables and then the drinks would be delivered.

To say I was light-obsessed put it kindly. In addition to installing ceiling fans every few feet, I'd strung Christmas lights across the railing and on the bottom of the eaves.

"I need your help with Liam," he said as we both sat facing the interior of the bar, so we were able to see everything going on inside.

Originally, the plan was for Julie's son to stay behind and finish high school. He planned to go to the University of Miami and wanted to retain his resident status. It was to be a short separation, the first movie projected to take two months to film. Liam had opted to stay with Mother in the interim.

"What's Mother done now?" I asked.

"Mother's being all protective and weird. She interferes in any plans I make, as if I'm a bad influence, which is highly insulting. Look at me – an up-and-coming pillar of the community." He puffed out his chest.

"Did I mention that you're looking smokin' these days? New girl in your life perhaps?"

He blushed slightly, snapping his fingers. "This conversation is about Liam. Has Mother forgotten that I spent more time than anyone else with the kid before Julie went to Hollywood? Now," he said in frustration, "I practically have to sneak him out."

"You're a step up on me. When I want to hang out with Liam, Mother has to come along." Noticing that Brad had finished his bottle of beer, I signaled Phil for another.

"Bullets have been known to fly around you."

"There's a big difference between taking Liam

on a job and out for ice cream," I said in a huff.

He squeezed my shoulders. "I'd trust my kids with you. I know you'd stop at nothing to protect them."

"Kids?" My eyes widened. "How many will be coming for a play date?"

"Enough to field a football team," he said with a straight face.

"That's a raft-load of kids. If they're anything like the two of us, I suspect you'll stop at two and borrow the rest for any games from your neighbors."

Brad laughed. "That's an idea."

"Back to your problem," I said. "I'll talk to Mother, and in return, you stay seated until you tell me what's going on with you."

"Been busy. I enjoy getting up in the morning; that's more than most people can say. Didier and I want to take the real estate partnership big league. After much reflection, I decided it was in my best interest to be more badass and less nice guy."

"Don't get so busy that you don't have time for your little sister."

"Not going to happen. Sorry I missed the last couple of family barbeques at your house, but I wasn't up to an evening with couples and me dateless."

Fab arrived, tray in hand, and served the drinks, setting down one for herself and slipping into a chair across from the two of us. "You look really nice, by the way." She smiled at Brad.

"You are one nervy chick," he responded. "You can stay until your first rude comment."

"Did you forget I'm like a sister?" Fab reminded him.

"That's a good one." Brad snorted.

"What's up with you and Julie?" I asked. "I thought you were going to pop the marriage question."

"I'm very proud of what Julie's accomplished. Her career is important to her, and she's worked hard to get this break. That said, bi-coastal isn't going to work; we're already growing apart. I'm afraid that in one of our conversations, she's going to ask me to relocate to California." He patted my hand. "Don't worry, not doing that. Life here is good, and my family's here. Besides, Los Angeles holds no appeal."

I sighed with relief that he wasn't considering a move. We had always been a close family. After our father died during our teenage years, Mother had turned into a mother hen with a watchful eye on her chicks, which reined us in from the typical bad decisions that kids make. It had pulled us apart when I'd gotten married and moved away and Brad moved to Florida. I didn't want that to happen again. After the divorce, I wanted my family together, where visiting was only a short drive and I could pound on their door at any time.

"Maybe it's time to have the 'let's be friends'

talk," Fab suggested.

"I'm doing the guy thing, waiting for her to bring it up. It's coming, but since neither of us has anyone in our lives, it's not urgent. Julie let it slip that she doesn't want any more kids. I don't see a compromise there; one of us is going to be unhappy."

"It's better to agree upfront about your expectations for the relationship," Fab said, a wistful look on her face. "Why marry and find out afterwards you're more compatible as friends? You've got to accept that most of the time, being friends after being lovers doesn't work out so well."

"What did you do with my friend?" I asked.

Her eyes narrowed. "I can do sensitive."

"Yes, you can." I smiled at her, then turned back to Brad."Now that Julie's gotten a second gig, will she want Liam to join her?"

"Liam enjoys visiting," Brad said, "but he doesn't want to move there. He's been out there a couple of times already and says it doesn't take long to miss Florida. I know for a fact that Julie doesn't worry about him; she knows that we're taking good care of him. I make it a point to see him every day, and if something comes up, we talk on the phone. I wanted him to come live with me but thought Mother's would be more stable."

"We'll get this worked out with Mother. Tell her you're taking him alligator hunting; she won't want to come along."

"Thanks, I'll owe you one. You need me to run interference, say the word."

"Too bad all problems aren't solved that easily," Fab said. "I saw you having a drink with that cretin, James Bordello, when I stopped for coffee the other day. Every single Bordello brother is an ass. Just so you know." She stuck up her aristocratic nose. "I know them all."

"I had a meeting with James today. Didier and I are in discussions to partner with him on a condo site in South Miami. It's looking good."

"I met James at one of those fancy dinners the Miami PD holds once a year," I said. "He demanded I call him sir. Thought he was kidding and laughed at him. He wasn't amused. And even less so when Creole ribbed him about not every woman dropping at his feet. His snotty reply was 'My women do what they're told.'"

"The Bordello brothers." Fab shook her head. "There's always an unsavory rumor or six floating around about one brother or another. Some free advice—and you know how I hate to do free—check them out and see if their skeletons are going to be trouble for you."

"That's a great idea," I said. "Before signing contracts, give me the names of any potential partners, and I'll have them investigated."

Fab observed Brad intently, a smile curving her lips. "I've been watching the changes you've been making—from easygoing to wound rather tight. Your new kick-ass persona will cause some to make an adjustment or two. Any reason at all you need backup, we're here for you."

I hit the table with my fist. *Ouch!* "I've always had your back, and that's not changing. Got it?"

"You're still my favorite sister. Sorry," he said to Fab. "You're still family. If we'd grown up with you, I suspect Madison and I would've been grounded all the time and you'd have skated."

"But she'd have broken us out." I laughed.

"I'll take you up on your offer to check out the Bordello brothers." Brad took a business card out of his pocket, scribbling on the back. "Don't get too snoopy. I hope you can do this without them finding out. I want to know if they have any kind of pending legal problems, personal or business. Check out all three brothers, even though I'm dealing with James."

"It's actually Grigorio," Fab said. "James is his middle name."

Brad nodded, clearly surprised.

"You need us to ransack his home, office?" I asked. "We offer that service. Fab does, anyway."

Brad shook his head. "I hope I don't regret this little request. Whatever you do, don't do anything to get arrested, or I'll bring Mother along to bail you out."

I shuddered at what a long ride home that would be.

Brad's phone rang once. He pulled it out of his pocket and read the message. "Family dinner at

Mother's." His mouth pulled into a tight, hard line.

"What did she do?" I asked.

"She knew that Liam and I had plans for a guys' night out – hamburgers at Roscoe's."

I refrained from licking my lips. They served the best burgers in Tarpon Cove and were regularly featured on dive hamburger joint websites.

"I don't get the fascination with that greasy spoon." Fab made an inarticulate sound of disgust.

"Stop. For as much as you complain, you eat every bite." I held out my hand to Brad. "Give me your phone." I called Mother, putting a finger over my lips.

"Mother," I said in a conspiratorial tone. "This needs to be quick. I'm at Jake's with Brad, and he's not going to be gone long."

"That's nice," she said, although her tone belied her words.

"You need to call Brad and cancel the family dinner plans."

"Why would I do that?"

"Because Brad and Liam have a boys' night out planned. You don't want to disappoint both of them, do you? You know that they'd never say anything to upset you, but this has been planned for a while—not something last minute. And your dinner can easily be changed."

"I'll make hamburgers here, and there won't

be any difference."

"You need to stop interfering in their relationship... unless Julie told you she doesn't want Liam and Brad together, which I highly doubt."

"I worry about Brad, and I've gotten to see him a lot more lately," Mother whined.

"Meddle some more, and the next thing you know, Liam will want to move out. I know you worry, but you need to lighten up. Brad's back." I handed him the phone. "Mother wants to talk to you." I knew she could hear every word.

The conversation was short. Brad disconnected. "Thanks, we're back on. I owe you one."

"That was impressive." Fab gathered up the empty bottles, setting them back on the tray.

"Mother knows when she's being heavy-handed, and at that point, it's easy to guilt her into doing the right thing."

Chapter Seven

Dragging my eyes open, I threw my hand out, fingers fumbling about, trying to find the source of the irritating noise. After a moment, I realized that it was my phone. Nothing good ever came from middle-of-the-night phone calls.

On the screen, Shirl's face smiled back at me. She was an RN at Tarpon Cove Hospital, once a tenant favorite. Knowing she was only a phone call away kept me sane.

"What happened?" I answered.

"Fab was admitted earlier. She got hurt tonight and seems to have lost her short-term memory." Shirl snorted.

"Is she going to be okay?" I asked, stumbling out of bed, opening a drawer, and pulling out a pair of crop sweats and a sweatshirt.

"She'll be fine. It's a minor head injury. She growled when I told her she wouldn't need surgery, perhaps because I was a bit overly dramatic."

"If you're going to provoke her, I suggest you remind her that you've been useful to her in the past." I already felt sorry for the hospital staff, knowing Fab would be at the top of the list of worst patients.

"We're holding her overnight for observation. I hid her clothes so she wouldn't run out the door. Damn shame, her silk blouse was covered in blood."

"I'm on my way." I hung up, tossing my phone on the bed and continuing to stagger around, getting into my clothes. "So my wily friend has once again snuck out in the middle of the night," I murmured. "One of her secret jobs that went wrong." It wasn't the first time she'd gotten hurt on a job, but she'd never landed in the hospital before. On the way out, I grabbed my bag off the bench in the entry.

This was one of those rare nights that I had the house by myself. The driveway was empty except for my SUV. Where was Didier? I remembered that he'd had a meeting up in Miami and was due back at any time. I jumped behind the wheel and slammed the car door. I'd wait until I saw Fab before calling Didier.

I kept to the speed limit. This was a small town, but law enforcement was always out in force and eager to hand out tickets to those with lead feet.

The hospital lobby was empty when I raced through the doors; instead of a receptionist, there was a telephone and a placard of instructions. Having been here more than a few times to visit people, I punched the elevator button and rode it to the ninth floor, where Shirl had her cubicle.

Shirl glanced up from a pile of paperwork. "Could she be a bigger pain in the ass?" Her mouth formed a grim line. "I know she's your friend, but to put it nicely, she's not a favorite on this floor."

"That's a good sign." I managed a weak smile. "That mean she's going to be released soon?"

"Fab needed you here earlier when she uttered some convoluted nonsense about what she did remember. Slipping, tripping... She changed it to falling, but it didn't make any sense and didn't match her bruising. She finished it off by grabbing her head and pleading amnesia. I couldn't help it; I laughed, and she shot me a dirty look. Dr. A laughed at her and whispered something in her ear, and her cheeks burned red."

Dr. A was short for Dr. Ardzruniannos, whose name no one could pronounce. He was by far the hottest doctor in this hospital and a good friend.

Shirl escorted me down the hall to Fab's room. "Good luck," she whispered.

I took a breath, opened the door, and closed it quietly behind me. The bed was a jumble of sheets... and empty. The bathroom door stood slightly ajar, with no lights on. There was no place to hide.

"Fabiana, what the hell?" I hissed. I turned and reached for the door handle, deciding to sneak out myself and ask Shirl not to tell anyone I'd stopped by.

"I'm here." Fab came out of the darkened

bathroom, tying a second hospital gown on backwards to cover her behind.

"That's a fetching outfit; now get back in bed."

"Didier just left. He's not happy with me."

"That's surprising." Even in the dim lighting, I could see that her eyes were red-rimmed from crying. "Unless you came up with some BS excuse, like you gave to the doctor, which Didier saw right through and stomped out of here. As your friend, I'm going to stop nagging you to tell the truth the first go-round, and I'm also not going to remind you that the man knows you better than you know yourself."

"That's crappy sympathy." Fab tossed her long brown hair and hopped up on the bed, crossing her legs primly, her hands curled into fists under her armpits.

Fab had scrapes all over her face. On the right side, she sported an impressive shiner that encircled the entire eye. Her arms were covered in bruises, with some on her lower legs. It was clear she'd lost the fight, assuming there was one.

"Tell your *bestie* what happened, and I'll help you come up with something that smacks mostly of the truth. Although it would be my second choice."

Fab fidgeted across the bed. "I want to go home. Now."

"I'm not taking you anywhere." I shook my finger at her. "You can stay one night. If I have to, I'll sit by your bed all night." I blew out a breath of frustration. "Stop stalling. What the hell happened? And don't leave out the part about why you thought it was a good idea to leave me behind."

"This was supposed to be a quick in-and-out job for one of my special clients."

"You mean rich and not willing to commit their own felonies but happy to pay handsomely for you to." I gritted my teeth. "Let's speed this along and jump to the good part."

"Getting in was easy," she said, a faraway look in her eye, as though she was imagining how she might have changed the outcome.

"It always is. Getting out is the problem. Why were you there?"

"My client left her ten carat diamond ring at her lover's house, and he refused to return it unless she left her husband. Which had zero chance of happening since the husband is filthy rich and the boyfriend is of moderate means."

Stupid man, what was he thinking of doing? Live off her alimony?

"Lover boy needs to get a grip and come to terms with the fact that he was a sexual fling. I could've been more careful." She paused. "But I had one day to get the ring before the husband got back from his business trip."

"You get the ring?"

"That's where my plan went awry. The damn thing wasn't where she said it would be and not in the near vicinity. I'd already blown my allotted time. I tossed the place and didn't bother with discretion. The ring was nestled in my palm when I heard creaking on the stairs, and I didn't make it out to the balcony before he saw me. Damn lock." She stopped and took a long sip of water.

I pushed her gently back against the bed, covering her with the sheet.

"He stormed after me, firing questions, threatening to call the police, all the while shoving me backwards. In an attempt to get away, I kicked out and made contact with his thigh, which slowed him, but only a little. He laughed when he caught up while I was straddling the railing. I don't think he gave a damn that we were on the second floor. He backhanded me. Before he could take a second swing, I jumped, hoping for a cushy landing in the bushes. Turned out to be not so cushy."

"This is where I would've come in handy, but I won't rub that in."

Fab grimaced. "He reappeared before I could get myself out of the bushes, kicked me a few times, and that's when I threatened to scream rape if he touched me one more time. Classy fellow. Hocked spit at me, which landed on my lower leg, and calmly walked off."

"How did you manage to avoid jail and end up in the hospital instead?"

"Last thing I remember was crawling across the grass to the parking lot. Apparently I passed out." She held out her hands, palms wrapped in gauze. "I did try to use the trunk of a palm tree to stand – big mistake. I'd forgotten about the prickly parts."

Tired of standing, I pulled a chair over from across the room. "The cops will probably want your story tomorrow."

Fab shook her head. "They were here when the ambulance arrived. I told them I didn't remember anything about the evening. Their body language told me they weren't amused by my bold lie. Dr. A came in and ran them off, said he had doctor things to do to me. Something like that anyway."

That had me smiling. "So all that and no ring?"

"Stuffed it in my pocket before taking my swan dive. Passed it off to Shirl, reassuring her it wasn't stolen and threatening bodily harm if she told anyone or, worse, lost it." Fab kicked her sheet off. "Wonder what the thread count is?"

I laughed. "Not up to your standards?" I asked in my snooty voice. "At least they're clean." I laughed again.

Fab leaned back against the bed. "My damn head hurts."

"I'd ask you to promise not to do this again—at least, not without a parachute—but I know you can be impetuous. If you don't want to do it for yourself, think about the Westin family. Every one of us would be devastated if we had to go to some celebration of life at Tropical Slumber."

Fab wiggled her fingers, pointing at her cup.

I flipped the top off and filled it from the pitcher sitting nearby. "Would you like me to adjust the straw, maybe hold it for you?"

"You can go now." Fab tilted her head toward the door. "I'm going to sleep. Besides, first thing in the morning, preferably at dawn, you need to bring me some clothes. Mine were trashed. Shirl offered to let me go home in this ugly gown, and I get to keep the socks." She shoved her foot out from under the sheet, showing off a bright-red nonskid sock. "Left one shoe behind at the scene of the crime."

"We need to get it back. I'll go in the morning."

"You will not," Fab said emphatically. "Before you start, I'm not going either. Not one word to Spoon. I'm hiring Billy. No one screws with him."

Billy was a non-descript man who blended in as an everyday Joe. Looks were deceiving. He had a soft side for a good cause, especially if it had to do with animals, which made him one of my favorites.

"Not that I'd ever wear the shoes again, but why leave evidence? Just in case a-hole decides to call the cops," Fab mused.

"It surprises me he didn't call immediately. My guess is he has something to hide."

A nurse came in the door, pushing a small machine attached to a tripod on wheels. "I'm here to take the patient's blood pressure." She eyed me. "Visiting hours were over a long time ago."

I stood and leaned over, whispering in Fab's ear, "Behave." Raising my voice, I said, "See you in the morning. I'll bring coffee." It was hard to believe, but not totally impossible that she'd give in gracefully and stay until morning. I blew her an air kiss.

Or maybe it was. As I headed for the elevator, I changed my plans. I'd head home, but instead of sleeping, I'd pack a change of clothes for Fab and come back. She'd have the nurses in an uproar before the sun came up.

Chapter Eight

The streets were still deserted; traffic in the middle of the night was non-existent unless a call for evacuation went out. The sight of Didier's Mercedes in the driveway made me squirm. As I pulled in beside him, I could see the living room lights were on, so there would be no sneaking in and out. It hadn't occurred to me earlier to figure out how to retrieve Fab's clothes if Didier was asleep in their bed. Sneaking around in that nervy way was more Fab's specialty than mine. For once, I was relieved Creole wasn't home. Two alpha males to deal with was two too many.

I groaned inwardly, realizing I was out of time to pretty up the story and still essentially stick to the truth. Unfortunately, both Creole and Didier were on to that trick; sometimes they laughed and other times growled their displeasure.

I quietly opened the front door, slipping inside and closing it softly behind me. I turned to find a pair of flinty blue eyes staring at me. Didier was stretched out on the daybed, which doubled as a couch and was the perfect spot for watching the comings and goings through the front and back doors. He snapped the lid on his laptop closed. "Did Fab come home with you?"

"She's still in the hospital." I dropped my purse on the entry bench.

Didier raised a challenging eyebrow. "Are you sure?" The air tingled with the annoyance that radiated off the man.

"Just left her there. I'm headed back with a change of clothes." I took a short breath to slow the babbling. "I'll stay until Dr. A releases her; hopefully, that will be first thing in the morning." I gave him a smile, which he didn't return. His irritation only went up another level.

He stood. "I'll take her what she needs." He brushed past me and headed up the stairs. He took three steps, paused, and turned. "What do you know about what happened tonight?"

My hand already by my side, I crossed my fingers. *Okay, it was childish, but I did it anyway.* "You know how she is with her 'special clients,'" I said, the air quotes audible in my tone. "She left without informing me about anything." That sounded better than "snuck out," which was what she did. "I got a call from Shirl and raced over to the hospital." *I almost smiled, proud of myself; so far, I'd told the truth.*

"What happened to the promise that the two of you made not to go out alone?" He didn't wait for an answer; his eyes darkened, boring into me. "I'm tired of the dangerous games you two play, putting your lives on the line, and for what?

64

Money? And I end up with a dead girlfriend. How many times do we have to have the same conversation, the promises to change, and nothing ever does? So much for your word."

I smiled sadly, hoping this conversation wasn't going to degenerate into something we couldn't come back from. "We've made a lot of changes," I defended. "We do our best to check the cases out ahead of time." I watched as he fought some kind of silent battle that made his jaw clench. "Since you came into her life, Fab's changed a lot. Quite frankly, you knew what you were getting into from the beginning. She was upfront about the kind of work she did."

He nodded in dismissal and started up the stairs. "Fab and I will work it out." After a moment, he added, "Or not."

"Factor in how perfect you are together," I called after him. "She makes you happy, laugh, smile. That's a damn lot. I'm sure you don't need me to remind you how much you love Fab and she you."

He stopped to listen but didn't turn around. Once I finished speaking, he stomped up the stairs. I heard the bedroom door click closed.

Although afraid they wouldn't, I hoped those two would work out their problems. Fab happy and in a stable relationship beat her going wild.

I bounced onto the daybed that Didier had vacated. I'd chosen each piece of furniture in my house for comfort, and this one delivered. Piling it with brightly colored pillows and throw blankets had only added to its welcoming appearance.

It didn't take long for Didier to come back down the stairs, clothing bag over his shoulder.

He looked in my direction but didn't make eye contact. "We'll see you in a few hours." He didn't slam the door, but it was damn close.

I was debating whether or not to climb the stairs to bed when Jazz made the decision for me, falling asleep on my chest, with Snow doubling as a foot warmer. Jazz, my long-haired black cat, geriatric by human standards, had been my only feline for years. When I rescued Snow, all white and long-haired, she fit into the family with her first sniff. The two had hooked up immediately, forgoing the "getting to know you" stage.

Having dozed off, I wasn't sure how much time elapsed before the click of the door woke me. Not wanting any kind of confrontation, I peeked under my eyelashes. My eyes instantly flew open. "What the hell are you doing home? More importantly, how did you get here?" I stole a look over Fab's shoulder, waiting for the door to re-open and Didier to follow her in.

"It's called a cab."

"At this time of the morning?" I groaned; it was still dark out. "Where's Didier?"

"Why are you asking me?" she snapped. "I told you he got mad and stormed off. Haven't seen him."

"You're in so much trouble." A lump as big as a boulder landed in my stomach. "He went to the hospital to take you a change of clothes and sit with you the rest of the night, or maybe squeeze into that skinny hospital bed."

Fab dug her sock-clad feet in, crossed her arms, and stared at me.

"Let's go." I sat up. "We'll sneak you back in and say you went for a walk."

"I'm going upstairs and take a bath. I'm filthy." She swept her hands over her hospital gown.

"Do they even know you left?" I struggled to keep from yelling. "No. You know how I know? No emergency calls from Shirl." I picked up my phone, which I'd dumped on the table earlier. "Hmm... no missed calls. When Didier finds an empty bed, he's going to flip." I knew he'd be more than livid but decided not to point it out since she appeared pale and had gently brushed her forehead twice since she moved to the foot of the steps, one hand on the banister. I sat up and scooted over, patting the vacant spot next to me. "Sit."

"I couldn't stand it there," she said in a pitiful tone as she flung herself down next to me. "I'm supposed to be sleeping. What do they do? Come into my room every hour to take some test or another, mostly blood pressure. Then the nurse complained it was going up. Then stop waking me up every hour."

I flinched when I heard tires squeal into the driveway. Leaning over, I brushed the hair back from Fab's face. "You're on your own." I shook my head at her when she grabbed my hand. Halfway up the stairs, I offered a tidbit of advice. "Milk your condition and tell him how much you missed him. A tear or two might help, if you can squeeze them out." I heard the key in the lock and ran the rest of the way to my bedroom.

The front door closed with a bang. Didier's voice could be heard down the block, unleashing a tirade in French. I closed my door quietly, not wanting to get caught eavesdropping on a conversation that I didn't understand. Judging by their voices, it was going to be a long night for those two.

Chapter Nine

The house was quiet the following morning as I crept past Fab's closed door and down the stairs, licking my lips at the thought of making a quick cup of coffee and taking it out by the pool to enjoy. Only thing better would be a pink bakery box on the counter from Mother, full of yummy and not-very-healthy breakfast pastries. Since her marriage, she'd cut back on early morning visits.

Fab's phone and a car key I didn't recognize sat in the middle of the kitchen island. Knowing that she didn't go anywhere without her phone, I crossed to the patio door and craned my neck, only seeing two wild parrots on an electrical line overhead. Another sunny day had dawned in the Keys: blue skies, fluffy white clouds. The scent of salt hung in the air.

Returning to the kitchen, I leaned over the sink and took auto inventory from the garden window. The key on the island was no longer a mystery; Spoon had dropped off his Mercedes for a backup ride until Fab made up her mind about replacing her car. I knew he really did it for me so I wouldn't be stranded if Fab jetted off without a word. Like now. Didier's car and my

SUV were gone. It annoyed me that Fab had helped herself to my ride when she had a luxe auto to drive. Also irritating was that she'd deliberately left her phone behind so I couldn't demand that she bring my car back.

I filled a large, sea green measuring cup with water, another find from Junker's, sticking it in the microwave. Waiting for the buzzer to ding, I picked dead leaves off my African violets.

Movement near the driver's side door of the silver Mercedes caught my eye. My mouth fell open at the audacity of some kid attempting to gain entry to the renovated 380SL with a slim jim, a thin strip of metal. Spoon would choke the life out of the kid if he got his hands on him. Now would be a good time to call the police, but he had the door open and was crunched under the steering wheel, his tennis shoes barely touching the ground. Four steps to the junk drawer, I withdrew my Beretta from the back and headed straight for the front door to scare the wits out of the car thief.

The kid, early twenties, had honed his skills; this wasn't his first car-theft rodeo. The engine caught, and he climbed into the driver's seat and, for the first time, made eye contact over the steering wheel. Instead of being scared when I leveled my gun, he shot me a smirk, along with his middle finger. Damn, he was going to call my bluff. He put the car in reverse and shot backwards, tires squealing into the street. Before he could change gears, I blew out the front tire. One flat tire didn't deter his getaway attempt; he hit the gas, but metal screeching against the asphalt had him rethinking his exit and slamming on the brakes. The car came to a stop in the middle of the street, engine running; the door flew open, he jumped out, and screamed, "You're a flippin' nutjob," and took off running down the street.

Before a neighbor could call in a nuisance report about the auto blocking the street, I got behind the wheel and inched it slowly back into the driveway, not wanting to ruin the rim.

Someone needed to call Spoon. After a short back and forth argument with myself, it was decided that it wouldn't be me. It didn't matter that there wasn't anyone else home. I'd think of something.

As I was running my hands down the sides of the Mercedes, inspecting for additional damage, a car approached. From the noises it emitted, it was on its last gasp. I concealed myself behind the trunk of a palm tree as an old minivan paused at the corner. Catching its breath, it lumbered into the driveway next door.

Ruby, the dead guy's girlfriend, jumped out, opened the side door, and began hauling out plastic containers, stacking them in the driveway. The man behind the wheel watched her, and when she'd unloaded the last of her belongings, he got out and shuffled to her side. He tugged on his short-sleeve button-down, covering most of his stomach but leaving a hairy strip exposed.

My attention turned to Ruby, wondering what she was up to. If only Fab were home, she'd go confront the girl. I knew Ruby hadn't taken up residence, as Scotch had stressed the point that he lived by himself in our first, "Hi, neighbor" conversation. In my experience as a landlord, I'd put money on her becoming a big headache for Scotch's family. However, possibly having the house occupied would stop the random break-ins from continuing. I could door-knock the neighborhood, find out if anyone else was having problems. But that had a real possibility of bringing out a sheriff's deputy, and how would I answer why I hadn't bothered to report any of the incidents? Especially the latest. I hoped, when I related the incident to Creole, that he'd reassure me that shooting out a tire fell under protecting hearth and home and not a felony.

I went back in the house and upstairs to retrieve my phone. I messaged Billy: "Car has a flat. Can you fix? Parked in the driveway." And then sent Creole a message so we could skip the lecture on not keeping him up to date. "Shooting in the driveway. Only fatality – a tire."

I went back downstairs and stared out the garden window, standing guard, since I'd had to leave the hot-wired engine running.

Billy messaged first: "On my way."

The phone rang immediately afterwards. I answered. From the frustrated sigh, I knew it was Creole.

"What the hell happened?" he demanded.

I gave him a stripped-down version of events.

He groaned, and the line went silent, then he asked, "You sure you're okay?"

I reassured him and proceeded to update him about the hospital drama of the night before. "Fab left her phone behind, and I have no way of getting ahold of her. I hate to call Didier."

Another long pause. "Didier broke up with her early this morning."

"I'm the last to know," I shrieked into the phone.

"Babe, my ear."

"We have to find her."

"She's a tough one. She'll be fine."

"You don't want to help. Fine. I'll find her myself," I said evenly.

"I'll get back to you. I just don't think meddling in their love life is a good idea."

"And how long do you think it will take before Fab moves another man in? One like her ex-husband, perhaps, criminal and insufferable to be around."

A long-suffering sigh came through the line. "I'll get with Didier and give you an update tonight. Now promise me you won't do anything to risk your safety."

"I'm going to Mother's. I'm debating whether to tell Spoon about the *flat* or let it be a surprise, hopefully when I'm not anywhere around."

Creole laughed. "I wish I could be there when he figures out you were less than truthful."

We exchanged kisses and hung up.

Chapter Ten

Billy parked in the front, opened the door, stood on the door track, and frowned at the car. He jumped down and circled the auto, sticking his head in the window. "You couldn't tell me that the flat tire in question is on the boss's cherry, big bucks, classic Mercedes?"

I waved and shrugged.

He opened the car door and bent down, reaching under the steering wheel. The engine shut off, and he came back up with a handful of wiring, which he tossed on the ground. Squatting, he inspected the tire and shook his head. "What the hell happened?" Before I could answer, his finger slashed across his throat. "I know nothing and want to keep it that way. There's something to be said for ignorance."

"Would you like something cold to drink?"

He rolled his eyes. "I'll take one of them fancy beers you got stocked."

I hustled into the house, thinking I should've warned him up front. I didn't think he would have turned down my request for help—he hadn't in the past—but I didn't want today to be the first time. Popping the top off a bottle of Red

Stripe, I hurried back outside.

I overheard the last of his phone conversation and knew a flatbed had been ordered. He ended with a curt, "Hurry it up." He turned to me and took the beer from my outstretched hand. "A little tip, and of course, you didn't hear it from me. Your story better be award winning."

After Billy loaded the Mercedes, he followed the flatbed back to JS Auto Body. I went back inside and changed into work attire, shoved my lockpick in my skirt pocket, and put my Glock in my bag. Back downstairs, I threw Fab's phone in my purse. I laughed at what had unfolded; one of those situations that was intense at the time and sort of funny later. The guy who thought I was nuts should be thanking me; little did he know that I'd saved his life. Spoon would've tracked him down and wrung his last breath out of him.

I gave the cab driver directions to Mother and Spoon's condo. He dropped me off at the security gate. I didn't have to wait, as another car drove out just then, and I hiked over to their building, bypassing two opportunities to announce my visit over security intercoms.

I had my lockpick in hand when I approached the lobby door and, thanks to Fab's tutelage, had the door open quickly. I rode the elevator to the top floor. Once outside their door, about to knock, I lowered my hand and opted to use my lockpick once again. When I stepped over the threshold, I knocked and shouted, "I'm here."

"How about knocking before unlocking the door?" Spoon stepped into view, narrowing his eyes at me down the long hallway.

Mother came from the direction of the kitchen to stand next to her husband and wave from the living room.

I breathed a sigh, happy they were both clothed. It was one thing to joke with Fab and another to catch them in the act. "I did," I said and winked at him, heading down the hallway. "Ready for a good story?"

Spoon met me halfway and enveloped me in a hug. "You've come to the right place. Plenty of drama here today."

It surprised me to find my whole family gathered in the living room. "Someone forget to invite me?" I waved to Brad and Liam and bent down to kiss Mother's cheek. Being the last to know was a running joke in our family, and today, I was taking my brother's usual place.

"Fab's asleep in the guest room," Mother whispered in my ear. "Fab and Didier broke up. I've got some tricks in mind, some ideas to get them back together. We'll just keep it between you and me. Some people think I meddle."

"No, not you." I made a face. "But…" I started and was immediately shushed. I wondered what kind of plan she had concocted.

I made myself comfortable in a chair next to my brother and across from Mother and Spoon, who sat on the couch.

"Does that mean my car is here?"

Mother nodded.

"Good. I'll be taking it when I leave." I turned to Spoon. "Fab needs another loaner. Your ride was slightly assaulted today." I gave him the details and didn't bother prettying up the facts.

"Fab's already signed the paperwork on her new ride; it's being delivered tomorrow," Spoon said.

Spoon's lack of response to the almost-theft was unnerving. Only the twitching of a cheek muscle signaled he'd heard every word.

"Damn. I miss all the good stuff." Liam shot me a cheeky grin from the floor, where he lay stretched out.

"You've had enough excitement." Mother looked daggers at him.

"Not so supportive now, are you?" Brad's words, directed at Mother, dripped with sarcasm.

"What's happened to the service in this joint? Can I get something to drink?" A bottle of water appeared over my shoulder. I smiled up at Spoon.

"Go ahead, tell her." Brad directed a stern expression at Liam and pointed to me.

"It's nothing," Liam mumbled.

"Oh, let me," Brad said, in a show of more sarcasm. "I'll enjoy being the bearer of atrocious news." He paused. "Liam's engaged."

"What?" I squealed and jumped to my feet. "You're not even eighteen."

"It's not that big a deal," Liam protested.

Spoon grumbled something unintelligible, and Mother smacked his arm.

Brad kicked the bottom of Liam's foot. "You forgot to mention that your intended is in prison."

I turned on Mother, hands on my hips. "You allowed this... whatever it is?"

"I'm sure you remember how sneaky and tight-lipped teenagers can be." Mother's lips compressed in a straight line.

"Everybody sit," Spoon ordered.

Looking around, that meant me, since I was the only one standing.

"It's not prison," Liam reasoned. "It's jail." He turned his attention to me. "I'm happy you showed up; planned to call you. LaLoose can get out as soon as bail gets posted. Not quite sure how it's done."

"Who the hell is La... what? Jail?" I struggled not to raise my voice. "That's a stripper name."

Liam looked seriously like he wanted to coldcock Brad for telling on him.

Brad spoke up. "La called last night. In addition to bail, she popped the question. She's such a romantic."

"She's twenty-two." Spoon's eyes glittered with amusement.

"I suggested that they wait until Liam turns

eighteen." Mother's face was pinched with concern.

"You *look* like my mother…" I told her. "Did you even attempt the 'hell no' speech?" When she didn't answer, I got up and changed chairs, pushing Liam's feet out of the way. "No!" I held his gaze. "First off, she's a perv. Secondly, you're headed to college, and loser felon chick isn't going to derail that."

Liam mumbled, "…nice girl."

"I'm afraid to ask what La is in for. If you're too nice to tell her to get lost, I'm not and neither is Fab." Liam shook his head. "You think I'm not handling this well, tell Fab. Be prepared to never hear from La again."

Mother leaned against Spoon, a satisfied smirk on her face.

"Oh, I see. I'm the bad guy? What would you have done if I hadn't stopped by?" I shook my head in annoyance. "If his mom gets wind of this, our favorite family member will be in smoggy Los Angeles before any of us can even blink twice."

"Really, Madison. Can't you keep your voice down? You interrupted my beauty nap." Fab slid onto the arm of the chair I'd vacated in a pair of black skinny jeans. Her long hair had that slightly messy look, which made her look hotter than ever, especially with a broken heart, which she would never admit to. She'd give most women a complex, but we'd never had that drama between us.

"Just broke the news about the upcoming nuptials." Brad smiled humorlessly.

"The one with the outstanding warrants?" Fab cracked her knuckles, earning a glare from Mother.

It shouldn't have surprised me that Fab already knew, and I was definitely not surprised that she'd already run a check on the woman. "Man hands," I tsked at Fab. That was always the threat from Mother when I cracked my knuckles growing up.

"Not happening." Fab's eyes bored into Liam.

I bent down and dug to the bottom of my purse, pulling out Fab's phone. "Catch." I tossed over her phone, which she easily caught. "Don't ever leave home without it again."

The sadness that swept across her face was quickly replaced with detachment.

"When you're legal and start hooking up with women," I told Liam, "you need to talk to Creole. He can give you pointers on how to avoid the ones with stability issues. Sorry, bro."

"We already had that talk. I gave him hair-curling examples of why it's not worth the fun and games," Brad said with finality.

Liam got up, stretched, and headed to the kitchen.

Mother went to the kitchen and came back with a stack of to-go menus. Her idea of home cooking. Both of us used to cook and gave it up when we relocated to Florida. Either the men barbequed or Mother ordered in.

Fab moved to a chair next to mine.

"How did you leave it with Didier?" I asked.

"He says we need a break," Fab said with little emotion. "My recklessness is too much for him to handle. Leaving the hospital with a head injury was the last straw for him." She stared out the window. "He suggested I give up my investigation work. Do something else. Except I'm good at what I do."

"Maybe there's room for compromise."

"He gets to do what he loves; why not me?" After a long pause, she added, "I think a clean break is what's best."

"Not if you still love him. I'm sure he still loves you. I don't imagine you'd be an easy woman to forget."

"I never thought I'd fall for a really good man." The last few words were little more than a pained whisper. "Look how that's turned out – terrible."

"I'm here for you." I shook my finger at her. "No dating without pre-approval."

"I assure you, I'm not interested in dating."

Since none of us could agree on what to eat, Mother placed an order from Jake's; she knew everyone's favorites.

I went in search of Liam and found him outside on the patio, hanging over the railing. Warm and humid, the air smelled fresh. Rolling waves crashed onto the rocks below. I moved across the patio to stand next to him.

"You upset that no one is supporting your relationship with your new friend?" I asked.

"Oh, heck no. I met her at a game of beach volleyball; she's a friend of a friend who knows Kevin. She asked for my number, and I thought what the heck, kind of flattered, older woman and all. Didn't expect her to call, and especially not from jail. I thought it was funny and told Spoon. Madeline eavesdropped."

"She better not hear you calling her by her first name, and I don't suggest 'Mrs. Spoon' either."

He laughed.

"What do you want to happen?" I asked.

"I want the whole drama to go away. No more phone calls," Liam said emphatically.

"That's an easy one. I'll take care of that tomorrow, no bloodshed."

"You wouldn't… uh…" He hesitated.

"No bodily harm. But yes to scaring her out of town." I winked at him. "What was your answer when she popped the question?"

"I hesitated at first. She started crying, and the next thing out of my mouth was 'sure.' I really need a crash course in women."

"You figure us out, write a book; you'll make a ton of money."

He wrapped me in a bear hug. "Thanks."

"You need anything, call me, and I mean it."

Chapter Eleven

Fab had spent the previous day stretched out by the pool, a towel over her face, and when she finally came back inside, she went straight to her bedroom, pleading a headache, and didn't come back downstairs.

Not even the delivery of her shiny black Porsche 911, which had been delayed by one day, perked her up. She signed on the dotted line and went back in the house.

When it appeared that she had another day of moping around planned, I insisted we go to lunch. Which she declined. I threatened to call Mother.

"Fine," she said sullenly.

My phone rang, interrupting my attempt to drag her out to the car by her hair. Mac's face smiled back at me. "Yeah, what?" I answered.

"You better get your butt over here. I quit!" Mac said.

"I suggest that you re-read your contract. You aren't allowed to quit. What's going on?" I closed my eyes, thinking that today was my day for a headache.

In the background, I heard pounding,

followed by Mac screaming, "Get out here, you weasel bastard."

"We're on our way." I scooped up my purse, tossed the car keys at Fab, and pushed her out the door.

Fab brooded the entire way to The Cottages. I made several attempts at conversation, which were ignored. I was about ready to tell her to pull over and let her walk home when she pulled into the driveway, parking in front of the office.

We both got out of the car, and Fab headed to the office. Turning the doorknob and finding it locked, she pulled out her lockpick. "Do you want anything to drink?" she asked over her shoulder.

Mac flew across the street from her house, a sheet under her arm. "Cops are on the way. Don't blame me. You can thank the nosy woman across the way." She pointed to the two-story apartment building on the other side of the property line. "Second floor bathroom window, third one over, where the telescope just disappeared."

Fab halted. "Cops. Peeping is illegal but do you think they'll actually arrest her?"

The window slammed shut as the three of us gawked.

"Depends on what she finds so fascinating, I suppose. If asked, she'll probably say the beach. That's what I'd say," I said.

Mac snorted. "She's disgruntled that her one

night in the sack with Crum didn't turn into a hot romance. He sees her coming, he picks up those bony knees of his and runs. Says she played rough with him."

I crossed my arms, telegraphing to Mac, "get to the point."

Mac motioned for us to follow her, turning slightly as she whispered hoarsely, "Crum and Joseph went man-whoring last night and came back with…" She pointed to the pool area and punched in the gate code. "That's Crum's new business. Teaching old guys or whatever how to get laid. They brought their conquests back here and passed out."

Despite my best attempt to squeeze my eyes shut to block out what I was seeing, it didn't work. I counted at least three naked bodies.

Joseph, in all his scrawny skinniness, was sandwiched between two sturdy women on two chaises pushed together. One woman's butt hung over the side, resting against a chair. I bet the old war veteran couldn't believe his luck and wasn't worried about breaking a bone if one of them rolled over on him in their sleep. I wondered what his doctors would think after writing him off for dead.

"That bastard, how did he get back out here without me seeing him?" Mac pointed to Crum, who was lying next to an also-naked woman. He had a beach towel wrapped around his middle, hairy legs and back on display.

"I suppose they're drunk?" I pushed Mac forward to make use of the sheet she'd brought over from her house. "Get the trio covered up. What about Crum's, uhm... whatever?"

Fab had stayed close to the gate, one eye on the driveway. "You're out of time; Kevin just pulled in. Unwrap the towel and drape it over the two of them. Course, you'd have to reach under him." She grimaced.

"Where are their clothes?" I asked Mac's retreating back.

Mac flipped the sheet over the threesome, ran to the other end of the pool, grabbed a pink plastic ring, and placed it over the rear end of Crum's companion.

"I drew the short straw again." Kevin banged open the gate. "Get out of the way," he said to Fab. He surveyed the area. "High five to Joseph; didn't think he had it in him."

"Nothing to see here." I pasted a phony smile on my face.

"I disagree." He waved his arm around. "Public indecency and engaging in sexual activity in public are illegal."

"They're perfectly covered," I snapped.

"I bet that only happened after you got here. The neighbor that called in gave a pretty detailed report about the drunken debauchery that went on."

"You're going to pile all that nakedness in the back of your car and drive them through town, hoping they don't pee on themselves or worse?" I said with an unmistakable challenge in my words.

Fab's eyebrows shot to her hairline. I bit back a laugh, knowing that later I'd have to endure a lecture on the use of the word "pee." I'd have to ask what word a well-bred woman such as herself would use. My guess: in her world, it would never come up.

"Looks like you got things covered." Kevin laughed at his own joke. He walked over to Crum's chaise and kicked his foot.

Crum rolled over. "That hurt." He glared at Kevin and shook his foot.

"You've got five minutes to get your hairy ass and your 'friends' dressed and off the property or you're all going to jail. You, for sure." Kevin's eyes narrowed, skimming the pool area once more.

Crum grumbled under his breath and stood up, clutching his towel. As he passed Mac, he slowed and whispered something that made her smile, then continued behind the tiki bar, reaching down.

"Couldn't let anyone steal our duds." He tossed a black garbage bag over the bar top.

"Are you sick?" Fab asked Kevin. "Just asking. You love to arrest people, and you're letting an opportunity slide by."

"There's always you." He took a step in her direction.

She laughed. "I have it on good authority that your hands have been cuffed; you have to have an airtight case to arrest me or Madison."

"Sooner or later." He wagged his finger.

Crum's friend woke up on the crabby side of the chaise and unleashed a naughty tirade about being disturbed, which roused the other three.

Joseph spotted Kevin and pulled the sheet over his head.

Mac joined Fab and me. "Let's go to the office."

I turned to Crum and said, "This whole unseemly episode smacks of you. When you get rid of your friends, you and Joseph come to the office."

I detoured over to Miss January, who sat on her front porch, newspaper in hand. It surprised me that a woman who passed out every day from drinking stayed up on current events. Stick thin and wild-haired, she was slumped down in her chair in a buttoned cotton robe.

"Honey," she slurred, her glassy eyes meeting mine. From the other side of her chair, she produced a thermos filled with vodka, the only liquid that passed her lips. Her liquor delivery had arrived early.

Her butt was about to slide off the seat, and I hurried up the stairs and reached out to grab hold of her arm. "Let me help you."

"I've got it." She grabbed the armrests and bucked back against the seat, maneuvering herself somewhat upright.

"What's in the news?" I bent down to pick up the newspaper, which turned out to be only the center sheet.

"Ollie Badger died. He was an old fart. There were a couple of others, but I didn't recognize their names. I like to keep up on who dies and my horoscope," she said in a serious tone.

Unsure of what to say, I handed back her reading material. "You need anything, yell."

The driveway was deserted as I crossed to the office. I barely got the door closed when it opened again. I turned and bit back a groan at the sight of Kevin filling the doorway. "That was fast." I claimed the chair on the far side of Mac's desk, wiggling to get comfortable. Fab was sacked out on the couch, her eyes closed, but that didn't mean she wasn't listening to every word.

"Rumor has it that Crum is running a sex business out of his cottage." Kevin smirked, enjoying imparting that morsel. "As long as he's not engaged in prostitution or indecent exposure, it's probably not illegal. But even if it's legal, he still needs a business license." He pointed to the snack bowl. "I'll take the chocolate chip cookies." He held out his hands to catch.

Mac sent them sailing.

"Anything else?" I snipped.

"I thought we were working on becoming friends," Kevin managed to say with a straight face.

A loud snort came from the couch.

"Fabiana, so unladylike," I said, mimicking Mother's voice.

"Hey, Deputy Dog," Crum's voice came from behind Kevin. "Can you move your…" He paused. "…out of the way?"

Kevin turned, and I couldn't see what transpired from my vantage point, but Crum stepped back. Kevin took the only available chair, which was next to me, pushed it back, and stretched out his legs. "I'm not missing this."

"We're here, as ordered," Crum said, swinging out his arm and almost hitting Joseph, who leaned against the jamb.

Joseph never looked the picture of health, but today, his skin tone was grey and pasty and made him look closer to the death his doctor had been predicting. I tended to forget that I had two terminal tenants, as they kicked along, doing what they damn well pleased, which included all the things that weren't good for them.

"What's wrong with him?" I asked Crum after Joseph groaned.

"Belly ache." Joseph clutched his abdomen.

"If you're going to get sick, go home. At least keep it out of the bushes. That's what the sidewalks are for." I jabbed my finger at Crum. "If he does get sick, you're hosing it away."

"That damn horny goat weed," Joseph moaned.

I squinted, taking a breath, not wanting to ask

questions.

Fab rolled to her side, staring him down. "What's that?"

Crum cleared his throat and stared down at his mismatched tennis shoes, toeing the laces he hadn't bothered to tie.

Mac, an obsessive gum chewer, blew a large bubble and pricked it with her fingernail. "It's an herbal stimulant that you get at the gas station," she said, cleaning the pink mess off the lower part of her face.

"What the hell happened to you?" I asked Crum. "How do you go from being an esteemed college professor to a... what? What are you doing? Don't give me that innocent look; I've got it on good authority that this man-whore idea is your brainchild."

"Whores? Hardly." He raised his eyes; instead of focusing on one person, they shifted around the room. "I'm providing a service to us older gentleman to facilitate our meeting fun women."

"What are you charging?" Kevin asked over the sound of Joseph getting sick in the bushes.

I interrupted before Crum could answer and get in more trouble. "Go help Joseph back to his cottage and then come back and clean up the mess; get rid of the smell before it kills my plants and creeps into this office."

Crum nodded and stepped backwards.

"Hold it," I said. "New rules: All nakedness goes on inside your cottage. Keep the shutters closed. Refund Joseph's money. Unless you have the necessary licensing, your entrepreneurial spirit could be considered illegal and land you in jail. Keep in mind that we have one member of law enforcement living here."

"I thought he was moving," Crum grumbled, lacking the nerve to make eye contact with Kevin.

"Here's your opportunity to ask him his move-out date," I said. "He keeps promising, and yet here he is."

"You're family," Kevin said with a straight face.

Fab belly-laughed.

"Well, sort of, maybe not." He glared at Fab. "I'll take a Coke," he said to Mac. "The place has grown on me. Go ahead, evict me. Once word gets around the station, Mac and Shirl will stop getting inside information."

Mac frowned at Kevin, ignoring his soda request; she crossed her arms across her ample bosom, middle finger sticking up over her arm.

"Joseph's done." Crum backed over the threshold. "I'll be back and take care of everything." He slammed the door.

"It probably smells out there." Fab pinched her nose.

"This has been fun, but I'll take another bag of cookies and the drink I requested and leave." Kevin held out his hand to Mac. She turned in her chair, getting a bag out of the bottom file drawer, and threw it over her shoulder, then handed him a can from the refrigerator.

"Let's do this again." Fab waved. "Next year would be good."

Kevin waved over his shoulder, banging the door.

"The first person to break the glass buys a whole new door," I yelled. One of the many things I'd done to put my stamp on the property was replace the solid wood door with a glass French door. It made the room feel bigger, and the addition of shutter blinds had a dual use: spying and keeping out unwanted stares.

"Do you think you can keep the guests from running naked?" I asked Mac.

"If I'd only known what was going on last night, I could've made some cash on the side, renting fold-up chairs to peepers."

Chapter Twelve

This was getting old!

Morning coffee by myself. The house had been eerily quiet of late, and I hated the solitude. An hour was enough alone time, days of it... too much.

No Didier and again no Fab. Last night after we got home, Fab waited until I was in the shower, then left a note that she had a date and would see me tomorrow.

"Date." I snorted, betting it was excuse.

Once again, she'd driven off in the SUV, even though her Porsche sat in the driveway; it still hadn't been on its maiden drive. If Fab was going to continue taking my car, I needed to get a key made for the Porsche. I immediately winced at the thought of getting even the smallest scratch on the car.

Fab's breaking up with Didier affected the entire family. When Fab was around, she moped; most of the time, she just snuck off, leaving behind a note void of details. It wouldn't surprise me if she was packing herself off to a hotel so she could brood without people fussing over her.

Mother did lecture her on safety, but Fab only laughed at her.

The first meow came from between my feet, where Snow sat waiting for tuna; behind her, Jazz entered the kitchen howling. It took a minute for me to satisfy them both. I'd had hopes that Snow's good manners would rub off on Jazz, but that hadn't happened; instead, Jazz spent his time trying to turn his girlfriend into a hoodlum. So far, she'd resisted his attempts.

I rested my cheek on the island counter, thinking about my day; nothing couldn't be shifted to tomorrow. Before coming downstairs, I'd put on a red tankini, and my original plan to go out to the pool still sounded like a good idea.

"Ahem."

My head flew up. Two men stood inside the French patio doors. I didn't recognize either man. They were opposite in looks, dressed in wrinkled shorts and shirts reminiscent of beach riff-raff. The pair attempted a casual air and failed; the menace in their eyes spoke loud and clear that they were up to no good. I cast a glance sideways, wanting to reach into the junk drawer for my trusty Beretta, but on second thought, it seemed like a bad idea; not enough time. One had a distinctive bulge under his left arm, and I didn't want to initiate a contest of who could draw and shoot faster.

"I prefer that my guests ring the *front* door bell," I said, trying to affect a calm I didn't feel.

The dark-haired one, who appeared to be the ringleader, flicked his eyes across my chest and back to my face; his tongue slithered out and then disappeared. "We won't be here long. We're here to collect the money you owe for a job well done." He nudged his friend, and they laughed.

"I don't know what you're talking about."

"Don't play stupid. This visit is a friendly reminder. If you haven't got the cash together…" The man tsked. "We'll allow you one more day. But if we have to come back…" He paused and made eye contact with his friend, then turned back. "Let's just say it will be painful. Have you ever stopped to wonder how many bones you can break before you pass out or die? If you pay up, you'll never have to find out."

The front door opened, and Fab stuck her head into the kitchen; she was disheveled, not her usual put-together self.

"Easy, boys," I said as the ponytailed blond sidekick reached behind his back. Flicking my gaze briefly in Fab's direction, I asked her, "Do you owe these nice men money? What was the amount again?"

Fab pulled her Walther from her waistband; shielding it to one side of her leg, she crossed to stand next to me. Always prepared, that girl.

So much for friendly. The blond drew his gun. But not before Fab had hers pointed at his head. "Drop it," she said calmly. "Now."

"You're making a big mistake." He inclined

his head towards Fab. "It's not like we tied up your friend and she's missing her fingers."

I clenched my hands, grimacing at the gruesome thought.

"You screwed our boss—" The blond leaned in. "—and there will be no easy ticket to the afterlife for you. Such as one well-placed bullet."

"I don't owe you a dime," I said. His dark smile didn't go unnoticed, nor did the calculating gleam in his eyes. "I'd introduce you, but this is the first time I've had the honor of your presence." I tugged on a strand of Fab's hair. "What about you?"

Fab shook her head. "Can I shoot him and his little friend?"

I almost laughed and inquired which friend, then decided it was the blond-haired partner, since he was a good foot shorter.

"The law is on my side," Fab continued. "Trespassing, breaking and entering, being a general ass—"

"I'll call the police," I cut in.

"Don't you know who you did business with? Do either of us look like that person?" Fab asked. "Here's a business tip: next time, get your money up front."

The blond snapped, demonstrating a surlier attitude than his friend. "We're collectors. Just doing our job."

While sliding my phone across the counter, I put my hand into the junk drawer, withdrawing my Beretta. I waved the gun around, enjoying the narrow-eyed response I got from the two men in return. "You're lucky I'm the reasonable one. I'd prefer she not shoot you, but only because blood is so messy to clean up. The police can deal with you and impress upon you never to come back here without an invite, which you'll never get."

I hit speed dial.

Creole answered the phone. "Hey babe, thinking about you."

"I'd like report two intruders. They came with guns, attempting to extort money, and wouldn't answer the 'who the heck are you?' question."

"Cops are on their way. Call you back." He disconnected.

"Don't move," I instructed, leveling my gun. "Law enforcement just got invited to the party."

The dark-haired one leaned down to whisper to his sidekick.

"None of that," Fab barked.

They turned and ran out the door, heading down the path.

A shot rang out.

One man uttering the F-word was confirmation that Fab's bullet hit him or came close.

I jerked on Fab's arm. "If the sheriff's deputies got the call, with our luck that means Kevin, and shooting a lowlife in the back will at the very least get you hauled in."

"I plugged his ass while he was still in the house."

"Go out the front and get a license number. Or a description of their bicycle." I laughed, which released some adrenaline. "I'll kick their gun under the chair and let the cops take custody. It will also strengthen our defense that we were scared and helpless."

That got a smile out of Fab. She flew to the door, letting it slam behind her.

My phone rang again. "That was quick."

"Help's on the way," Creole said.

"I thought you were sending real law enforcement."

Creole snorted. "Wait until I tell him you impugned his character; he won't respond next time."

"He's not that thin-skinned."

Help was Creole's undercover partner. The name was an aka that Fab and I had assigned him upon meeting the scruffy, jean-clad man. He typically used what I suspected was another alias, Stephen something, and claimed to be an insurance salesman.

"I forgot to tell you to have Fab shoot if one of them moves."

"Too late. They ran out the back, and who knows where. Fab gave one a parting gift – a plug to his backside on the way out the patio door. She's trying to get a license number."

"You okay?"

"Unnerved. Never seen them before. No clue what they were talking about, except that they wanted money. They apparently didn't make the initial contact, as they didn't know they had the wrong house and didn't believe me when I tried to tell them." I crossed to the sink and hung over it, peering out the garden window.

Creole demanded that I go over the details one more time. After a pause, he asked, "How did they get in the gate?"

"When Fab gets back, I'll send her to check that out. I'll hang over her shoulder."

"Where's that damn detective?" Creole grouched.

"Help just came face to face with Fab in the driveway; she looped her arm in his, and he doesn't look happy."

"The man doesn't know happy. He's a surly sort but damn good at his job. Don't skimp on the details. Help will track those two down; there's no hiding from him. He'll ferret them out, even if they take up residence in a mole hole. Before turning them over to Harder, we'll have a little one-on-one chat. I'll call the chief and tell him what happened."

Chief Harder was Creole and Help's boss and a well-respected member of the Miami Police Department.

"Do you want to talk to Help before I hang up on you?" I asked as I got to the door before the other two got there.

"Put him on. I want to figure out why your house has become so popular of late."

I passed my phone to Help. "It's for you."

He scowled, and I turned away slightly so he wouldn't see me smile. Turning back, I motioned with my fingers. "Just hold it up to your ear and talk." It took very little to annoy the man.

Instead of a greeting, he grunted, then turned his back, headed for the patio, and made himself comfortable on a chair. He sat on the far side, where he had a view of the pool area, house, and exits.

I raised an eyebrow at Fab.

"I got three letters of the license plate, and the make and model." She nodded towards the patio. "That man's not normal." She withdrew a notepad from the drawer and copied down the information.

"Start by not asking questions you know he won't answer."

Help didn't stay on the phone long. Good thing, since it appeared to irritate him. He silently slipped back inside, laying my phone on the counter top, and headed to the front door.

"Hold on," Fab barked. "What's next?"

"I'm going to find your two extorters and find out what they want. I have enough information. Then I'll be real hospitable and get them some free room and board."

Chapter Thirteen

Didier blew in like a gale-force wind, banging the door behind him. "Fab!" he bellowed.

I had camped out in the living room, piling up the pillows on the daybed, where I could stake out both entrances, waiting to catch Fab sneaking back in after another so-called date. I'd about given up, but she couldn't avoid me forever.

"She's not here," I grumped over my laptop. "Do you want to leave a message?" My voice was laced with sarcastic sweetness. "You look like sh... like a dog dragged you around and then left you for better prey."

The narrowing of his icy blue eyes made him look impressively menacing. Undaunted, I held his gaze and returned a glare of my own.

"I'd appreciate your not mentioning I stopped by." He continued to stand there.

"Don't come into my house and ask for squat. Which means nothing, Mr. Proper. You're a dick." His eyebrows shooting to his hairline only spurred me on. "You break Fab's heart, and for what? Now she's acting really reckless. Satisfied? She's not perfect and never was, you f..." I took a breath. "And you knew that from the beginning."

"Out of control is nothing new for her; she never thinks about the consequences. How many times has she skirted death?"

"Fab's a private investigator, which isn't a news flash since you knew from the beginning. Not quite perfect enough for you when you met, and you thought you'd change her. Into what? A simp at your beck and call?" I struggled not to indulge in an all-out yell fest. "If anything happens to Fab, watch your back. I just might shoot you, in my grief and all."

His face was set in a stern expression, his mouth firm and unsmiling; he glanced at his watch. "I have to go."

"Next time, knock."

* * *

The next night, I was prepared for Fab's antics. She hadn't gotten home until almost noon and then hid out in her bedroom, pleading her twenty-fifth headache. I waited until after the house was dark, then crept silently downstairs to wait for her to sneak out again. I didn't have to wait long.

"Where are you going in the middle of the night? Again!"

Fab startled, grabbing the handrail. "You sure know how to scare a girl."

Even in the dim nightlight, I could see her lips pulled into a tight line as she stared down at me where I was stretched out on the daybed. I eyed her up and down; she was dressed in jeans and a sexy midriff top that showed her rock-hard abs. The tennis shoes told me she had a job.

"You're in luck." I threw the blanket aside. "I just need to put on some shoes, and I'm ready to go with you." Anticipating another night of sneaking around, I'd donned a pair of sweatpants and a cropped t-shirt that read Key West. There were two pairs of shoes to pick from under the table: flip-flops and sneakers. A sweatshirt stuck out of the top of my purse.

"I just need some time to myself. I'm going for a drive." Fab came down the stairs, standing on the bottom step.

That mopey voice of hers grated on my ears. I needed to get with Mother and find out the details of her reunification plan.

"I realize it's rude of me to call you a liar, so why don't you try again."

She crossed her arms and served up her mean stare, which I returned.

"A better friend wouldn't make it about themselves, but I'm tired of your sullen and moody self." I cut off her attempt to speak with a wave of my hand. "Instead of sneaking out and doing what lost you the greatest boyfriend —"

Fab held her throat and gagged.

" — suck it up and get Didier back. He's a mere

man; he'll fall at your feet again – just turn on the charm. You need someone to point out you're miserable? Fine. I nominate myself. You are. This nonsense about dating other men isn't going to mend your heart and turn you back into the snarky friend I adore."

"Too late," she said forlornly. "Didier's got a new girlfriend. A model."

I shook my head. Could there be two dumber people? I kept the sentiment to myself. "Like you? Although I suspect yours is complete fiction. You two – hooking up with people that you don't give a damn about; it's called rebounding."

"I've got to go."

"You wouldn't want to keep your client waiting," I said in disgust. "Can't take the SUV," I told her as I watched her bypass the entry bench and cross to the island, looking for the keys. "Your new Porsche would like its engine cranked."

The door opened as Fab reached for the knob, catching her off guard. Creole took one look at her and stepped back; she stomped past him.

"My lucky night – you're not going with her." He leaned down and brushed my lips with his, scooping me into his arms.

"I've missed you." I clasped my arms around his neck as he carried me upstairs. "What are we going to do about Fab and Didier?"

"We're going to stay out of their love life and

let them figure it out."

"They're both already dating other unsuitable people. Or so they say."

"I tried, but Didier refuses to talk about it. Just said he's tired of wondering if the next call he gets will be to inform him she's dead." He opened the bedroom door. "Call me selfish, but I came here with other things on my mind." He set me on the floor and stripped off my clothes, flinging them in the direction of the chair. His followed.

"You're good at this."

Creole flexed his muscles. "That's because I enjoy it." He pulled the bed coverings off in one yank, laid me down, and got in next to me, pulling the sheet over us. "No more talk about those two. We've got other stuff to do that doesn't require speech." He leered.

* * *

The bed bounced under me. I opened my eyes one at a time, watching Creole put on his pants, his hips swaying side to side, so seductive, I blatantly stared.

"You're late. The sun is up." I made a kissy noise.

"It's all your fault." He leaned over and attacked my lips. "I've got two meetings this morning."

I leaned over the bed, eyeing him up and

down, and looked back up. "Shoes optional?"

"If I had my way, my desk would be on the beach. Behave." He shook his finger. "What's the number one rule?"

"Call if anything happens, no matter how insignificant. You'll decide if it's important." I smirked. "And your rule?"

He laughed. "That's an easy one. Don't get hurt."

"Have a good day at the office. If I have to behave, then so do you."

"Love you." He brushed his lips against mine.

"Me too." I wanted to smack his backside, but he twisted out of range with a laugh.

As soon as I heard his footsteps on the stairs, I reached for my phone and texted Spoon. "Coming over in a half hour. Be decent." And scrambled into the shower. My plan was to sneak out without being confronted by Fab; that is, if she had come home.

* * *

The door opened before I could knock for a change. Spoon grinned at me. "It's early. You in trouble?"

I flashed a "who me?" look. "Just stopped by for coffee with Mother."

He crossed his arms and scowled. "You better not be getting my sweet wife into trouble. You two are up to something, and don't bother to deny it."

"I didn't know you drank in the morning."

He tapped my nose with his finger. "Don't think I won't tell on you." He kissed my cheek. "Work calls. Tell my lovely wife I'll be checking on her later."

Spoon owed JS Auto Body, down on the docks. He specialized in the repair of luxe autos and didn't take customers off the street, appointment only.

"If you think you're going to control Mother, good luck with that."

"I've got my ways." Sinister smile on his lips, he winked, and closed the door behind him.

I walked down the hall towards the kitchen, where Mother turned from the counter and handed me a cup of coffee.

"What were you two talking about?" Mother asked as she led the way to the patio. We sat side by side in chairs facing the water.

The patio ran the length of the condo, and each of the bedrooms had access. In addition to the large wooden table off the living room, there was additional seating all along the patio. I'd been along on a couple of the shopping trips and encouraged comfortable furniture and plenty of pillows. Hard as I tried, I could only talk her into one string of lights, which ran along the railing. Spoon had added his touch; he'd hauled up several varieties of potted palm trees.

"We have to be careful," I said quietly, turning

my head from side to side, checking for uninvited guests. "Your husband is as suspicious as Creole."

"It's just the two of us here. We haven't done anything. Yet."

"This plan of yours better be a good one; I'm ready for whatever you've got cooked up. I want my friend back. Didier stopped by, and he didn't look all that great either, and I was rude to him." I smiled sadly, putting my arm around Mother.

"I don't have all the details completely figured out." At my groan, she continued. "So far, we lure them down to Spoon's boat and lock them in the stateroom until they come to their senses."

"That's kidnapping." My inner voice was shouting, *I told you this would be a bad idea.* "And a felony."

"You got a plan?" Mother sniffed. "It's not some hell hole. We're talking king size bed, en-suite, and we'll stock it with champagne and food."

I squeezed my eyes shut, ticking off the ways this would blow up in our faces. Kidnapping Fab! Good luck to that. Yeesh! "What if something goes awry?"

"Got that covered. We'll take turns guarding them."

"This has 'unhappy Creole and Spoon' written all over it. Not to mention Fab and Didier when they get out and track us down. You know, when I get on Creole's last nerve, he disappears for days and no… well, anything. It's lonely." I held out my mug. "I need more coffee."

"You're the biggest prude in the family." Mother leaned in. "It's called sex. Spoon tried that tactic, and it backfired," she said smugly and stood.

I followed her into the kitchen, sliding onto a stool. "Mother, I love you, but I can't hear about your sex life. See, I said it."

"Don't worry about Fab and Didier; they'll soon be back together and happy again," Mother said with confidence. "You lure Fab, and I'll take Didier. The gentleman in him won't be able to say no to me." She sighed. "Might not work in the future."

"Does the door to the stateroom lock from the outside? A regular lock isn't going to hold Fab; she'll have it open in half a second."

"Took care of that already. Got a new lock installed, and it will hold the lovers until they reunite." Mother mumbled, "Hopefully before Spoon finds out."

Unsure what kind of lock she meant, I asked, "Where did you get these connections?" That would be one of Fab's first questions; that is, if she was still speaking to me.

"Really Madison, I called a regular locksmith." She shook her head.

I wasn't sure whether to believe her or not. "Spoon will pry it out of you, and it might not be pretty."

"You let me take care of my husband." She smiled. "I'll offer up something he can't refuse."

"I love that you're both so happy. Let's hope he doesn't get too mad." The guilt of her being unhappy would kill me. "Maybe we should take some time to hone this plan."

"Stop worrying. My husband isn't a stick. He's a man I depend on; he'd never let me down, and he feels the same about me. We had each other's backs long before getting married. His unhappiness over my meddling will be short-lived. Fab and Didier will get back together, and we'll all be happy."

I squeezed her in a bear hug, which she returned.

"Don't worry about me and Spooner. We have a lot of fun. A lot of laughter. He loves my children. Doesn't get any better than that." Mother beamed at me. "Look how happy you are. I wish my sister was here to see the two of you together. Elizabeth loved Creole and loved you, and she'd be ecstatic that you're together."

"Back to the plan," I said. Mother handed me back my coffee cup, and I forced myself not to gulp it down. "You lure Didier first. I'll show up with Fab and make an excuse about needing to do a favor for Spoon. What's your bait?"

"Same as you, and I want to discuss it in person."

"Are you prepared to lose both their friendships if this backfires?"

"You're such a worrier. Think positive."

"When do we do this?" I asked.

"Day after tomorrow. Spoon has morning meetings, which will be perfect. I'll take the day watch."

"We can't leave them in there for days. This scheme has a one-day expiration; if they can't kiss and make up by then, they're not going to."

"I'm leaving a burner phone so that either of them can call, but only me. I decided I was the best choice; Fab might trick you."

"Burner phones? You're becoming a hoodlum." *Brad better not find out.* "Mother, one more thing: if Fab or Didier calls and wants out, then we spring them. Agreed?"

"This is going to work."

Maybe. It was better than anything I'd come up with, which was zilch.

Chapter Fourteen

Oh great!

Kevin had parked his police cruiser at the curb and sat his backside in a ratty beach chair on the sidewalk. My guess was it was a trash treasure he'd somehow got Crum to part with. If he left it behind, I planned to call 911 and report nuisance littering.

The driveway was empty when I pulled in, and childishly, I wanted to hog the entire space. Fab could park in the street.

I slid out from behind the wheel, turning to meet the man before he got up the driveway. "Before you start, look around. See a dead body anywhere? No," I answered for him. "If by chance you ferret one out, I didn't do it."

Kevin nodded. "Just a friendly visit." He clearly saw disbelief wash across my face. "Really." He snapped the chair closed and threw it in the trunk of his car.

"Let me guess. The sheriff's department now issues junky webbed chairs as necessary equipment?"

"I'll be sure and let Crum know his taste sucks."

"I hope you used disinfectant. You do know that it came out of the trash?" I shivered at the thought of bugs. "You amaze me; you harass my tenants and then show glimpses of humanity."

He grinned. "Although I don't consider you a prime suspect, I do have a few questions about your dead neighbor. If you know who did it, that would save me a lot of time."

It irked me to invite him inside my house, but I refused to stand out in the humidity and drip sweat. Worse, there was a possibility he might figure out a way to give me a free ride to the station. I waved my hand for him to follow.

"Would you like something to drink?" I asked, heading to the refrigerator.

"Coke, something sugary. You're making me feel special. Just like when you invite me to one of those family dinners, where one of you feels the need to air grievances and a fight breaks out."

I tried not to laugh, knowing that I was usually in the middle of one of those memorable moments. "Don't get used to the hospitality. Pull your list of questions out of your pocket, and let's get started." I put a can of soda onto the island, grabbing a water for myself, and hopped up on a stool.

"You forget to relate anything about the departed?" Kevin cocked his head in the direction of Scotch's house. "Fight? Argument? Any unsavory sorts hanging around? Family as chummy as they say they were?" He took a notepad and pen from his shirt pocket.

"That's a lot of questions. No to all of them except the family, whom I never met. Scotch wasn't a tenant, so I'm not up on every piece of minutia regarding his private life. The man kept to himself, friendly, but no overtures to be pals."

"The girlfriend?" he asked.

"Ruby moved in a few days ago, as in after his death. I did see her coming and going before Scotch's demise, but he made a point of telling me he lived there by himself."

"You sure about that?"

"I had an unobstructed view when a junky van pulled up the other day. Man I've never seen before behind the wheel. Who, by the way, didn't lift a finger while Ruby unloaded boxes." No need to tell him I used one of my trees as cover.

Kevin tapped his pen. "Anything out of the ordinary going on in the neighborhood?"

I had zero intention of informing him about the attempted break-ins at my house and the gun-toting intruders. Creole had that under control. He'd told me he called in a couple of favors from "friends," and I now got regular drive-bys. My hesitation turned into a stare down. I wondered whether he thought that tactic would elicit more information or was coming up with more questions.

"Thinking…" I weaseled.

"Did you know that winning the lottery can

shorten your life? A lot of greedy people out there. The latest case happened up north. The killers turned out to be the niece and her criminal boyfriend. They're both on death row."

I shuddered. "If Scotch has nieces and nephews, you can cross them off the list; they'd be kids."

"This went well." He picked up his soda can, looking around.

I held out my hand and took the can from him, a weak smile plastered on my face.

Kevin's phone dinged. He took it out of his pocket, glancing at the screen. He stood up. "If you hear or see anything, you've got my numbers."

"I've got a question. I know it's none of my business, and I'll understand if you can't answer. Who inherits the money?"

"Didn't leave a will. Probably thought he was too young, and he didn't have the money long." Kevin waved and left.

He'd barely had time to make it to the end of the block when the doorbell rang. The short hairs on my neck ruffled. Friends called first, even if they were sitting in the driveway. Family had keys.

I pulled my Glock from the holster that I had tucked inside my bag, which was sitting on the entry bench. Concealing it in the folds of my skirt, I looked out the peephole. A dark-haired, scraggly thirty-something shifted from foot to foot, eyeing the courtyard.

"What do you want?" I yelled.

"Delivery."

"Hold on. Let me get the key." I ran across the living room, across the patio, and down the side path to the front. "Go away" would've probably been a better idea, but I wanted to know what he really wanted.

He saw me come around the corner, Glock raised at chest level.

"Hey, man." He raised the box to chin level.

"Who's it for?"

"Mary Smith. I'll just leave it on the step; I don't get paid enough to get shot."

"Where's your delivery truck?"

He threw the box in my direction and ran for the street, heading to the corner. I ran after him; he slowed before turning the corner, not looking back.

This is a bad idea. I stopped, panting, then turned back to the house. The first thing I noticed was a lockpick lying next to the non-descript brown box that had no address label. Now I wished I'd pursued him further, but I highly doubted I would've been able to catch up to him without shooting him. The man Fab shot hadn't showed up in an emergency room, and there'd been no news items about a dead body. My luck, this one would have turned me in if I'd attempted a shot. With our last unwelcome guests, Fab had showed up just in time for all the excitement. Where the heck was she now?

Maybe it was due to watching one too many television shows, but I had no intention of picking up the box. It wasn't rigged to explode, as demonstrated by the so-called delivery guy's willingness to throw it. Creole could decide what to do before I added to the fingerprints.

I went back in the house via the side path, making sure the gate was securely closed and locked. I glanced around, spotting my phone on the coffee table; my call to Creole went straight to voicemail. I left a message, then flicked through my phone numbers, contemplating my next call for a few seconds before calling Help.

This latest intruder: what was he up to exactly? The chances of this man not being related to the other two seemed remote. Odds were that sooner or later one of them was going to get lucky, corralling us into a situation neither Fab nor I could get out of.

The phone stopped ringing, and ambient noise hummed in the background. Help had answered his phone but didn't say anything. I complained, "You're annoying. It wouldn't kill you to say hello."

"You only call when you want something; you should be a little nicer."

I knew he enjoyed the sparring, even though he wouldn't admit to a feeling about anything. "I'll just hang up," I sulked.

"Don't you dare. Then I'll have to drive over

there."

I told him what happened in painstaking detail.

"I'll take care of it. You did the right thing, staying away from the box and calling me. The boyfriend will be happy too. Where's the hot Frenchie chick? I hope she annoys Creole as much as she does me." He laughed and hung up.

"Good-bye to you too," I mumbled.

* * *

"Help just turned the corner," Fab said as she came through the front door, throwing her bag on the floor, where it landed with a thud. "He have an update on the two extorters?"

"Look who blew in." I looked over the top of my laptop, Jazz and Snow stretched out beside me on the daybed. "There was a little excitement." I went on to tell her about it.

"Sorry I wasn't here. We need to figure out what's going on."

"Hopefully, there's fingerprints on the box that will identify our latest intruder."

Fab threw three black garment bags over the chair and bounced down on the couch, stretching out her hands behind her head. "I had a great night."

"Happy to hear the 'job' went well." I used air quotes. "At least you're in one piece. Don't give me some BS about a date."

"What's wrong with you today?" she huffed.

"You're lying to me, to my face I might add. I'm not Mother; I know a lie when I hear one. Except with Mother, you have the tendency to only skirt the truth. Why lie? It's not like I'm judgmental."

"I'm not a sharer; you know that. I've had a hard time since breaking up with Didier, reliving the whys and what-ifs." Sadness engulfed her face, and she closed her eyes.

"That's some shopping spree you went on." I eyed the bags. "You can model the clothing for me. I won't tell you how hot and sexy you look."

She laughed, a low, sultry chuckle. "I, uh… you don't want to know. That way, you can claim ignorance."

"What have you done? Tell me now." Fab remained silent. "I'll find out myself." I set my laptop on the table.

"I stole Didier's clothes."

"You what?" I couldn't believe I'd heard her correctly. "Bet he's pissed, to put it mildly."

"So far, no reaction," she said sadly. "No phone call. No note. Nothing. He has to know it was me."

"Then what? You go straight to romantic reunion while holding his underwear hostage?"

Fab stuck out her chin. "Where is the flaw in my plan?"

"Besides the fact that it sucks? Did it ever once occur to you to share it with your best friend?" I unleashed my temper, which had been building for a while. "Why would you want my input now? You're sneaking around, keeping me in the dark, lying, and leaving me worrying every night about where the hell you really are and what you're doing."

"You're yelling," Fab whined.

I lowered my tone a smidge, not that it would be noticeable. "Why don't you address the issues that make Didier unhappy, starting with taking jobs where you end up in the hospital? Isn't there a limit to how many times you can jump out a window before you end up dead?"

Fab glared at me.

"Wipe the snotty look off your face," I said, imitating Mother. "You've got a couple of choices. Choose the great guy that loves you, if you haven't blown that damn option all to hell by stealing his clothes…" I let out a long breath. "Or continue taking jobs from clients that don't care about your personal safety as long as they get what they want. The rush hurts like hell when accompanied by a bullet. I'm giving you notice: I also like the edge, but I'm over getting shot at."

"If it were up to you, we'd rescue animals." Fab sniffed.

Fab had put a hole in my frustration level; the pure irritation on her face had me cracking a smile. "Return his damn clothes. Suggest a compromise, with the two of you working out rules you both can live with." They'd been down this road before, but I wasn't about to point that out. Anything to get them talking. "You stopped lying for a while. Get back on the wagon. Rearranging the truth just to pretty up an ugly situation is also a lie."

When I'd had enough of Fab ignoring me, I said, "I'm disappointed in you, Miss Sexy; you could have come up with something more enticing. Like, oh I don't know, seducing him."

"It's too late. He's already moved on," Fab whispered.

"I don't believe that. How do you know?" I asked suspiciously, mentally crossing my fingers that her explanation didn't involve three-way nudity.

"A couple of nights ago, my date and I showed up at the same restaurant as Didier and his date."

"Nice coincidence." Another plan of hers gone awry. "Your date? Thuggish looking, bulge under his jacket?"

Fab ignored me. That meant I'd hit the mark; maybe not exactly, but close enough.

"His date – a hot and upcoming model, and they were draped all over one another. The next day, the tabloids labeled them the newest 'it' couple?"

Fab continued to ignore my needling.

"Your stories of working – my behind. You've been following Didier. Your date... some associate who thought his lucky card got punched and agreed to show last minute?" Only Fab would know someone who could appear in ten minutes. "Date night, was that the night you ripped Didier off?"

"I'm going to bed." Fab stood and, without making eye contact, headed for the stairs.

"It's not even dark outside."

"You know what I mean."

I didn't, but getting an explanation might take all night.

Chapter Fifteen

Today was the day! I wasn't completely sold on Mother's idea and had concluded that no matter how our scheme played out, whether Fab and Didier got back together or not, there would be hell to pay. I was sitting by the pool, feet in the water, when the ringing of my phone startled me. My nervousness ratcheted up when Mother's picture popped up.

"Didier's locked in the stateroom," Mother whispered. "I feel sleazy tricking him. I hope he speaks to me again."

I groaned, my stomach in a nervous uproar. "It's not too late to just arrange dinner at a restaurant and force them to sit together."

Mother snorted. "Don't you think I already thought of that? They'd just head for the exit."

"It's not too late to abandon the plan," I said, reluctantly adding, "I'll go along with whatever you want."

"How long will it take you to get Fab here?"

"Ten minutes." I hung up and flipped my legs out of the water, drying them off and slipping my feet into nearby tennis shoes. I smoothed down my skirt, drawing a stabilizing breath.

"Fab," I yelled, walking back inside the house. I fished my car keys from the bottom of my purse, which I'd left by the door. She sat sullen-faced at the island, rubbing her ears. "Catch." I sent the keys airborne, and she easily caught them.

"Gee, I get to drive."

"Sarcasm is unattractive." I practically ran to the SUV, not wanting to answer any questions, thinking ahead to how I would ward them off in the car.

Fab slid behind the wheel, her usual calm, collected self.

"Spoon's boat," I directed. "Someone is camping out. Absolutely no guns."

"He's big and scary, why not deal with it himself?"

I needed to make up several vague responses, memorize them to be trotted out when needed. "He's got a meeting or something today." *Something.* I winced.

"What does he want us to do? Push him or her overboard?"

I turned to the window to avoid her scrutiny. "We convince whoever it is to come up with a healthier living solution."

"A better plan would be to threaten the person with certain death if they come back. Faster that way."

"Hmm." I nodded, toying with the window button.

"You okay?"

"All's good." I flashed a phony smile and wanted to add how much our friendship meant to me. But that would alert her "something's going on" radar, and I'd never get her out of the car.

Thankfully, traffic was light, and we made it to the dock in record time, cutting off conversation. Fab parked in the first aisle to the side of the gate, which stood open, a crew stocking a boat for a trip.

I needed to deter Fab from a search; finding Mother first would elicit questions for which neither of us had prepared good answers.

I told Fab as we climbed the steps, "Another boat owner told Spoon he'd seen some people coming and going and lights on in the main stateroom. I'll follow you," I said.

Fab pulled her Walther. "Where's your Glock?"

"Left it at home," I said lamely. Her explosion would be huge when she discovered that I'd emptied the bullets out of her gun earlier.

Fab shot me a dirty look. "If I needed backup?"

Mother stood in the galley, a finger to her lips. I winced; so much for keeping Fab from spotting her. But Mother had it all under control. She held up a key. "Spoon forgot to give you this," she said, handing it to Fab.

I attempted to follow Fab down the hallway, but Mother pushed me out of the way, stepping in front of me and almost treading on the backs of Fab's shoes.

Fab unlocked the door, kicking it open. "Didier?" she said, her confusion clear.

In mid-turn, Mother put a hand to the small of her back, shoved her in, slammed the door, and locked the top lock. To my untrained eye, it looked like a one-way lock with key-only access. So much for top-secret connections—my guess was her locksmith story was true.

All was quiet for a minute, then Fab yelled, "Open this damn door." She beat on it. "Don't think I won't kick your ass. Yours too, Madeline Westin Spoon."

Full name, that always meant big trouble.

I whispered in Mother's ear, "How long do we wait?"

Mother shushed me, ear to the door.

Fab and Didier's voices were low, nothing that I could overhear and probably in French, the two knowing Mother and I would eavesdrop.

Judging by the jiggle of the lower lock, Fab had taken out her trusty lockpick. "You two are dead," she yelled. "I don't care if you're married to the scariest guy in the Keys, Madeline; he's dead too."

"You two listen to me," Mother barked in a voice I recognized from childhood. "You *will* kiss and make up. I'm tired of your unhappy faces."

"Madison," Fab yelled. "Open up." Followed by a loud bang to the bottom of the door.

"I agree with Mother," I yelled back. "Stop thinking about yourselves. Mother and I went to the trouble of coming up with this bold plan; the least you two could do is try a little kiss and make up."

"Cherie, open the door." Didier sounded tired.

"Madison doesn't have the key, I do," Mother said. "Tell me that you don't love each other and getting back together is never going to happen."

"I realize that you're trying to help," Didier said. "But forcing the situation isn't going to work. This is our decision to make."

"You two are *stubborn*," Mother said in disgust. "I'll be back later to see if you've come to your senses." Mother grabbed my arm and pushed me toward the galley, loud voices in French following us down the hallway.

I sank into one of the leather armchairs. "This plan stinks. Time to release them and let them figure it out themselves, while we still have a chance of not completely ruining our friendships."

"Give it some time to work," Mother snapped.

"Creole's not going to be very happy with me. He told me to stay out of their relationship, and I should have listened."

"Spoon thought my plan stunk. He wanted to know when I was going to stop meddling in family members' love lives."

I half-laughed. "I'm sure you told him never."

"I can hardly get away with anything, or at

least, I haven't so far." The twinkle in Mother's eyes belied her tone; she wasn't upset in the least. "I know he's on to me when I catch him staring in that beady-eyed way of his."

"Give me the key." I held out my hand. "You can make a run for it. When you reach the parking lot, I'll unlock the top lock, and Fab can take care of the rest."

"They're not fighting anymore."

"That's because Fab's probably wiggling out the porthole. Be prepared for her to come rushing up the stairs and wrestle us both to the floor."

Mother tapped her temple with her finger. "Thought of that – too small."

"Maybe. I've seen the woman in action." I snapped my fingers. "The key. I'll take the first watch."

Mother's phone pinged. She hesitated. "Do you promise to give them a few hours?" She smiled while reading the message.

Hours? I didn't respond, instead crossing my fingers where she couldn't see. "Of course I do."

"Spoon wants to meet for lunch, and then I'll be back." Mother dropped the key in my hand, stood, and brushed a kiss on my cheek. "You'll see, this is going to work."

I knelt on the seat cushions on the back bench, leaning over the side to watch Mother as she made her way down the dock. At the gate, she turned and waved. I waved back. I flipped the lid on my silver seashell watch open, giving Mother two minutes to get to her car. Since I'd never set the time, I'd have to hope for some patience.

Unable to sit still any longer, I stood and paced the deck, going back inside, listening for voices. In fact, after a few angry words, they'd lowered their voices. Now all was silent. I taped a piece of paper I found in the drawer to the door, writing 'lock up' on it. I slipped the key into the lock as quietly as possible. Once it was unlocked, I hustled off the boat. Before heading to the parking lot, I checked out the aft side to make sure there wasn't a body hanging out of the porthole.

Chapter Sixteen

Awake most of the night, I caught a random hour of sleep here and there. Fab neither showed up nor called. At daylight, I drove down to the docks, checking for Didier's Mercedes. I circled the lot twice, even though it didn't hold many cars; he was gone, and he was too much of a gentleman to leave Fab stranded without a ride. They had to be together; she'd at least want to retrieve her car from the house.

I pulled into the driveway and studied the front of the house. It looked the same as when I left. I took my phone and a cup of coffee, went outside to the patio, snatching up a towel on the way, and claimed a chaise.

It was mid-morning, and I hadn't heard from anyone. I finally sucked up some courage and called Fab. It went straight to voicemail. Then I called Mother, and her phone also went to voicemail. That neither woman had called didn't bode well, but how exactly, I was unsure. Bad news traveled fast. I was sure I'd have received that call already. I'd given previous thought to all the ways the plan could go wrong and gone along anyway. I refused to think Fab would stop being my friend. I'd figure out where she was living and go steal her shoes.

I jumped when my phone rang. Spoon's picture popped up, which sent a shudder down my spine. Now what? My relief when the call went to voicemail was short-lived when it rang again. He was persistent today. I waited for a text message, and it never came, so I told myself that his call couldn't be that important.

Closing my eyes, hoping to ward off a headache, I drifted off to sleep. A loud banging noise on the front door jerked me into a sitting position, unsure of the time. The banging continued; whoever it was was insistent. I crept into the house and moved towards the door, stopping at the entry bench to remove my Glock from its holster, then tiptoed to the peephole. The smartass had put something over the hole, probably their finger. I'd never liked "who's there?" – I wanted to know without having to ask.

"Open the damn door, Madison Westin," a male voice bellowed. "Don't get crazy and shoot me; left my weapon in the truck."

Recognizing the voice, I yelled, "That was stupid." And opened the door.

"Would you really have shot me?" Billy eyed the handgun at my side.

"I still might if you damaged my door."

"Boss wants to talk to you." He pushed past me and headed into the kitchen. "You were ignoring his calls."

I held up my hand to ward him off as he pulled his phone from his pocket. "Tell Spoon you couldn't find me."

Billy closed the space between us, a glint in his eye. "He signs my paycheck. Lying to his face would get me fired. I have fudged the truth for you in the past, and I know he knows when I do it. He gets that secretive smile of his."

"Want something to drink?" I pointed to the refrigerator. "Help yourself."

"Humidity stinks." He fished out one of the sodas that I stocked for Liam and pulled out a stool, then turned his attention to his phone, pushing a few buttons and then thrusting it at me. "Stop being stubborn and speak to him."

Squeezing my eyes closed, I took a breath. Maybe this wouldn't be so bad. Who was I kidding? Spoon had gone to way too much trouble to get in touch. "Hi," I managed to say calmly.

"Hi yourself. I won't mention all the calls you ignored." A deep noise rumbled in his throat.

I mumbled under my breath.

"Family dinner at our house tonight. Your mother would be disappointed if you were the only one to not show up."

Family dinner? This was a trap. "Put Mother on, please. I'm not feeling well; I'll explain it to her."

Billy groaned.

"Suck it up, sweet cakes. I'm redeeming one of those IOUs you like to toss around."

"Wasn't it you who said that all the favors you've done for me are out of the goodness of that big heart of yours? No IOUs involved."

He growled out a laugh. "Be here no later than six. Earlier works. I'll reserve the couch for you so you can stretch out."

"Can I speak to Mother?"

"Madeline's tied up right now."

I was sure that it was an innocuous comment, but it made me squirm all the same. What the two of them did in their personal life wasn't any of my business, and I didn't want to hear about it. If he put a toe over the line, he knew he was a dead man without my having to threaten him.

"I'll try to make it."

"Do you need Billy to drive you?"

"No," I muttered, which he accepted and hung up, a cheerful note in his voice.

I handed Billy back his phone. "I have a question to ask, but I need your pinkie promise that you won't mention it to another soul. If you can't, say so. Don't screw me."

"This isn't some deal where you confess to where the body is buried, is it?"

I shook my head.

He held out his little finger; I wrapped mine around it.

"What does Spoon know about what happened yesterday?" I asked.

"About the part you played in locking your best friend in a closet and leaving her to die?"

"You've got the details wrong, and in case you didn't know, you're not funny."

"Well, damn." He smirked. "I suspect that the boss knew quite a bit before your escapade went down. Any pesky details he was unaware of got revealed when Madeline came by the shop and narced on herself in full, glorious detail."

"Mother's dead. That's why he wouldn't put her on the phone."

"Pretty much. Lordee, you're dramatic." He rolled his eyes. "The boss shook his finger and expressed some disappointment that didn't sound sincere to my trained ear. Madeline giggled, and the boss couldn't get her out the door fast enough. He called a little while later to tell me he was taking the rest of the day off. Would you like me to speculate?"

"Please don't." I rubbed my temples.

Chapter Seventeen

I arrived at Mother and Spoon's early, giving me time to call Fab again. I found a place to park that wasn't in the direct line of sight from one of Mother's windows. I laid my head back against the seat, punched in Fab's number once more, and once more got voicemail.

A tap on the window. I squealed, and my smile at seeing Creole grinning at me was short-lived, knowing I'd once again left him in the dark. I had no intention of letting him find that out from anyone other than me. I opened the door, and he reached in to hit the unlock button, then drew me into his arms. My legs wrapped around his waist, he lifted me out, opened the back passenger door, and slid me across the seat, climbing in after me.

"We have time for a make-out session," he said, a mischievous glint in his eyes. "Word has it you've been very naughty."

I groaned and tapped my head against his chest. "I wanted to be the one to tell you."

"Listen to me." He caught my chin in his hand and held my face still. With his thumb, he gently traced my lips. "You weren't hurt; no bullets, or did I miss that part?"

I shook my head.

"Blame it all on your mother."

"So mean."

He caught my mouth in a kiss, and anticipation shot up to my lips. It was a kiss without finesse, demanding; I leaned in closer and kissed him back.

"What I want to know is: did it work?"

"I don't know anything," I said, annoyed. "You know anything? I take it you're here for the family dinner. Did Spoon demand your appearance like he did mine?"

"Spoon doesn't demand, he asks. He isn't quite sure if I'd arrest him or not, or pull a Kevin and hassle him on jaywalking or some punkass thing." Creole chuckled.

"I have a great idea."

"I bet it's not, but I want to hear it anyway. I'm certain it's something that will get us both into trouble with your mother. She can be scarier than her husband."

"Don't tell her, even though she'd love to hear it. Let's go to your house, get naked, and you can tell me how your day went."

"Oh no, young lady." He tweaked my nose. "We're not missing out on the fun. After dinner, I'll sneak us out of there, and beach house here we come."

"Let's hope Mother didn't forget to order dessert. But Liam will have reminded her," I said with confidence.

"In your family?" Creole snorted. "Sorry folks, no dessert? That would start a revolution."

"Didier's here." I perused the parking lot. "Fab's car is still in the driveway at home. Fingers crossed, they're here together. Unless Fab jacked his car and left him on the roadside somewhere."

"Your brother or I would've gotten that call already. Brad's car is over there." Creole pointed in the opposite direction from Didier's car.

He pushed me back on the seat, tickling my foot.

"Nooo," I squealed.

He climbed out of the car, reaching over the seat and taking the keys out of the ignition. Then he grabbed my ankle, dragging me across the seat to the door, and picked me up, setting me on the pavement.

We strode toward the lobby. At the secured door, I withdrew my lockpick. I could feel Creole's frown before he said anything. "There's something to be said for the element of surprise," I told him.

Having the elevator to ourselves, we made the most of it, kissing until we arrived on the third floor.

"It annoys Spoon when you pick the lock," Creole reminded me.

"I know," I said with a devilish smile and slid the lockpick in place, shoving the door open.

Fab looked up first. I returned her scowl with a wave. Didier sat next to her, his arm draped across her shoulders. She whispered in his ear, and he didn't look in our direction.

"Looks like we're all here," Fab said loudly, pointing to Creole and me.

Liam waved from the corner before his attention returned to his phone.

Spoon handed me a margarita and Creole a beer. "The doorbell works, you know."

"What fun would that be?" I asked.

I walked over to Fab. "Kiss?" She turned away. "Fight?" I held up one fist and gulped my drink with the other.

"I'll take the kiss." Didier's eyes bored into mine, letting me know all hadn't been forgiven – yet.

"Always the gentleman." I brushed his cheek.

"Did I hear fight?" Brad air-boxed. "Five bucks on Fab."

That broke the tension.

"Bro, you've got to support your sister, even if you lose money," I said in faux disgust.

"Between me and Didier, who's your money on?" Brad flexed his muscles.

"Creole beats all of you, including you, big guy." I winked at Spoon.

Didier stood. "We have an announcement." He pulled Fab to stand beside him.

She didn't look happy, which made me tense.

"We've decided to work on our relationship,"

Didier said.

"Oh good." I clapped. "I missed you cooking breakfast. Shirtless was an added benefit."

"I never noticed." Mother blushed bright red. She was one of his biggest fans, and everyone in the room knew it.

"We're back together, and we're working on our relationship, but I won't be moving back in," Didier announced.

"Don't worry." Fab smiled; one of her scary versions that worried most people. "You'll be seeing him every day. He'll have to come by the house if he wants a change of clothes."

"Cherie, what have you done?"

The duo had captured everyone's attention; no one said a word.

"All of your clothes are hanging in the closet. I even dropped off your dry cleaning."

"I packed them up and took them to the hotel," Didier said.

"And I moved them back."

I wondered if he still had a hotel room. Up to her old tricks—right after they met, she'd packed his belongings and checked him out of his hotel.

Didier lifted her chin to face him. "You did what?"

"Seriously, you're surprised?" Fab said without an ounce of remorse.

He spoke to her in French in low, clipped tones; she just smiled at him.

"Your first breakfast back," I said, "I have a

new recipe for a breakfast smoothie."

"Will you be joining me in a glass?" Didier asked.

"Of course not."

Chapter Eighteen

I walked in the front door, dumping my packages on the kitchen island, then did a double take over my shoulder, drew my Glock, and backed up to the entry, peeking around the corner.

"Don't shoot; I'm not armed."

My eyes locked on the large man sacked out on the daybed, the overloud sound of raspy breathing whistling from beneath the arm covering his face. His frame filled the daybed, his filthy feet pressed up against the side rail. It surprised me to see a pair of deck shoes on the floor, although they appeared to have been mauled by a dog. His black shorts and shirt didn't appear all that worn, but they were a good color choice since hygiene appeared to be lacking at the moment.

"Bad place for your firearms." I pointed to the two guns lying on the table. "Unless you tell me why you chose my house to take a nap in and how the hell you got in, I will shoot you."

"Fabbie isn't the only one who can pick locks," he wheezed.

"You and I both know that you're not a friend

of hers, or mine either." I reholstered my Glock.

He rolled to his side to get control over a coughing attack. Unsuccessful, he flopped on his back. "You owe me," he gasped out. "I just need a place to rest for a day or two."

"Casio, what are you doing here?" The sun streamed into the room, casting shadows on what appeared to be fresh bruises on the left side of his face, which were in the stage of turning from red to purple.

Casio Famosa was Brick's older brother, a decorated Miami police detective who currently looked like he'd had the stuffing kicked out of him.

"I was in the neighborhood..."

I retrieved my purse from the entry and dug my phone out.

"Who are you calling?" he rasped. "Hang the hell up. Now."

"I'm calling 911."

Casio raised his head to shoot me a glare. "No, you aren't. Tell them your ass dialed or something so law enforcement doesn't show up."

"You need to go to the hospital."

He started shaking his head before I got all the words out. "Who are you calling now?" he demanded.

"I'm making two calls." I searched my address book, finding the number I wanted.

"Yeah," a grumpy voice answered on the other end.

"I have a houseguest who's, uh... not feeling well."

"Am I the only doctor you know?"

"For these kind of calls, you are."

"On my way." He hung up.

"What's with you men and your inability to end a conversation politely, rather than just hanging up?"

"It's efficient."

I called Creole, and it went to voicemail after a few rings. I hung up and texted, *We've got company.* I glanced up at Casio and wagged my finger. "The boyfriend's going to find out sooner or later, and it would be better if it didn't come as a surprise. Want something to drink?" I asked over my shoulder, heading to the kitchen.

His hand flopped down, and he held up a bottle of beer. "I helped myself on the way in."

I returned and sank down into a chair across from him. "So what's your story?"

"None of your business." Casio leaned back and closed his eyes.

"You're an arrogant son of —"

"Yes, I know." He grinned like a wild man. "We're friends – mi casa... in this case, your casa."

"You have a head injury? Saying we're friends doesn't make it the truth, nor do a couple of brief encounters qualify. Your brother's not a friend either, but I do know and dislike him. In case you're not up on the latest, Fab doesn't do his dirty work anymore."

"Heard some glossed-over version that ended up with Fabbie leaving town. When she gets back to the states, I want to facilitate a kiss-and-make-up reunion." His lips curled up, highly amused with himself.

"Mind your own business. And in case that wasn't clear enough – stay out of it. Most of Brick's slimy jobs end up in an exchange of bullets. I've always wondered why Brick doesn't avail himself of your services instead."

A knock on the door saved him from having to answer.

I looked out the peephole. *What does he want?* I cracked open the door, shoving my head out. "I'd invite you in, but I'm sick and wouldn't want you to catch anything." I covered my mouth and coughed several times.

Dr. A lounged against the doorframe.

"Good thing I'm here. Look what I brought." He held up his doctor's bag. "Having a hard time coming up with another way to politely tell me to get lost?" He shot me a raffish, lopsided grin. "I'm filling in for my godfather, Doc Rivers. He's a bit under the weather, or so he says. I'd call it a hangover after drinking and gambling for hours last night. Your mother cleaned him out, by the way."

I'd assumed that once Mother got married, that would be the end of her running a gambling den. I was wrong. Pleasantly so, as it was good for Jake's bottom line. The original intent had been to fix up the extra space and turn it into a rental room, and without the gambling, it would have been a flop.

"I know that you have some degenerate inside who's in need of medical help and wants to avoid having the cops show up."

I felt like asking for my clothes back—while he spoke, his intense dark eyes had stripped me naked and checked me over from head to toe. "If he was an outright criminal, I wouldn't have called." I opened the door, stepped back, and swept out my hand.

"Hey, Casio." Dr. A dropped his bag on the coffee table. "I suppose I should ask how the other guy fared."

"Casio got his big ass kicked," I said in a stage whisper. "Before you ask, no, I didn't invite him here." I bounced into the chair. "He broke in and made himself at home."

"I'll take him with me when I leave," Dr. A offered.

Casio sniffed. "You and what army? I'm not dead."

"Well…" He snapped open his bag. "I've got this…" He pulled out a Ruger handgun.

"That's so hot." I smiled.

"I carry guns, and no one ever says that about me." Casio frowned.

"That's hard to believe." I gave him an exaggerated eye roll.

Dr. A laughed. "Roll over, and I'll take your temperature." He motioned to Casio.

Casio shot him the middle finger. "Do you mind?" he said to me. "I'd like some privacy with my doctor."

"Since you apparently don't know it, this is my house. And you haven't been forthcoming, so I'm sitting right here in the hopes of learning *something*."

"Women." Casio sniffed. "Got a big family of them; the men are outnumbered. They're a pain, every one of them."

The Famosa extended family was huge. They procreated in large numbers, mostly females. Casio could joke, but I knew the men in the family kept an eagle eye on every member, especially the women. Every time Brick put up a new family picture, their numbers had increased.

"What happened?" Dr. A took out his stethoscope, listening to Casio's chest. "Breathe." Casio did and grunted in response.

"Fell," Casio said curtly.

Dr. A frowned over his shoulder in my direction. "You wasting my godfather's time? He's an old man and doesn't need to spend his energy being jerked around."

"Ignore him." I tossed my head in Casio's direction. "The last thing I want is for Casio to die or be permanently injured and it be all my fault. Does he need to go to the hospital or can he be dragged to the curb?"

Dr. A asked him a few questions and had him lift his shirt. "It's one of those times that he looks worse than he actually is. Since you're not on the verge of death, I recommend going to see your own doctor," he said to Casio, then turned to me. "Do you need help dragging him out of here?"

"I can do it." Creole stood inside the French doors, arms crossed. "What the devil are you doing here?" he asked Casio as he cut across the room and sat in the chair next to me. He raised his eyebrows at Dr. A in acknowledgement – so they had met, no need for introductions.

Made me wonder if Dr. A was part of the boys' club that I'd once thought only included Creole, Brad, and Didier. Brad had let it slip one day that there were a couple of others but refused to give names. Supposedly, they got together to engage in grueling bike rides and runs along the beach. I'd have to broach that subject again.

"Didn't know you and Madison were friends," Creole said to Casio.

Casio shook his head.

"You can speak cryptically without giving out harmful information. You do it all the time."

"In the neighborhood. Not feeling all that well. Didn't think Red would mind me stopping by. She owes me."

I huffed. "No, I don't. Stop saying that."

"You know who kicked the crap out of you?" Creole asked.

"Am I getting any good drugs out of this house call?" Casio asked Dr. A. "If not, you can leave now."

"I'm not going anywhere; hopefully, you've got a good story. It's probably lame, but I'll make up my own mind." Dr. A moved to the couch. "I am bound by doctor-patient confidentiality. No worries about me spreading all over town that you got your ass kicked."

"Do you know who did it?" Creole asked.

"Not one hundred percent, but I've got a good idea. I'm on vacation, so you need to keep your mouth shut."

"Got it. You're doing something off the books, and we both know how the chief hates that. If you need backup, there's another guy in the area that will help you out."

Dr. A checked his watch and stood. Before snapping his bag closed, he pulled out a business card and scribbled on the back, handing it to me. "Next time you need a doctor, call me directly. Doc's too old for this kind of stuff. He needs to concentrate on fun and that younger girlfriend of his."

"Thanks." I retrieved the card from his fingers and shoved it in my pocket. "I've got your number in my phone already."

Dr. A gave a short wave and headed out the door.

"You need a place to stay?" Creole asked Casio.

"Just for a day or two."

"Don't you have a house, wife and kids to go see?" I asked.

"I show up like this, and she'll know I'm a big liar and didn't have a conference out of town. Once she gets an eyeful of my bruises, she'll know what I've been up to, and once she's done unloading on me, she'll want to kill me." Casio sat up with a grunt.

"I've got an empty cottage," I offered. "You can stay there. Keep to yourself, and you'll have your privacy."

"No, thanks. This couch is comfortable. I'll stay here. Gives me and Creole bonding time." Casio's smarmy smile rattled my nerves.

"No, you won't," Creole said emphatically. "I've got a local place you can stay." He looked at me. "And it's not The Cottages."

"Thank you," I mouthed.

Creole gave Casio a hand up and helped him out the door. Before it closed, he said, "We're going out for dinner."

I nodded.

Chapter Nineteen

"They're back." I stared out the kitchen window, noticing Didier's car parked next to Creole's in the neighbor's driveway across the street and Fab's Porsche in our driveway next to my SUV.

I reached into the refrigerator, pulling out several containers that held a variety of green vegetables and fruits that I'd cleaned, piling them on the counter and reaching underneath for the blender.

"Making me something special?" Creole wore a pair of black jeans and a black t-shirt that hugged his abs. His dark hair had that slightly messy look.

"This is a big welcome back for Didier."

"That might be premature." He shook his finger. "You're up to something." He poured water into the coffee maker.

"Me?" I flashed him a wide-eyed stare. I pulled a sticky note out of my pocket and consulted it before adding the ingredients.

Creole grabbed me by the arm and pulled me tight against him, running a knuckle down my cheek and kissing me.

"You wouldn't lie to me, would you?" He

stared down into my eyes.

"I might." I jumped when he pinched my butt. "But I have no reason to at the moment."

Didier appeared in the kitchen. "Good morning." He was barefoot and wearing only sweatpants, his broad chest bare. He hadn't combed his hair, instead leaving it tousled, a bit of scruff on his cheeks.

"Bon jurio," I greeted with a smile.

"Please don't butcher my native language until after I've had coffee," he grumped.

"No coffee for you." I gave him an exaggerated finger shake. "I've got a little something special for you."

He crossed his arms, eyes narrowed, and stared down at me. "You've done enough lately."

I blushed and turned on the blender, cutting off whatever he was saying. Within a few seconds, I had created a slimy green concoction reminiscent of one of Didier's own.

"I'm not entirely back, but I might as well be. My clothes tend to disappear as soon as I take them off. I don't know how Fab does it. I've tried to catch her in the act."

Creole laughed at his friend's frustration. "Just accept your fate. You're smiling; can't be all that bad."

"It's just a little rough patch." I poured the goo into a glass and handed it to Didier with a flourish.

"I better not be missing anything," Fab said,

crossing the kitchen to stand next to Didier.

Didier took a long drink. He swallowed and choked, or the other way around; I couldn't be sure.

"Yummy?" I asked.

In two long strides, he reached the sink and threw the rest of the drink down the drain. "What in the hell was that?" he boomed.

Fab ran her finger inside the blender container, licking it off. "Ick." She screwed up her nose. "You tried to kill my boyfriend!"

"How many times has Didier made drinks for me? I wanted to reciprocate and got this recipe off the internet." I pushed the sticky note across the counter.

"She make anything for you?" Didier scowled at Creole.

"She loves me." Creole smiled, pulling me to his side.

"You like green drinks," I said indignantly. "It was made from organic ingredients from your favorite grocery store. I have the receipt. There's not a single item in there that will hurt you. The signs at the store didn't say anything about death, or even sickness, connected to anything I bought."

"Did you even taste it?" Didier asked.

"Of course not."

"Thank you for the thought, I think," Didier said.

"Friends again?"

"That's a lot to ask after trying to kill him," Creole said.

I nudged him in the ribs. "I missed you both." I blew a kiss to Fab. "I'm very happy you're back."

"I'm doing the cooking tonight; you'll be safe," Creole said. "Let's go for a run and stop for breakfast."

I pushed away from Creole and walked around the island to hug Didier. "The foursome is back together. It's nice to see you first thing in the morning. In the future, I'll let you handle all the vegetables."

"It was terrible." He made a retching sound. "You're lucky you're not mine. I'll have to have a talk with Creole."

"Oh no you won't. You keep your ideas to yourself." I still remembered a conversation during which Fab told me, stupid smile pasted on her face, that Didier used a mixture of evil methods and sweetness that made her toes curl.

Fab took a bag of fresh-ground coffee from the refrigerator. She and Didier got a special roast only obtainable at a French café they frequented. Didier prepped the espresso machine.

"What did the gravediggers want?" Creole asked. "Another job?"

I ignored Creole and faced Fab. "I've been meaning to tell you that Dickie called and wants us to come for a wedding. He's worried. Every time they branch out, something goes wrong.

We're being hired to make sure everything goes smoothly."

"A wedding!" Didier said. "That's a good one."

Creole snorted. "What did they really want?"

"Raul mentioned it to me, but I didn't realize it was happening so soon." Fab reached for two cups, and Didier filled them to the top with their special brew of muck. "I didn't know how to tell him that the whole idea sounded ghastly, so I kept my mouth shut."

"Really!" Didier hugged Fab to his side. She nodded and kissed his cheek.

"There's another thing… incident… You know how stuff happens," I said to Fab.

"Get to the point," Fab said in exasperation.

"Something happened yesterday that you don't know about… yet." I went on to tell Fab and Didier about Casio's impromptu visit.

"About Casio," Creole said. "I got out of him that the case involved a friend and murder. Why he ended up in the vicinity is unclear; he needed help, and Madison lived close by. Told him not to bring his problems to your door or all bets were off. Also warned him that this house wasn't available as a flop house."

"If Casio sees you, Fab, he'll tell Brick. So if you're not ready to go back to work for the man, you'll need to keep a low profile or tell Casio to keep his mouth shut. He thinks I owe him; well, he really owes me now."

"Brick has a brother?" Didier's mouth thinned.

"Casio's not as big a dick as his brother," Creole said, which fell short of an endorsement. "You definitely want him on your side if the shit hits the fan." He poured himself another cup of coffee. "Casio did ask a bunch of questions about the murder next door. Wanted to know what we knew."

"That's weird," I said. "Tarpon Cove is a long way from his usual jurisdiction up in Miami-Dade County."

"Did you happen to mention the attempted break-ins here?" Fab asked.

Creole nodded. "I gave him the rundown, asked him to keep an eye out and not to knock unless it's a real emergency. Told him if he withheld information that would bring harm to any of us, I'd personally kick his ass and make his current round with someone's boots look like child's play. He assured me that the cops had nothing new." His cell phone pinged. "Stephen left me message; so far, nothing new."

"Is that his real name?" Fab asked.

"You know I can't tell you that. He likes the nickname that you two gave him."

"Don't forget that I can kick an ass or two." Didier flexed his muscles. "Now that I have a carry permit, I don't go anywhere without my trusty firearm. Unless I'm with Fab; we've agreed she can do the shooting."

It was fun to have us all back together again,

and if it took stealing Didier's clothing to make it happen, then I'd be helping Fab.

Chapter Twenty

"Smirk all you want," I said to Fab as she squealed into the parking lot of the Tropical Slumber Funeral Home, sliding into a space across from the red carpet that led into the entry. "Payback can be painful."

"I knew that dress would look hot on you." She smirked.

Getting out of the shower this morning, I'd wondered what to wear to a wedding for which I didn't receive an invitation and didn't know either the bride or the groom. I discovered that Fab had come into my bedroom while I was in the bathroom and laid out a dress that I'd never seen before on the bed. It was hot pink, with a fitted top and flared skirt that backed up her admonition that we weren't attending a funeral. She'd also left a pair of black stilettos, which I kicked under the bed, replacing them with lower heels that I could at least stand in.

Her sleeveless, black mid-thigh sheath hugged her hips and bared her arms, showing off long legs and toned biceps.

"I changed my mind; I don't want to go. I'll

wait in the car," I told her, hitting the doorlocks for effect.

"I'll drag you out." Fab smoothed her hands down the front of her dress. "I get dirt on me in the tussle, and you owe me a new dress."

I shook my head. "We both know you're hot air on that score. Mother, Didier... those names ring a bell? I'd whine so long and loud that they'd wring your neck just to shut me up. If you don't give me the details, I'll get out and walk home."

"It's a wedding. We'll have fun," she said, barely keeping a straight face.

"Who gets married at a funeral home? I mean, eww..."

"You've reached your question quota. Now smile, and let's get out." Fab forced a wide smile.

"Mother would say, 'That will give you wrinkles.'"

"She thinks everything gives you wrinkles." Fab turned her head, grunting at me. "Ask the boys your questions. Something about the building being rich in history."

The funeral home got its start as a drive-thru hot dog stand, which had since undergone major remodeling and add-ons. The locals claimed that, on humid days, the aroma of greasy food was revived.

"I don't think it's ever going to be designated a historic site," I said. "Did you get a present? A cheap toaster, perhaps?"

"You make my head ache."

"Ohh…" I pouted. "Don't worry about the gift. I'll take a tag off a nice big package, scratch out the names, and scribble in ours." Her look of horror-shock forced me to bite my lip so I wouldn't burst into laughter, cutting off this perfect moment of pranking her.

"Behave," she said sternly and got out of the car, shutting the door with a bang.

I got out and joined her, linking my arm in hers. "Aww… don't ruin one of our special kettle/pot moments." Before she could strut the red carpet, I jerked on her arm. "The bride or wedding party must be here; I see two limousines parked at the far end, a foot away from the crematorium." I shivered. "Do you suppose the guys cleaned out one of the viewing rooms to use as a changing room?"

Fab squirmed and ignored me, stepping on the red carpet and working it like a pro all the way to the entry. "Did you remember your Glock?"

"Of course." I patted my leg.

Fab hated it when I forgot her number one rule. The times I did leave my firearm behind always turned out to be when I needed it.

Dickie and Raul, dressed in tuxedos, greeted us as we came through the open doorway. Dickie was well over six feet, painfully thin and pale-complexion; his partner, Raul, was a foot shorter, with an athletic air, muscled and buffed. Both got called away before we could speak with them.

Cars started arriving as we crossed the threshold. The entry was decorated in white stock flowers and baby's breath in a style that bordered on funeral arrangements, which made me wonder who did the ordering. The viewing room doors were all closed, with discreet "Do Not Disturb" signs tied to the knobs. Unless they were locked, Fab would soon have poked her head into each room.

Rather than claiming my usual plastic-slip-covered brocade chair by the door, I followed Fab as she gravitated to Raul, who had moved inside the entrance to the main room where all the services took place.

"Tell us what you want done," I said.

Dickie, who had been speaking to the pianist, ended his conversation and joined Raul. His frown deepened, arms crossed. "A wedding." Lost in thought, his agitation level grew.

The man didn't like anything that interfered with his dressing-the-dead skills. I knew without a doubt that this new brainchild was courtesy of Raul, who was always on the lookout for a quirky idea to set them apart from the competition. I knew that he often encouraged Dickie to give his plans a try before vetoing them. Knowing the two as I did, they could be talked into just about anything short of illegal.

"How about some details?" I asked Raul. "Your friend here either didn't know or wouldn't share. I suspect the latter." I nudged Fab.

Fab and Raul had bonded when she stayed in their house several years ago, some would say hid out. That she was abrupt and tended to rudeness never seemed to bother the man; he always smiled indulgently, even when it was aimed at him.

"The bride chose this venue because her father got his first job here as a teen, working the drive-thru window. Now that her father is deceased, she thought it would be a nice way to include him and that he would enjoy it."

"Why were we invited?"

"Dickie and I talked it over. These people aren't locals, so we don't know them like we do our regular clientele, where we typically know the deceased or a family member. We've had much more peace of mind since the two of you agreed."

"That was nice of *us*," I mumbled.

"Excuse me." An older woman walked out of the main room. "Could you remove the mannequin at the front? The man is quite disconcerting to look at and not appropriate for wedding decor."

Raul paled a little. "We'll remove him right now." He and Dickie engaged in a glare-off.

"Raul, you're the one who forgot." Dickie waved his hand in a dismissive manner and trailed after the woman.

"I'll be right back," Raul said. "Dickie can't carry Mr. Burns by himself."

Fab, who had disappeared momentarily, returned. "What's going on?"

"A tiff between the guys as to who does what," I said to her back as she peered into the main room. "If asked, what do we tell people – bride's side or groom's?" I waited for a response and didn't get one. "I'm going to say the bride is your friend and I'm your date. What's her name anyway?"

"You know I don't remember names."

Raul and Dickie came back through a side door that I hadn't known existed carrying the "mannequin" on a chair. He appeared to my untrained eye to be a recently deceased man of about sixty. The boys had obviously been sucked into another theme funeral. The gentleman, one leg crossed over the other, was dressed in a plaid suit with suspenders that dated back to an era before I was born. There was a cigarette in his hand.

I need an aspirin.

Dickie lowered his end of the chair to the floor, opened the first viewing room, and the two carried the man inside. When they returned, Dickie said, "Mr. Burns had a rather large viewing earlier, and at the last minute, we moved the mourners into the main room to accommodate them all. We were getting ready to move him back to his room when the wedding party started arriving. The funeral is tomorrow."

"Mr. Burns planned his own funeral," Raul

said. "He knew exactly what he wanted and even included pictures in his funeral plan."

Dickie checked his watch. "The wedding ceremony begins in fifteen minutes. Raul, will you check with everyone and make sure there aren't any last minute snags?" He whispered to me, "Some people think I don't make a good first impression."

"You're fine." I patted his arm. "We'll sit in the back."

Fab had a big smile pasted on her face, clearly enjoying the drama. I followed her to our favorite spot—seats she'd reserved next to the exit, with a clear shot to the front door.

"Do you think if I wrapped my fingers in your hair, I could swing you around, right off your feet?" I asked sweetly.

"You always suck the fun out of everything."

"Not always. Did you know about Mr. Burns?"

"Oh, heck no. But I did get a picture. Wait until your mother sees it."

"You're turning Mother into a ghoul, and I'm not sure I like it."

Chapter Twenty-One

The normally canned music used for funerals had been replaced by a pianist seated in the corner. The grey-haired woman with wire-rimmed glasses concentrated carefully on her rendition of *Here Comes the Bride*, but still threw in a few notes the original didn't have.

The bride was stunning in a backless, floor-length gown with a full skirt and full veil. A younger man, waiting in the doorway, extended his arm and led her down the aisle.

The ceremony started without a hitch, everyone seated and well behaved. Fab put her head on my shoulder, and I shook it off. If I had to be awake, then so did she.

I leaned over and whispered, "Can we leave as soon as they say their I-dos?"

She fidgeted in her chair and finally said, "We're staying for the reception."

"What happens when someone wants to know who we are? You never answered me before. Then what? The old 'friend of a friend' excuse hardly works in this setting."

The person in front of us turned, finger to her lips, and shushed me. I almost cracked a smile when the lime green feather fell from her purple velvet hat, an exact match for her dress.

Fab smacked my hand, shaking her head in faux annoyance. The woman smiled at her.

The preacher concluded the ceremony with, "You may kiss the bride." The groom lifted the veil and jumped back after a quick glimpse of her face, the veil falling back into place. He yelled, "What the f —?"

Silence descended over the room.

Fab shot out of her seat, motioning for me to guard the door as she hugged the side wall, where she wouldn't attract a lot of attention, and headed to the front.

The groom turned on the preacher, yelling, "This better not be legal. I'd never marry this bitch."

"Robbie, I love you." The bride swept the train of her dress over one arm and launched herself at him, wrapping her arms around his middle, grasping and clawing to keep from falling to the floor.

The groom loosened her arms, which she then wrapped around his neck. He tugged on her hands, prying her loose, and pushed her backwards. She stumbled to the floor in an ungraceful heap. He bent down. "Where is Leslie?" he screeched in her face.

Gasps were heard around the room.

"Leslie?" a woman screamed from the front row.

The woman raced forward. I guessed her to be the mother of the bride. She peered down into the face of the woman on the floor and suddenly collapsed beside her.

Fab flew to the woman's side. I held my breath, not sure what she intended to do.

"She's fine," Fab shouted over the voices that had begun to escalate. "Just fainted. Do we have a doctor or nurse here?"

The bride encircled the groom's legs in a death grip, causing him to tip forward. He caught himself and, instead of landing on top of her, fell to the side. He grabbed her shoulders, dragged her face to his, and unleashed a tirade of words that were unintelligible. In return, the woman clawed at his face.

The groom shrugged her off. "Call the police," he yelled. "We need to find Leslie."

Fab joined Raul, who was trying to calm down the groom. Fab laughed, which earned her two dirty looks.

I heard one couple say, "Who the hell is that woman?"

Fab helped the "bride" to her feet, turning her towards the guests. A few of them stared back in shocked recognition. Fab strong-armed her part of the way down the aisle before she twisted away and ran to grab the microphone from the stand.

Fab let her go and motioned me down the aisle. "She's not the bride."

"Figured that out by the groom's reaction," I said, the sarcasm unmistakable in my voice.

"Everyone, sit down," the faux bride screamed into the microphone, which reacted with ear-splitting noises of its own.

"Nobody noticed until now?" I asked.

Fab shrugged, as if to say, *these things happen.*

"I love Robbie," the woman started. "Leslie stole him from me, and I got him back. Serves the bitch right. We're married now, and there's not a damn thing any of you can do about it."

Deluded woman, there was nothing legal about this marriage. Tired of standing, I headed back to my seat, not wanting to be far from an exit. "I'm not missing a minute of this drama."

On my heels, Fab said, "You think the other bride is dead?" She motioned me to move over a seat, wanting to be on the aisle.

The lady in the row in front of us turned around again. "Shut up, you two. Stop your caterwauling. I can't hear a damn thing."

"You're overly dramatic." I stared back at the woman.

Fab lifted the skirt of her dress, showing her the Walther strapped to her thigh, then leaned forward and growled.

I loved her imitation of an unhappy dog about ready to chew a leg off.

"Gun!" the woman squealed, jumping up, tripping over the leg of her chair, and skidding into the aisle.

Fab climbed up on her chair and shouted, "False alarm. We're security."

When the woman shouted "gun," the new bride had run to Robbie and he'd wrapped his arms around her and appeared to be comforting her.

Guess he doesn't hold a grudge, even after "marrying" the wrong woman.

Raul grabbed the microphone, tapping the side to get everyone's attention. "We'll be making an announcement shortly as to what will be happening next. In the meantime, if you'd like to go out to the patio, we have a bar set up with wine and beer." He pointed to the sliding doors.

I tapped Fab's leg, pointing to the chair. Fab ignored me and instead went to confer with Dickie, who was waving frantically from the far side of the room.

She returned faster than I expected.

"Dickie spotted Leslie through the windows of one of the viewing rooms. She's tied up and the door's locked. He went to get the keys." Fab jerked on my arm. "Why wait?" She retrieved a lockpick from her bra and, without backward glance, headed to the viewing rooms.

I hung back, not wanting to get an eyeful of a dead person propped up in all their glory.

Fab started with the last door, opened it, peeked in, and put away her lockpick, motioning me forward. In the corner lay Leslie, bound and gagged, her face twisted with rage.

To say Robbie had a type put it mildly. The two women were similar enough that they could be sisters, and the crazy ex had somehow managed to get the exact same wedding dress.

Fab crossed to Leslie, speaking softly, introducing herself. She untied her, removed the gag, and helped to her feet.

Instead of saying "thank you," Leslie slapped Fab's hands away. "I'm suing this place." She pushed past us, hiked up her dress, and ran out the door.

I backed out of the room; no body inside but still creepy. "I predict fireworks. Since you've politely reminded me several times that you're the ass-kicker, you need to follow and keep the peace. I'll stay in the back and be the one to take pictures for a change." We hurried back into the main room.

"Leslie!" The woman who'd fainted sobbed, throwing her arms out.

Leslie didn't acknowledge her mother, shoving past people, her eyes on her nemesis. She halted in front of the other woman, checking her over from head to toe, and judging by her ice-cold glare, the first thing she'd noticed was that they had on the same dress.

"Marla, you bitch," Leslie roared. "I don't know what the hell is going on in that bat-crazy head of yours, but Robbie's going to be my husband." She swung her fist and missed her target, but clocked Robbie—who'd made the mistake of stepping between the two women at the wrong moment—a good one on the side of the face.

Word spread like wildfire to the guests who had gone to the patio for free drinks. They crowded the doorway, and others joined those that hadn't left their seats.

Marla reclaimed the microphone, panting heavily. "He's mine." She blew a kiss to Robbie. "Aren't you, babe?"

Robbie stood mute.

Marla turned her attention back to Leslie. "Ask Robbie where he slept last night. Ask him about how he told me it was the best sex of his life. Wait." She stuck up her hand. "And ask about the night before and the one before that." She turned to the crowd. "Where's Robbie's family? See them anywhere? They hate her. She's crazy."

Plenty of crazy going around.

Marla had no intention of giving up the spotlight. "The only reason Robbie asked you to marry him was we got in a stupid fight." She waved her finger at Leslie, nose scrunched up as though she smelled. "Robbie's weakness is money, and let's face it, hon; your family has plenty. You think he was going to give me up? He wasn't about to, and certainly not when Husky Robbie didn't like you and couldn't get it up half the time. You frigid bitch."

Men needed to stop naming their dicks; more

often than not, it came back to embarrass them.

Clearly, no one had the desire to shut the woman up, the spectators remaining mute. Robbie, looking shell-shocked, took it all in, obviously unable to comprehend how ruined he was—no woman but Marla would want him now. Leslie stared, with no idea how to stop the trainwreck.

"Robbie likes it rough, but you don't do that, Miss Vanilla," Marla continued with zeal. "You lie there like a frigid stick. I couldn't get Robbie to see that money isn't everything; he needed my help, or he'd be living out his life in complete misery. Hell, he already is. I love him enough to save him from himself."

What rubbish! I rolled my eyes. If Fab had been the real bride, she'd have shot Robbie already, the heck with witnesses.

Leslie roused herself from her stupor. "You're a liar. He was with me last night."

Marla smirked. "Not all night he wasn't." She gripped Leslie's dress in her hands and ripped it down the front. "This is my dress. My husband. And guess damn what—we're married."

Robbie stepped between the two.

Leslie sidestepped him and hurled herself at Marla, sending them both to the floor, where they rolled around, pulling hair and landing the occasional slap.

Raul and Fab let them get a few punches in before simultaneously jumping into the fray, each tugging a woman to the opposite corner. Neither wanted to cooperate, and they slowed the process by kicking and screaming. When Leslie started to crawl away, Fab planted her foot squarely in the center of her backside. She should be thankful Fab had left her stilettos under the chair.

"I should've known you'd be here." Kevin sat on the seat next to me.

"Shouldn't you be up there breaking up the fight?"

"Chick fight? The new guy is right behind me; he can do it. Last time I jumped between two brawling women, I damn near lost something I cherish." He flashed a boyish smile.

"You wouldn't sacrifice your… or one of your… for the sake of the job?"

He snorted. "Not if I can help it."

Another uniformed deputy walked through the door and paused next to Kevin. "You take the one on the right; I'll take the left," he said.

"Put a bullet in the ceiling; it won't be the first." I pointed upward at several patches. "Free advice, by the way."

Kevin sighed and stood up. "Don't leave. I have questions for you."

"Good luck," I chirped.

At the first sign of law enforcement, Fab let the women start brawling again. She appeared at my side. "Let's go."

"Can't. I'm being held for questioning. Before

you start arguing, I'll remind you that it beats a jail cell."

"Kevin again!" Fab knelt in the chair in the row ahead of me, leaning over the seat. "Two women fighting over loser Robbie when they could go out and get another man who'd keep it zipped."

The two officers pulled the women apart, and everything quieted down up in front. The new deputy announced that the wedding wouldn't be happening and told everyone to leave through the nearest exit.

Someone in the crowd grumbled, "What about the one that already happened? That one legal?"

Another said, "Is Robbie married?"

"You can go home, and I'll get a ride in the hearse," I said, tired of watching Fab punch the back of the seat.

Fab ignored me, scanning the room. "Don't look at him." She motioned to Kevin, who was moving in our direction. "We could get lucky and he'll pass us by.

I glanced up. "Don't think so."

"We caught a break. They were tired and ready to stop fighting." He waved to his partner. "They each threatened to press charges, and when I informed them that in that case they'd both be going to jail, they stopped talking."

"You need to arrest Robbie," I said.

"Being a douche isn't a crime." Kevin appeared amused. "Besides, once I finished questioning him, he snuck out the side door. Judging by the squealing of tires that I heard, he left the property rather quickly."

"The brides?"

He shrugged. "I'm just happy they decided to leave without further incident."

"What do you want with me?" I asked. "If you make it short, you can get a free meal at Jake's, the protect-and-serve discount."

"Just wanted you to stick around in case I couldn't get a straight story out of anyone. And I never get a discount."

"Says who?"

"Phil."

I wondered why and then remembered. "That's what you get for having her car towed."

"That was years ago. She needs to get over it."

"You display a certain amount of charm at times; use it on her, smooth things over already."

"I'm certain that was a compliment." Goofy smile on his face.

I stood, happy his partner had reappeared and needed his attention. "This has been a wedding to remember." I went into the entry, where a couple of the guests were grabbing presents and heading out the door.

I resisted the urge to move the gift tags around, instead frowning at Fab, who ended her conversation with Raul.

"Whose idea was this dumb job?" I asked Fab. "Oh yeah, you."

Chapter Twenty-Two

I walked down the stairs very slowly to give myself maximum eavesdropping time. There was more going on with the night's upcoming events than I knew about, and no one appeared to be planning to enlighten me anytime soon.

I vaguely remembered Didier and Brad mentioning a dinner party to schmooze a business contact for a real estate deal that had them excited, but that wasn't tonight. Technically, every deal got a hand vote by all investors, mostly perfunctory. This would be the biggest deal yet.

"I thought tonight was about family," I said when I reached the bottom of the stairs. I'd envisioned a barbeque and a swim, sneaking off to bed early with Creole. "Who exactly is coming? And who the heck is Richards?"

Mother and Spoon had already bailed; if they even knew what the plan was, she hadn't mentioned it when she called to tell me that she and Spoon had plans to sneak out on the boat to haul in a fish or two.

Creole glared at Didier. I wasn't the only one who didn't get the memo; we were both dressed in bathing suits.

"I didn't think to remind you; thought you'd have it noted on your calendar," Fab said from a nearby chair, legs draped over the back, patented smirk firmly in place. "This is a business dinner for the partnership. There's a new project on the table, which is where Benton Richards comes in."

Apparently, Fab was still annoyed at me for locking her up with Didier. It didn't matter that they were back together; she didn't like being bested by anyone.

"We have reservations at The Grill, the trendy new place on the water in Marathon." Didier looked apologetic. "Brad ordered a limo for all of us. Minus Richards—he called and will be meeting us at the restaurant."

"Dress-up." Fab flashed a big smile at Creole, knowing he preferred casual.

"In the Keys?" My eyebrow arched. "I'll call and double check."

Creole crossed to me and hauled me against his chest, tucking me to his side.

"We're meeting Richards and his date at 6:30," Didier said.

"See you guys later." Creole turned me back towards the stairs, his hand on my lower back.

* * *

Coming out of the bathroom while loosely tying my bathrobe, I spotted a dress hanging from a hook over the closet door. So much for pool attire. I wondered how many more surprises there would be tonight.

"You picking out my clothes now?" My attention turned to Creole, standing there in a pair of Calvin Klein's. I whistled, wondering how much time we had.

He snorted. "I grabbed up my towel to cover myself when your friend, knowing we were in here, picked the lock and marched right in."

I tried to bite back a laugh, but it came out anyway.

"Laugh now. Wait until it happens to you. You'll be demanding a beatdown."

"Won't happen again. I'll have a talk with her," I assured him. "How did you get rid of her?"

"I pushed her out of the room, right into the arms of Didier. When he asked what the hell, I handed him her lockpick and shut the door in their faces. Then I heard an angry male voice moving down the hall and another door slamming." His lips quirked up.

"I vote that we drive ourselves." I untied my robe and let it fall to the floor.

"Oh, babe." Two steps later, he had me in his arms. With one hand on my hip and the other curled around the nape of my neck, he lowered his mouth to mine. "Later…" he murmured, kissing me again. "We have to get dressed." He pushed back and slapped my ass.

"You're no fun." I pouted.

"You'll take those words back." He pointed to the dress. "We have ten minutes."

"Ten?"

I took the dress bag down, shoving it to the back of the closet, and instead choosing one that Mother had bought me for my birthday. A curve-hugging, sleeveless black dress, the bottom half leather, the top suede. It might surprise some people to know that I could pick out my own clothes. Although, if I'd had something totally hideous, I'd have been tempted to wear it. Fab must have learned her lesson about making my shoe choices, since none were lying on the bed. I pulled out a new pair of low-heeled black suede slip-ons that I bought to match the dress.

"Did I tell you how incredibly hot you look tonight?" Creole growled possessively.

I twirled around, blushing furiously. "Your favorite?"

"My fave is the strapless bra and that bit of lace you call underwear."

I didn't think it possible for my cheeks to burn even more. "You're pretty smoking yourself." I ran my hand across his chest.

He wore a white button-down shirt that stretched across his chest, the top two buttons undone and the knot in his tie lopsided. His black suit pants hugged his hips.

His gravelly laugh sent a chill down my spine. His deep-blue eyes bored into mine, knowing I was thinking naughty thoughts of which he was the star.

"Ready, love?" He held out his arm.

We came down the stairs together. I hip-bumped him as we went. He laughed at my attempt to mess up his usually windswept hair, which he'd succeeded in combing into something manageable.

"No drinks?" he joked with Didier, who looked like he'd walked out of an Armani ad in his black suit.

"There's a well-stocked bar in the limo."

Voices from the hallway announced Brad's arrival. He escorted a woman I'd never seen before into the living room. The man posing as my brother had the air of a man to be reckoned with. He'd replaced the easygoing version of himself with a sterner one. His jacket hung from his frame as though it was made for him, and he and his date could model for a magazine cover.

Another reminder that I need to check in on my brother more often.

"Pamela Stone, this is my sister, Madison, and her boyfriend, Creole." Brad followed that up by introducing Didier, and then Fab, who'd just came down the stairs behind us in a sexy black dress that molded to her frame.

Pamela, a six-foot brunette goddess, had surely been poured into the curve-hugging red dress. Her breasts about ready to pop out of the low neckline, she appeared bored. She extended her fingertips. "If we get to be friends, you can call me Pammy." Her eyes swept over me in a dismissive fashion, then lingered on Creole until I thought about putting my fist in her nose.

I knew the slight choking noise next to me came from Creole trying to disguise a laugh.

Jazz and Snow, who'd been watching from the daybed as the room filled up with people, jumped down and wandered over to Brad for their obligatory ear scratch. When he bent down, Pamela wrapped her hand around his arm and jerked him back. "You don't want to get hair all over you. Dirty fat things."

I hissed, and Creole tightened his hold on me. "We don't want to be late," he said with insincere cheerfulness. "We'll toast to a good business deal in the car." He steered me away from them. "If we're lucky, one of the cats will heave up a hairball on her stilettos," he whispered.

"Pammy does not make a good first impression." I glared at her back. "She checked out my house like she'd stepped into a third-rate motel."

Creole and I were the last to leave, locking up and following everyone to the limo. The last to climb in, we sat on the far end of the bench.

Chapter Twenty-Three

The Grill was a small, intimate restaurant overlooking the water and decorated in high-end beach chic. The hostess announced with an apology that it would be a few minutes before the table was ready and directed us to the bar.

"Drink?" Creole asked.

"Tequila, straight-up."

Creole laughed in my ear. "I don't think so. This isn't the kind of restaurant that would appreciate you dancing on the table." He joined Didier at the bar.

Brad whispered in Pamela's ear and headed over to me. Pamela scowled and quickly latched onto Fab, who stood nearby.

Brad held out a chair for me and sat opposite me at the small table.

"New girlfriend?" I asked.

"Behave." His brown eyes sparked.

"I can kick your butt. Okay, maybe not, but I can irritate the hell out of you."

The corners of Brad's mouth turned up.

"Oh look, a smile."

"Pamela's a friend. And doing me a favor." He leaned forward. "We'll talk about it later."

Creole returned, handing me a glass of red wine.

Brad stood up. "If it tastes like swill, take it up with Frenchie; he pre-selected the wine."

"Lunch this week?" I asked.

"I'll call you."

"You better. Don't think I won't track you down." I watched as he picked up two glasses of wine and returned to Pamela's side. I almost laughed when, as soon as Pamela's attention turned to Brad, Fab used the opportunity to disappear.

"To us." Creole clinked his glass against mine in a toast.

"Let's sneak out of here." I took a drink and licked my lips. "I don't know why we're here; we're silent investors."

"Too late." Creole looked over my shoulder. "Didier's on the far side of the bar talking to a man—Richards, I presume."

Engaged in conversation with Didier and Fab, Benton Richards stood with his back to me. His head a mass of brown hair, his stance was tall and straight, and his wide shoulders were prominent in his flawlessly tailored suit.

The hostess reappeared, menus in hand, and led the way to the table. I looked around the room. All the other tables were filled with couples or small groups of people. We'd been relegated to one side of the main room, the table for eight covered in white linen, china, and gleaming silverware. If Mother were here, she'd be horrified it wasn't a window table.

Introductions were made before we sat.

"Nobody calls him Benton," Creole whispered. "It's just Richards."

There was an intensity to the man's brown eyes as they swept over the women in the group. He gave off the authority of a CEO.

Richards introduced his date. "Carly Simms."

The tall, stick-thin, ponytailed blonde wore a silver dress, the hem hitting her above the knee, a deep side slit showing off well-toned thighs. Before responding to our greetings, she looked up at her date. "Nice to meet you," she said softly, curling herself back into his side.

Two waiters appeared, wine bottles in hand, and refilled the glasses. Once our orders were taken, conversation resumed. The mood music, louder than usual in a restaurant, made it difficult to hear anything.

After two glasses of wine, which I slugged down with brutal efficiency, I decided my own dinner parties were better — the atmosphere was relaxed, nowhere near this pretentious, and I didn't have my sexy-girl bra digging into my sides.

Pamela soon bored Fab, and she stopped pretending to listen as the woman chattered on. The woman turned her gaze on me. "What do you do?"

"I'm her sidekick." I flicked my eyes in Fab's

direction. "I lend a hand when needed and keep her from getting killed." Brad would probably want to lock me away if I went on to detail just how many times I'd gotten Fab out of someone's house after the occupants had come home earlier than expected.

"Won't anyone hire you for an actual job?"

Fab answered. "I admire how many people Madison has helped when no one else would step forward."

"I'm very proud of you," Creole said, his lips brushing my cheek.

The food arrived, the two waiters serving everyone with efficiency. Everyone got busy eating, which slowed the small talk.

Pamela zeroed in on Carly. "Do you always have to get permission from your master before speaking?" She giggled.

I'd also noticed that Carly didn't answer any question without a nod from Richards but wasn't rude enough to bring it up.

"Pamela!" I interrupted, hoping to drag her attention away from the other woman, who now looked decidedly uncomfortable.

Richards held court at the other end of the table. The men talked business, excluding the women, and snippets of condo-development talk floated down the table: how some were rented and how would that alter the bottom line, the possibility of a quick flip bandied about, and so forth.

"You two are so different." Pamela looked between Fab and me. "Je suis surpris que vous êtes amis."

"Surprised you're friends," Fab translated for me. "Best friends, in fact."

Didier clasped Fab's hand in his, smiling at her.

"You only speak English?" Pamela asked in a pitying tone.

Carly shot me a look of sympathy.

I took another sip of my wine, considering whether to blurt out the handful of dirty French words that I knew or mention that I took Spanish in high school and could butcher that language as well, but I wasn't here to be entertaining.

"Do you two have other friends?" Pamela asked. When neither Fab nor I answered, she said, "How quaint."

Brad leaned in to her and whispered in a hair-raising tone, "Keep quiet."

She linked her arm in his and laid her head on his shoulder.

Fab and I exchanged raised eyebrows.

Richards stared at me from the other end of the table. I'd caught him a couple of times and stared right back; when his jaw clenched, I didn't bother to look in his direction again. He also checked out Fab, who'd thoroughly ignored him from the start.

Carly contributed nothing to the conversation. Whenever someone directed a question her way, she provided a minimally worded response, reserving her reactions to smiling at Richards.

Plans were made to walk the property in question. Didier told Richards that Fab and I were partners, along with my mother and Spoon, and that we'd be included. That revelation seemed to surprise Richards.

The waiter returned with dessert menus, and Richards waved him away without checking with anyone. My jaw tightened at his high-handedness; I'd been looking forward to dessert. And it was Richards who stood to leave first. The check showed up in front of Didier; he scribbled his signature and handed it back.

"Since you don't have a real job, you can get this field trip planned," Pamela said to me, out of everyone's hearing. "I'd do it, but my schedule is booked."

"You never said what it is you do," I said.

Pamela either wasn't listening or didn't care to answer. She continued, "We'll all meet at the property so as not to waste time."

"I'm a business woman with interests of my own. My biggest job is minding other people's business," I said sweetly. "I'll have my assistant check with everyone and set up a mutually agreeable time."

The men had headed to the exit, where Richards' laugh could be heard over the voices of the others. Didier and Brad appeared relaxed.

Creole hung back and put his arm around me,

and we walked out together.

The cool evening air swirled around me, smelling of salt and sand. The last thing I wanted was to get in the limo and endure the freezing air conditioner. My party manners had worn thin; as soon as we were inside, I'd check to see if the windows rolled down.

"Don't run off," Creole said in my ear. "Didier's waving to me."

We said our good-byes under the outside portico. Before I could step away, Richards kissed both my cheeks. He apparently didn't get the memo that I don't do touchy anything with strangers. "It was nice to meet you," he said.

I didn't believe him. True to form, his date remained mute, a fake smile plastered on her face.

The valet signaled to Richards, who took his date's arm and left without a backwards glance.

Fab appeared at my side. "Can't say I enjoy business meetings."

"The best part is we're best friends again. Don't deny it; I have witnesses who heard you say it."

"You're so weird."

Brad and Pamela were the first to climb into the limo. A brick wall appeared behind my back; I stepped back into Creole's arms and let him lead me to the car. "Let's sit in the same place; I can stretch out and use your lap as a pillow."

Fab and Didier got in last, and the doors

closed.

We claimed the back bench; I kicked off my shoes and turned to Creole. "You remember Pamela's last name?"

"What are you up to?" he growled in my ear.

"Nothing… yet."

"Put Richards on that list. Something about him I don't like."

Chapter Twenty-Four

"Slow down," I grouched at Fab. "You're going to make me sick, and I'm going to stretch sideways and do it in your lap. We didn't get into any trouble today; don't ruin it with vomit."

Fab scrunched her nose in a tight ball.

"How do you find these shoe outlets? This one had better prices than the last one." I'd found two pairs; not sure how many Fab's tall shopping bag held.

"One of those shifty connections that you complain about." Fab glanced in the rearview mirror and pulled around a car amidst a flurry of honking horns. "You get a report back on our dreadful dinner companion, *Pammy*?"

"That was supposed to be top secret; how did you find out?"

"You think I don't know you? I thought your brother had stopped thinking with his—"

"Don't finish your sentence; I get it." I blushed. "Enough of my brother and sex talk in the same sentence. Answer my question."

"I eavesdropped in the limo. It was a little hard to make out your words; you need to speak up."

I shook my head. "Phil's working on it. I made it a rush job. I'm arrange the next dinner party—beach attire and shoeless." I laughed at the pained look on her face.

"What has you suspicious? Pamela acted like any other snotty rich person that hasn't had their money long. Definitely not old money." Fab sniffed.

"I also put in a request for a check on Benton just-call-me-Richards."

"There's a cold one. If his date the Doormat had any personality, Richards squashed it out of her."

"What was her name? I'm getting as bad as you." I ignored her snort. "Carly, that's it. She looked at Richards like he was a god. Speaking of people thinking with their hoohah…"

"You better not be lumping me in that group."

"Hardly. You scored with Didier, and the family approves."

"Damn you. Okay, thank you. I was never mad about the kidnapping. Miffed that Madeline got the better of me. I was happy to be locked in a room with a big bed and Didier. Your mother thinks of everything." Fab laughed. "Food for days, and Didier couldn't hold out that long. Once I saw the deadbolt, I knew we weren't going anywhere and only made a show of attempting to free us."

"How did Didier take his confinement?"

"At first, his ego took a hit, tricked by two

women and all. In the end, we dissected your game plan and laughed. I won't say we immediately jumped into one another's arms but close enough. We missed each other; it wasn't one-sided, as I'd feared."

"Aww." I tugged on a lock of her hair. "So happy you're back together."

"Me too. Now stop touching me." Fab flung her hair over her other shoulder. "Didier wants me to work with him on the condo project. Schmooze the high-dollar clients, run the show room, and have a couple of employees to tell what to do."

"You're beautiful, intelligent, and classy; you'd be a hit at the schmoozy stuff. The problem, as I see it, is you don't like being in one place for long and you really don't like people." I also couldn't see her sitting in an office all day, no matter how opulently decorated. The woman had more energy than five people.

"I can do this. Didier made the position sound exciting," she said, sounding like she was trying to convince herself. "I'd rather set up the security in each unit and the entire building."

That's my girl!

Fab continued, "In the meantime, as part of my effort to compromise, I promised to herd cats and mentioned starting a ride service for old drunks."

I leaned back against the seat and laughed.

"Didier really didn't like the last idea. I got a

slap on my butt, a hard one." Fab made a face. "And you know… which led to stuff… It all ended well." She careened into the driveway.

"What the…" My mouth fell open, and I pointed through the windshield.

Fab hung over the steering wheel. "I'd like to see the tool that was used to wreak that destruction."

The garden window had been shattered. Shards of glass lay on the ground, every pane gone, the frame twisted and mangled.

I jumped out of the car and walked carefully through the glass. The six-foot-long window was one of my favorite renovations, replaced after a hailstorm cracked the previous, paned window. The inside shelf was missing, not a plant in sight. Glass littered the ledge, and I guessed there was more in the sink.

"This is the third attempted break-in," I pointed out. "Someone wants something really bad. What is it?"

"That's what we need to figure out." Fab unholstered her Walther.

"This one didn't have any lock-picking experience, much like the first one. Given a choice, I'd rather they beat the lock off." I wanted to pull Fab back, but she was out of reach and at the front door already. "Don't go inside; there might still be someone hanging around. Since I know you can hear me," I grumbled, "don't shoot up my furniture or get blood anywhere."

"We come face to face with someone we don't recognize, shoot fast. We'll each grab an arm and drag the carcass to the patio."

"Dead should be a last option," I cautioned her.

"I'll take the upstairs."

This time, she truly wasn't listening. I caught up and followed her. Fab poked her head into the living room before creeping up the stairs. Glock in hand, I cut left into the kitchen.

The kitchen looked like a war zone—broken flower pots, dirt, and flowers strewn around. I unlocked the garage door and stuck my head inside; nothing out of the ordinary. Fab would know at a glance, as that area was her domain.

I tiptoed across the kitchen and headed for the French doors, which were closed and locked, as they'd been when we left. I threw open the doors, preparing for the possibility of dragging a body outside.

Fab stood at the top of the stairs, shoving her gun in the waistband of her black skinny jeans. "Nothing up here."

"Careful," I said when she got to the bottom. I pointed to her feet; she'd kicked off her heels. "There's glass everywhere." I grabbed a pair of flip-flops from the boot tray by the door. "Don't worry, your feet won't fall off if you wear them for a few minutes." I handed them over.

"I hope I don't get feet cooties," she grumbled.

Seven-year-old-child antics made me laugh

every time.

"Who's going to clean up this mess?" Fab grumbled some more.

"Not you. I'm going to try to salvage my plants, because you'll just throw them out the window."

"It doesn't look like whoever it was made it inside." She whipped on some rubber gloves she'd retrieved from a side drawer and leaned over the sink, inspecting the window. "The metal bar in the middle is the reason. It held. Whoever it was had crappy tools or didn't know what they were doing, probably both."

"I'm calling the window store to come out and board it up. They'll know the dimensions, so I won't have to look anything up. First the police. Creole got annoyed I waited so long last time."

Fab went out to the front and snapped pics. Coming back inside, she handed me her phone. "Call Didier for me."

"Let's go outside." I grabbed two waters and headed to the patio.

I called the police. Since it wasn't an emergency, I bypassed 911 and called the main number. After calling the window people and being informed that they didn't do that kind of work, I called Billy. I texted Creole and Didier the same message: *Attempted break-in. All clear.* "You owe me." I dropped her phone in her lap.

Our phones rang almost in unison. Creole's picture popped up on mine, and since Fab answered in French, I knew hers was Didier.

"What the hell is going on over there?" Creole asked.

"Good question. We need to find out."

"Have I mentioned the L-word lately?" He lowered his voice to a sexy rumble.

"Oh yes, you have. Let's discuss it later at your house."

"Clothing optional?"

I giggled into the phone. "I'll bring the food. Your second-favorite: Mexican from Jake's." Hamburgers weren't as easy to heat up; if you weren't careful, they turned into shoe leather. I heard a voice in the background and knew the conversation was coming to an end. "Stay safe."

"I'll text when I'm on my way."

I hung up at the same time as Fab.

Fab turned and peered over her shoulder. "How did we get so lucky?"

I followed her hair toss and saw Kevin standing in the opening of the kitchen window. He waved. "You two touch anything?"

We both shook our heads. "Rock, paper... to see who lets him in?" I suggested.

Fab flashed her "you're nuts" look. "I'll do it."

"For your first security job," I said to her retreating back, "beef up the system around here. We haven't needed it before, but we do now." Fab turned at the door, and I added. "Don't get all high-tech and rig a gun to shoot when the door opens."

Fab poked her head out. "What?" She turned back to me. "Do you want me to let him in?"

I nodded. "He needs to write up a report."

Kevin glared at Fab as he came in the door. "You're popular lately." He bent down in the entry. "Footprints."

"They're mine. I got caught up in an emotional moment and forgot. It doesn't appear the intruder got inside."

I picked up the cat bowls, setting them on the counter and checking for glass, then dumped the contents in the trash. The cozy cat couple were curled up by the patio doors, asleep, clearly not bothered by the drama.

"Make my job easier: get me a list of the people that dislike you. If it won't take too long." Kevin grinned.

I made a circle with my fingers. "That's how many people I know that would break in and steal from me."

Fab stood by my side. "More people like me than they do you," she said to Kevin.

I laughed, which only raised Kevin's irritation level.

"The fingerprint people are behind me," Kevin said.

"They can do their job outside," I said. "Last time, they scattered fingerprint dust and left stains on an area rug that never came out. And got squat in terms of a lead."

"If you offer me a soda, I'll tell them to be

careful," Kevin said.

"Help yourself."

"Oh, let me." Fab crossed to the refrigerator and opened the door. "What kind don't you like? I'll give you that one." Before Kevin could answer, she handed him a can. "Don't expect seconds."

I hung my head to cover my laughter, but my shaking shoulders gave me away.

Kevin jerked the can away with no thank you. "Haven't seen you at The Cottages, and I have a few questions about the murder. One of your neighbors claims that you and your girlfriend here had a very friendly relationship with Scotch."

"I talked to him in passing a few times, but that's it."

"And what do you have to contribute?" Kevin asked Fab.

"I never spoke to the man."

"Knowing you, I believe that," Kevin said. "You should board up the window."

"Great advice," I said.

"What's he doing here?" Kevin pointed to Billy, who sauntered up the driveway, stepping aside for the forensics van and stopping to say a few words to the driver.

"He's here to board up the window."

"Criminals, are they all you know?" Kevin sneered.

"You know that's not true. You ever dream

about being fed to an alligator… alive?"

Fab grimaced.

"That's what I get for being nice," Kevin huffed and stomped out.

"I'm locking the door, in case he tries to get back in." Fab followed him.

Chapter Twenty-Five

Creole got off early that night, coming by my house to check out the damage to the window. Billy had boarded it up in record time and produced a vacuum to suck up the glass.

We stopped for mini tacos and ate them out on his patio, which overlooked the water. When we finished, we went for a long walk on the beach.

Phil called when we got back, and Creole urged me to take the call, even though I wasn't in the mindset to be interrupted by anything.

"Since you put a rush on this file—" Phil started.

I interrupted. "I'm putting you on speaker; Creole's here."

"Five years ago, Richards didn't exist. It's said that there's always a simple answer for everything, but I don't believe that. I'll keep checking if you want. Getting his real name would be helpful."

Creole leaned back against the patio chair, hands behind his head, pure annoyance on his face.

"Real name?" I groaned. "Just great. Forget

Richards. I'll let Brad know, and he can deal with the man."

"Pamela Stone's report should be back in the morning." Phil ended the conversation.

"Wonder what Richards is hiding from," Creole said. "We have to know the answer before going into business with the man."

"I agree. But he's Brad's connection. My brother can handle it."

"Enough business talk." He stretched and fake-yawned. "Time for bed." He wiggled his brows.

He stood, picked me up, and carried me into the house.

* * *

Another gorgeous morning in the Keys, the sun streaming through the window. I lay on the king-size bed, snuggled next to Creole, my legs stretched alongside his.

"What are you doing?" Creole peeked out from under his eyelids.

"Nothing."

"You're checking out my legs?" He ripped the sheet away.

"I'm comparing body parts." I rolled onto his chest.

"Why do I think you're up to something?"

I traced a line over his mouth and pressed my lips to his. "You wound me." I put my hand over my heart. "I do want a favor."

"Is it legal?"

I chewed on my bottom lip, pausing overly long. "Ouch," I yelped. He'd reached around and pinched my butt.

"The answer better not be no." His fingers stayed in place, brushing my skin. I tried to push back, and he tightened his hold.

"You're no fun. I want you to recommend Fab to oversee installation of security systems for any new projects."

"Why can't she take it up with Didier or Brad?" He raised a challenging eyebrow.

"Didier has another idea—he wants her to schmooze clients."

"Until one of them annoys her and she 'accidently' shoots them." He pulled the sheet over his head. Groaning, he said, "You should ask your brother. I'm not involved in the business except for writing a check. It would be weird, asking for a favor for Fab."

"Have you noticed the changes in Brad?" I asked.

"Don't worry so much; it's all good. I admire the guy. When he got tired of fishing, he turned himself into an urban dealmaker. He's hanging with new people – doing deals with influential up-and-comers. I know a couple of the guys in that tight-knit group, and Brad is well-liked, fit in from day one." He kissed my forehead. "More changes ahead on the business side. They'll be scheduling a meeting to bring everyone up to speed."

"Are they going to dump their investors?" I hoped not. Fab and I often talked about what a good investment it had turned out to be, with no worries about someone running off with the profits.

"Hardly, they need our money. Who else are they going to find who'll reinvest the profits and not be a pain in the backside, constantly looking over their shoulders?" Creole nibbled on my neck. "Enough about business. We've got more important things to discuss."

He pulled me closer, pushing my hair behind my ears and capturing my face in his hands. Warmth rolled off him and washed over my lips. My eyelids fluttered closed, and I waited for his lips to press against mine. His kisses were always a good way to start the day.

Chapter Twenty-Six

On the way home from Creole's, I detoured by the condo complex the guys were working on. One night while out drinking, the guys had decided on the name – The Inlet. The building was located in the docks area. The city had released plans to renovate the entire area and reap the rewards of more tax dollars. One of the problems they'd run into was that they didn't own all the parcels, and a few investors had stepped up to get involved in the project.

After Julie left town, Brad got tired of living at The Cottages, so he commandeered space on the top floor of The Inlet and moved in. The other half of that floor would remain office space until it got sold. I'd heard vague talk at the dinner that it would be the last unit to sell. I wondered if someone had already shown interest.

All of the renovations were complete, and they were now going through a floor-by-floor punch list. An open house had been scheduled for next month. The outside of the building had a modern exterior, with lights running up the front. The gardeners had finished, filling in the planters with low-maintenance plants.

Not having a card for the security gate, I parked on the corner opposite the building. Just then, Didier exited the building, his attention on the front of the building, where a black stretch limo was backing down into the underground garage.

Crossing the street to stand next to him, I asked, "What's the story?" I pointed in the direction of the car.

Didier looked at me quizzically. "That's your ride for the job tomorrow. Fab got the call to pick it up."

When I didn't say anything, he said, "You don't know what I'm talking about, do you?"

"I'm sure I do. It's just slipped my mind," I tried to cover, doing a terrible job. "I'm sure she told me and I wasn't listening. Or maybe she hasn't told me yet. You know how she is—loves the last minute. Tomorrow, huh? I just may tell her I'm busy."

Didier pulled me into a hug. "She can't go without you."

I rolled my eyes.

"That's a pet peeve of mine. The eye rolling." He shook his head. "Fab's not allowed to do it and neither are you. Can't have you being a bad example."

"Next thing you're going to tell me is that she does everything you tell her and is always well-behaved."

"I don't want her too well-behaved." Didier

laughed a deep, sexy laugh that I hadn't heard before. I felt the heat rush into my cheeks. "I'll have to have a talk with Creole."

"You will not, or I'll put bugs in your underwear."

He threw his head back and continued to laugh.

Fab came out of the underground garage, a smirk pasted on her face.

Proud she parked that fifteen-foot-long vehicle. I could never do it. I'd leave it where the previous person parked it.

"Bad news," I told her. "I'm busy tomorrow for whatever the gig is."

Didier stood back, a stupid smile on his face, enjoying the exchange.

Fab sighed and shook her head. "What do you want?"

"Fifty IOUs." Amongst my family and friends, we exchanged IOUs for favors; no weaseling when the redeemer came asking.

"One," she countered.

I barely glanced at Didier, knowing he was biting his cheeks to keep from laughing again.

"Will I be needed to drive or park?"

Fab rolled her eyes.

I pointed and said to Didier, "See, I told you so."

"Have you forgotten that you're in the middle of negotiations?" Didier reminded me. "Don't you want to know what the job entails?"

"Doesn't matter. After much consideration, my final offer is twenty-five IOUs," I said.

"Didier," she snapped.

He threw up his hands.

"I hate you," Fab said to me.

"I know. But you'll get over it; you always do."

* * *

The clock on the dashboard confirmed that it was morning and not the middle of the night. The day started going downhill from the moment I opened my eyes and saw Fab staring down at me. Assuring myself that it was only a bad dream, I rolled over, only to have the pillow jerked out from under my head.

In all-business mode, Fab ordered, "Get up. We can't be late."

Noticing her tuxedo uniform, I grumbled, "Don't want to go."

Fab yanked the sheet off. "Fifteen minutes. Your uniform is lying over the chair." She stomped out of the room.

Somehow, I managed to shower and get dressed and downstairs in fourteen minutes. Fab's uniform fit her far better than mine did me. I ignored the dumpy ensemble when checking myself out in the mirror. Fab wore a hat, another in her hand that she held out.

"Screw the hat; not wearing it." I didn't share

that hats made my head sweat.

Climbing into the SUV, I demanded we stop for lattes, preferably at the Bakery Café.

Fab gave me the once-over, as though purchasing cattle from an auction. I half expected her to ask to check my teeth.

"Too bad we didn't have time to get your tux tailored," she purred insincerely. "I had one of my own hanging in the closet."

If it were anyone else, I wouldn't believe they just happened to have a tuxedo handy.

Fab detoured to the condos, leaving the SUV parked underground, trading it for the limousine. I checked it out. There was leather seating throughout, and the back had S-shaped benches that would seat a gazillion. I checked the owner's manual, which said "occupancy 20." The bar, sink, and refrigerator area was built on top of a large aquarium with a sea-life background that held a few real fish. The ceiling had been fitted with flashing lights that, when turned on, gave it the ambience of a disco.

Having sucked down most of my coffee, my attitude improved. I stopped staring out the passenger window and instead closed my eyes and leaned my forehead against the window, the drive up the Interstate boring so far. Fab hadn't suggested an overnight bag, so I assumed we would be staying within state lines.

I turned my head slightly. "So far, I haven't gotten one detail about this job." I did know that were headed north.

"You're lucky I speak to you at all."

"Yes, I know that." I smiled at her scowl.

"We're picking up the daughter of one of my clients. She's away at college, and I'm driving her and a friend home for break."

"Wouldn't it be cheaper to pay for airline tickets than gas for this monstrous thing plus your rate, whatever that is? Another client rolling in dough, who I'm sure could afford that option." As many times as I'd been backup, I knew zilch about her secret clients. At one time, I'd thought she made them up. I revised my opinion after I had to come to the rescue a couple of times. "Throw in my expenses too."

"I pay you well."

"You never pay me."

"You don't pay either."

Point taken.

"We're picking up…" Fab shifted, reaching into her pants pocket and removing a sticky note. "…Chrissy Westmont and her friend Blaise in front of their sorority house at the University of Tampa."

For once, when Fab was ready to exit the freeway, she slowed down and used the blinker, not the horn. In fact, she'd driven just above the speed limit the entire way.

"I'll do the talking," Fab said. Several turns later, she pulled up in front of a two-story brick house in a well-manicured neighborhood.

"I'll hang out here."

"You're getting out. We're going to look professional, which means you need to put your shoes back on." She jabbed her finger in the direction of my feet.

The woman once again sported a pair of heels, though not in nosebleed territory like her stilettos. I swore she could do a back flip and land on her pointy toed, spiked heels. I'd originally held up a pair of tennis shoes for her approval, but her look of disgust was priceless, so I exchanged them for a pair of flats.

The walkway up to the Old Colonial home was littered with luggage. A bubbly blonde with shoulder-length hair introduced herself as Chrissy and informed Fab that it *all* had to be loaded in the back. "Try not to take any of our seating room."

I silently counted and wondered how two girls could come up with twenty-four pieces of luggage and where they stored it when it was empty.

Fab's eyes narrowed, but Chrissy didn't seem to notice. Fab motioned for me to join her off to one side.

"I don't suppose you packed some kind of luggage cart?" I asked. When she shook her head, I said, "Let's hope they all have wheels. You do know that if I had heels on, you'd be schlepping bags by yourself?"

Her look of disgust, which burned into the

luggage, didn't escape me.

As it turned out, most of the bags had wheels. I rolled them to the road, and Fab heaved them in, not giving a damn about the best use of the space. The remaining bags were heavy, and I left them for Fab. The problem was we had run out of room.

"Where did Chrissy go?" Fab demanded.

"She's your client. You should keep better track of her."

Fab's heels clicked impatiently up the walkway, where she pounded on the door and alternated with the bell.

The door opened wide, and a line of girls trotted out, following Chrissy, who led the way to the limo. She opened the door and ushered the giggling females inside. My count ended at ten! Ten coiffed, designer-clad college girls, mostly blondes, a brunette or two had snuck in. All with overly large shoulder bags that would have to be held on their laps or on the floor between their feet.

I rearranged the trunk to maximize the limited space and had to come up with a few creative storage ideas, which also meant taking away a small amount of leg room from the inside.

At first, I didn't think Fab would close the door, assuming even she knew that it was part of her job. I motioned to her, laughed, and ran around to my side. The plexiglass privacy screen was still down, and I heard Chrissy apologizing to her friends.

"I thought it would be fun to have a woman driver, but the downside is that they can't handle the luggage." She pointed to the bags sharing their space. "I'll tell Daddy not to pay the bill. That woman should have been told the Westmonts demand exemplary service."

Fab had slid behind the wheel in time to hear her. She ground her teeth and stared straight ahead.

I wasn't sure if Chrissy knew that her audience had grown by two, but judging by her covert glance, she did. She moved to the front, precise in her movements, and before pushing the button to raise the screen, said to Fab, "If you have something important to say, knock first or call my cell phone; we don't wish to be disturbed."

I'd already grown tired of her snotty attitude. "The order was for two girls," I said, which I hoped served as a subtle reminder that it wasn't our fault they'd exceeded the baggage limits. "Should we call and get an okay from your father?"

"Don't be ridiculous," Chrissy snapped. "Daddy loves it when I bring friends home." She closed the window.

"Thanks for standing up to her." Fab started the engine, pulling away from the curb. "Until we get back to Miami, we'll have minimal contact. Can't imagine Chrissy and her friends are going to want to hang out at gas stations, and those are the only stops we'll be making."

People made fun of my hair-tingling premonitions, but they'd never let me down. "I've got a headache."

Chapter Twenty-Seven

Fab signaled, arriving at the ramp to the Interstate. One of the girls had located the stereo system, and music blared through the speakers, so loud that the plexiglass rattled.

The intercom buzzed. "Bathroom break," one of the girls shouted.

"I'll pump the gas; you cut the wires to everything," I said.

Fab had just crossed the county line. She veered off the freeway and into the first gas station. Well, the only one, next to a deserted hamburger stand. The rest of the block was weeds. The rundown place charged "ha ha, we're the only station around" prices. On the side of building hung a crudely lettered "Bathroom" sign with an arrow.

"I'd rather pee on the side of the road."

Fab flashed her demented smile. The princesses in the back had met their match, but unfortunately, even if Fab won the war, she'd wind up being the loser.

"We're here," Fab announced over the intercom. "Might as well fill up." She stepped out from behind the wheel and sauntered around to the other side of the car.

I powered down the window to offer my help, but catching sight of Chrissy, I hesitated. She faced the building, hands on hips, working herself into an apoplectic state, her friend Blaise at her side.

Blaise marched up to Fab. "Is this your idea of a joke?" she hissed. "How dare you stop at a place like this? You don't look stupid, but these days, it's hard to tell. You should've taken us to a hotel."

Under normal circumstances, Fab would consider shooting her, or at the very least threatening her. To her credit, she maintained her cool. Even as a bystander, I was having a difficult time keeping my mouth shut.

"In case you haven't noticed, there's not much out here. Unless you want to rent a cheap motel room, I suggest you pee now or get your clothes all wet." Fab gave her a frozen glare.

I beamed with pride; my friend had dropped a bodily function word. Now I'd be the one to remind her that such references were unladylike.

"If you pee on the floor of the limo, you clean it up," Fab went on. "Chrissy's father will be picking up the tab for the damages, and I'll be happy to tell him that you girls refused to use the bathroom." Her eyes flashed a "don't mess with me" warning.

Blaise leaned in. "Bitch face."

To Fab's credit, she didn't flinch.

I leaned halfway out the window. "Problem, ladies?"

Blaise rolled her eyes and mumbled, "Another stupid one," then stomped around to the other side.

Half of the girls decided to brave the bathroom conditions and walked back to the car laughing and catcalling. They appeared to have been drinking. One had tucked a pint of spicy rum in the front of her barely butt-length skirt. I recognized the colorful label before she pulled it out and whisked it out of sight. She didn't buy the bottle here—Florida had explicit liquor laws and prohibited its sale in gas stations.

Fab stood ready to close the side door, and Blaise jerked on the handle. "Cut over to the coast; we've decided to have lunch in Ft. Lauderdale. You have a problem with that, call Chrissy's dad."

"I'm not doing it," Fab said as she got behind the wheel, slamming the door.

"Calm down." I handed her a cold coffee from the cooler bag I'd brought along. "We'll just say we forgot. Besides, I think we have bigger problems."

"What?" Fab eased back onto the road.

"They've been drinking, and a couple them are showing signs of being unsteady on their feet." I looked in the rearview mirror in time to see one of the girls pull the drape across the plexiglass window. "Is the bar stocked with liquor?"

"When I picked it up, I had to go through a checklist, and there wasn't a bottle of anything back there, including anything in the refrigerator."

"I'm not a lawyer, but I know a few. If we get pulled over and they're stinking drunk, or even smell like liquor, we're in big trouble. They *are* under age." I let out a long breath, trying not to let my anxiety run wild. "I hate jail and know you share the same sentiment."

"What do we do now?"

"With no authority to stop them, we don't have a lot of options. They'd laugh in our faces." I paused. "Call your client and rat out his daughter. Let him deal with it."

Fab didn't like that option.

"Or pull over and demand they dump out their bottles, but I believe they'd call our bluff," I said. "I vote for leaving them on the side of the road."

Fab smiled at that.

"I'd need to know that Chrissy is drunk; Milton Westmont isn't going to give a damn about the rest of the girls."

"We could lower the partition to eavesdrop, but they'd notice," I said.

"There's an intercom button." Fab pointed to the dashboard and flipped the button up. Rock music filled the cab, and she turned it off just as fast.

An hour outside of Ft. Lauderdale, she took the turnoff onto a road that ran through a Wildlife Management area to the coast. A shortcut, according to the map. The girls had come prepared to party hard, not caring it wasn't even noon yet. Those large totes of theirs held more than I'd imagined.

I kept a steady watch through a gap in the drapes. Tired of gyrating around in their seats under the disco lights, they finally lowered the volume on the music. Fab flipped on the intercom, but it was still hard to make out their conversation.

Blaise figured out how to open the sunroof, and several of them stood on the seats, heads hanging out the opening.

Gunshots rang out.

Caught off guard, Fab swerved, quickly regaining control.

"You pay attention to the road," I said. "I've got this." Glock in hand, I lowered the divider and demanded, "Get. Down."

One girl tripped into another, who was hanging out the window. She swayed, a Baby Browning dropping to the floor. I recognized the model, my brother having one in his collection.

"Put it away," I yelled.

The girl snatched it up, stuck it out the window, and fired several more shots.

Blaise, armed with a handgun, joined the girl,

firing indiscriminately.

"I'm not telling you again," I barked. "One more shot, and I'll call Chrissy's daddy. He might not give a damn about you, but he's smart enough to know that his daughter will go to jail along with the rest of you."

Two of the girls whispered and snickered.

Chrissy wobbled over and tugged on Blaise's shorts, looking up and shaking her head.

The drunkest of the lot, a redhead, took out a shelf of glasses with one shot and dropped her gun. "Oops, I had my finger on the trigger." She covered her mouth.

Only one girl took cover, wiggling under the bench; her dress rode up, bare butt hanging out.

"Sit down." I channeled Mother's no-nonsense voice. "One of you is going to end up dead, and the rest of you will spend the rest of your lives in prison, and that's if you escape the death penalty. Ten years is your life span if that happens. No mani/pedis, no designer shoes. Scratchy cotton and recycled shoes." I made eye contact with each girl.

They ignored me completely.

"Last call," I yelled. "Sit. Down."

Not a one of them moved.

"Ride's over. I'm calling the police." I tapped Fab's shoulder. "Pull over."

Fab screeched over to the side of the highway, slamming on the brakes and coming to a stop in a puff of black smoke.

"My tummy aches," one whimpered, clutching her stomach.

Blaise pushed open the side door and directed two of the others. Each one grabbed an arm and hauled the sick one out, where she dropped to her hands and knees and emptied the contents of her stomach.

"Retta, why are you always the one who ends up puking?" one of the girls asked unsympathetically.

Fab got out and stood by the driver's door, watching as the girls gathered and talked amongst themselves. I joined her.

"I'm not going to jail," I said to Fab, who nodded in agreement. I walked back around to the passenger side, leaned in and fished my phone out my purse, and texted Creole. I got in and rolled up the window.

My phone rang almost immediately. I skipped hello and relayed the events.

"Where are you?" Creole asked.

Looking at the GPS, I gave him our location.

"Don't move. You did the right thing, pulling over. I'll call in a favor and send an officer your way. I'll request that he scare the devil out of those spoiled girls. Then you have Fab hightail it to their destination, no stopping."

"Love you," I said before we hung up.

Fab, who was sitting with her butt on the seat, feet on the ground, made a gagging noise.

Blaise pressed her face to the passenger side

window and banged on the glass.

"Ignore her," I said to Fab, hurriedly relating Creole's side of the conversation. "You're pretty much screwed." I knew she wouldn't accept it lying down. "You've got choices to make, and my advice, unsolicited as it is, is to put yourself first. It's only money, and you have plenty of that already."

Thanks to her ex-husband, whose name was never mentioned. He was a gigantic... Well, not a nice man, a criminal in fact, but he did leave her well provided for.

"That's enough," Fab yelled. Chrissy had joined her friend in licking the windshield and banging on the glass. Laughter overcame them, and they paused for five seconds, then started up again.

I reached for Fab's arm, but she brushed me off and launched her body out of the limo. Fab rounded the front of the car and, in one move, dumped Blaise onto the dirt. Chrissy followed.

"Knock it off, you two," Fab said icily.

"You're buying me new pants," Chrissy whined, brushing her hands down her previously all-white outfit.

I got out of the car. "Hold your breath."

Blaise stood and helped Chrissy to stand, looping their arms together, appearing united.

"No more drinking," I said.

Unsteady on her feet, Chrissy confronted Fab. "You better not call the police. You do, and I'll tell them you bought the liquor."

My phone rang, and I was happy to step away. "Tell me something good," I said when I answered.

"Officer Tarlow's on his way," Creole answered.

"How do you know people out in the middle of nowhere?" I asked in awe.

"Not me. The chief. I was with him when you called; he's worse than Fab when it comes to eavesdropping. I could hardly say, 'Mind your own business.'" Creole half-laughed. "Turns out he golfs with Chrissy's father. The Westmont family is stinkin' rich and well connected. The brat can expect a call from Daddy."

"You tell Mr. Chief Sir that I said, 'Oh my gosh, thank you.' And a big hug."

"No wonder he likes you; you know all the right things to say to stroke his ego."

"What do I do in the interim?"

"Channel Madeline Westin Spoon."

"I did that once already; do you think it will work the second time?" I asked.

"Oh hell yes. Play hardball. They want to leave, let 'em walk; if you want to be nice, point them in the right direction. You can do this." He blew a kiss through the phone. "Do not let them get their hands on the keys. Tarlow's big and scary; they don't need to know he's a teddy bear. He'll give them a good scare, and after that, in addition to Westmont's call, you shouldn't have any further problems."

"Foot rub for you."

"And a back massage."

I laughed. "You drive a hard bargain."

"Anything goes awry, I'm your first call."

I shoved my phone back in my pocket. Before re-joining Fab, I checked to see what the other girls were doing. The sick one had crawled to a grassy strip to fend for herself, ignored by her friends. One unzipped her shorts, squatted, and took a pee. Two others, unfazed by the display, sat on the ground, leaning against one another.

"Are you two done with the name calling?" I asked in a bored tone. I'd heard Chrissy and Blaise's colorful words while I was on the phone.

They dismissed me with the briefest of glances and walked away.

"Shall I explain the new rules to the girls?" I asked Fab. "We'll switch roles; you'll be good cop, I'll be bad."

The corners of her lips briefly turned up.

Fab and I rounded the car to where the girls were gathered.

"I'll give you the same advice you gave me: 'Don't shoot them,'" Fab said, loudly enough to capture their attention.

They all stared, the three at the back of the huddle whispering to two others, then scurrying to the sides of their leaders – Chrissy and Blaise.

"Listen up, the rules have changed," I said, back to channeling Mother. "The police are on their way, since the lot of you seem content to commit felonies without fear of consequence. Which would be fine, if we weren't involved. We're not going to jail because rich girls think they can do what they want."

"You're both fired," Chrissy said, stumbling just a bit. Blaise clamped her hand on her shoulder.

I ignored her. "Second." I focused on Chrissy. "If you don't have your phone on you, you might want to fetch it. Your daddy is going to want to chat with you."

"You're full of it," Chrissy snapped.

"Am I? Call my bluff. Check your phone. I'm certain that *Daddy* takes the calls of Chief Harder and won't be happy when I call the chief back and he tells your daddy you're willfully ignoring his calls."

Chrissy paled a bit, which made me happy.

Blaise whispered to Chrissy and turned to Fab. "Since you're fired, give me the keys." She held out her hand.

"Come and get them." Fab jerked her shirt out of her pants and tucked it behind her Walther.

"You morally reprehensible bitch, threatening to kill college girls," Blaise shouted in outrage. "You'll never drive another limo."

"Thank goodness," Fab mumbled.

A police car whipped a u-turn across the median and pulled up behind us.

"That would be Officer Tarlow." I sauntered

off to meet the man.

The uniformed officer got out of his car. "Madison, nice to meet you."

"Creole gave you my description?"

Tarlow shook his head. "The chief. He speaks highly of you and mentioned that you don't do handshakes. Which endeared you to me before we'd even met. What's going on here?"

I related the events.

"Stupid girls. They don't know how badly their day could've ended."

"I tried to stress that there were no jail perks, but they weren't listening."

"You got that right, and some folks come back time after time."

I cast a glance toward the girls; to my relief, they hadn't moved. "They're sauced. The one lying face down is in the worst shape but hasn't passed out cold. Thank you for showing up." I smiled with relief, tired of the bad cop role.

"Don't run off," he teased.

"I really want to."

Stern expression on his face, hand on his revolver, he strode straight over to the girls. The more sober ones straightened their spines.

I motioned to Fab, who stood next to the back bumper. "Tarlow's working his magic. Then we drive them to Daddy Westmont's non-stop. If you have a return trip, I'm busy."

"I'd like a cigarette. Your mother says it calms her nerves."

"You two are a bad influence on each other." I arched my eyebrow. "We're almost home. Thankfully, the shots fired weren't from our guns." I flashed my crazy smile, mostly to get a laugh out of her, and it worked. "One more thing: you charge Daddy triple, and if he won't pay, I'll get it collected. For a fee, of course."

"Once we dump these brats off, you place an order for all our favorites from Jake's, have it delivered, and we'll get sloshed."

"I predict..." I rubbed my forehead in a circular motion.

"So cheesy."

"Daddy's on the line." I nodded in Chrissy's direction. "I'm certain he'll jerk her into line."

* * *

True to my prediction, the rest of the ride to Fisher Island was quiet and drama free. All of the girls dozed off. Tarlow had cleaned out all the liquor bottles, confiscated the guns, and helped the sick one back inside, where she stretched out on the floor, a pillow placed under her head. He even produced a garbage bag from the trunk of his car for her use. I thanked him and so did Fab. I handed him a business card and told him to stop by Jake's if he was ever in the area and show it to the bartender, so they'd know he was to receive special treatment.

For a weekday, the ferry was slower than

usual, but we finally arrived at the ostentatious mansion. Rather than ask Chrissy for a security code, I fished out my own card, which opened most gates in South Florida—a gift from one of Fab's more nefarious clients. When Mother found out, she demanded one of her own. She and her friend Jean used it to joyride in the private, keep-out neighborhoods.

The butler walked down the steps before we came to a stop. Made me wonder if he was on door duty. He opened the side door. Bleary-eyed and pale, the girls filed out, never saying a word, leaving their passed-out friend without a backward glance.

Chrissy paused and turned to Fab. "Unload the luggage. Leave it at the front door." Her nose straight in the air, she led the rest of women inside.

I counted the steps at twelve – straight up.

Fab jerked open the back door, and bags flew through the air, landing haphazardly on the ground.

I tried not to laugh but couldn't help myself.

Standing next to me, the butler glanced down, a stern expression on his face.

"It's been a long drive," I said.

"I heard," he whispered.

"Is Mr. Westmont at home?"

He shook his head.

"That's too bad. They need a lecture that burns their ears off."

He smiled slightly. "Don't worry. Chrissy will take the brunt for all of them, and I expect they will be perfectly behaved the rest of their time here."

"The tux must get hot." I nodded to his uniform. "You have to wear it every day?"

He shook his head. "The Westmonts are gone a lot. The household help runs wild then, and we dress as we want." He was clearly amused by his own answer.

Two men dressed in jeans strolled around the side of the house. I'd guess gardeners.

"I assume you're the problem solver." When he nodded, I continued, "There's a girl passed out in the back. They left her to rot. We don't want her. I have to warn you, she's already thrown up her guts several times. Don't know if she has anything left. Probably smells."

He grunted.

"You could get the gardeners to do it. Get Cook to make them something special as a thank you, cookies or something."

"You're an impertinent little thing."

"Thank you." I flashed my biggest smile.

The butler snapped his fingers at one of the gardeners. The conversation was short and out of eavesdropping range. The gardener shot him a dirty look and ran around the side of the house.

It didn't take long before he was back with a wheelbarrow and a pillow. The two men dragged the drunk girl out of the limo by her feet. One scooped her up and deposited her into her new ride. Then they wheeled her around the back.

Sick people didn't get to go through the front door?

The butler noticed my quizzical look and said, "She'll feel less drunk once she's had a shower and a nap."

"Come on," Fab barked. "Before I throw a match on the luggage." Once behind the wheel, she slammed the door.

The butler actually laughed.

"Thank you very much." I beamed. "Nice to meet you." I waved and ran to jump inside before Fab left me. She gunned the engine and drove off.

"You do make a cute chauffer," I told Fab.

"You should have held out for fifty IOUs."

Chapter Twenty-Eight

After returning the limo, Fab and I agreed that we'd indulge in a do-nothing day, and Didier took the afternoon off.

It was hard not to stare as Didier came through the patio doors in navy bathing trunks, pushing his wet hair back from his face as he headed to the kitchen. I'd been swimming earlier and came inside because I knew Didier wanted to swim laps at a punishing speed. It tired me out to watch.

"Where's Fab?" he asked, peering around the refrigerator door as he pulled out a variety of fruit, laying it on the island.

I jerked my thumb upward. "Would you like me to blend you up something special?"

"No, thanks. I don't want to die today," he said drily.

I clutched my chest.

Fab swooped into the kitchen and slapped down an envelope in front of me. "Don't wait too long to collect this; I don't want that bastard leaving town."

"Fabiana!" Didier gave her a long look.

"What happened? Do you need a hug?" I asked.

"Skip the hug business and get my money. I jacked up the bill to include your twenty-five percent."

"Done. I'm proud of you. Nobody died, no matter how much they deserved it—a couple of them anyway." I smiled at her.

"Madison Westin," Didier said in exasperation. "I thought Fab was the instigator."

"You've been away too long. We need to break you in again." I picked up the envelope, flipping it over, and was disappointed it was sealed.

"Westmont told me if I couldn't handle young girls that I'd overhyped my skills. He holds me completely responsible. Don't expect to hear from him again, and he said he'd be reporting back to the man who recommended me. There go two clients." She frowned.

"Did you happen to mention that because of you, his daughter and her underage friends didn't end up in jail? In addition to the liquor, what about the firearms? State law says they're 'not old enough to purchase.' Not to mention the mandatory jail time."

"He blew a gasket when I mentioned the gun antics. Told him I had a friend who'd give him a fair price for the lot of them. He had the brass ones to tell me that the gun shots never happened and if I knew what was good for me, he'd better never hear about the 'incident' again."

"That big prick," I said with venom.

Didier shook his head.

"I know worse words."

He turned away, which I'd bet was to hide a smile; he knew a little encouragement was all it took for me to ramp up the antics.

"I'm not only going to collect your bill, I'll also get an assurance that Westmont never mentions your name to anyone and stops with the threats. Anything happens to you, I'll use one of my connections down on the docks to contract his murder. I get a discount if it can be grisly, one body part at a time." I gave her my deranged smile, which I'd been working on.

Fab laughed, so I knew I'd improved.

"Cherie, how do you know these people?" Didier asked.

"Finally, we're back to the frenchy words I like so much."

"Come here." Didier held out his arms. He hugged me tight. "I should've said this before: thank you for always looking out for me and Fab."

"You're family." I smiled up at him. "We stick together." After a moment, he released me and I went back to my seat.

Didier used the lag in the conversation to turn on the blender. I twisted around on my stool, stood, opened the cupboard, and retrieved a glass. I looked over my shoulder at Fab and arched my eyebrow. She shook her head. I set the glass in front of Didier and got a smile.

I stared out the new garden window. Turned out the owner of the glass company was a friend of Spoon's, and my order got bumped up to a rush job. "What's he doing here… again?"

Before I could get to the door, it opened, and Casio filled the entryway. "Honey, I'm home," he bellowed. Turning towards the kitchen, he flashed his signature smarmy smile.

"There's no 'honey' here, and this isn't your home," I said.

Damn, the last thing I wanted was for him to know that Fab was back, or worse, that she never left town. It was just an excuse she'd used because she wasn't ready to tell Brick to go to hell but needed a break.

"How's my little French morsel?" Casio wiggled his eyebrows at Fab.

It surprised me that Casio didn't burst into flames from the intensity of Fab's glare.

"So, you must be the boyfriend," Casio said, barely acknowledging Didier. "I come with felicitations and greetings." He threw out his arms.

I bet you do.

If he misinterpreted the complete silence as some sort of acceptance, he was in for a rude awakening.

"Who beat you up?" Fab asked.

Casio's bruises had grown faint but were still

234

noticeable.

"I heard it was a girl," I said.

Fab and I laughed, and even Didier cracked a smile.

Casio clenched his jaw and turned his phony charm on Fab. "Brick needs your help." He held up his hand. "Just hear me out."

Fab nodded.

"Brick has a client that ordered a 200K custom Ferrari, one of the fancy models." Casio helped himself to beer from the refrigerator, ignoring Didier's scowl. "The car disappeared from a locked storage unit at the back of the car lot. Brick's got a wild hair that the client might be in on it. He's stalled as long as he can, but the client wants the car or his deposit back, which I understand is hefty."

"What about his spiky haired bodyguard? Or whatever she is," I asked.

"Everly's only a bodyguard. His wife would nut him if it were otherwise." Casio grimaced. "After the third time someone tries to kill a man, he can get a little paranoid. She signed up for beck-and-call duty, so he's ecstatic." He stepped closer to Fab. "Brick does miss you. He's unhappy with the way things shook out between you two."

"I'll bet he does miss you," I said to Fab. "He's found out you're not as replaceable as he thought."

"Your comments are not helpful."

I stuck up my middle finger.

Didier gave me a thumbs up.

"The pot is being sweetened." Casio's hand swept out in a flourish.

All eyes turned to the window. A car hauler blocked the driveway, unloading a shiny black convertible.

"Is that the same hauler that took the Porsche away?" I asked.

Casio slashed his finger across his neck and focused on Fab.

"Guess I already let the happy news out of the bag. I told Brick you're back. I don't need to tell him you've been home for…. how long now?"

"You and your brother can go to hell," I said. "If she works for Brick again, it will be her decision and not because she's strong-armed into it."

"Say the word." Didier moved to Fab's side, his arm around her shoulder. "I'll throw him out."

"You and what army?" Casio hissed.

I stepped in front of Casio. "You start anything in my house, and I'll shoot you."

"What kind of car?" Fab asked.

"Lexus. Mostly new – a bit of a problem with the title, but it all got worked out."

I bet that's an interesting story.

"It's not a Porsche." Fab turned up her nose. "We need a backup car?" she asked me.

I shook my head.

"Could you hurry it up? This really is a rush job."

"I need a couple of days. If it's that big of a rush, he should call someone else," Fab said.

"You dispensed your greetings, and the unwanted bribe arrived; is there anything else?" I asked.

"Can I least have another beer before you kick me out?"

"Where are my manners?" My words dripped with sarcasm. "You know where they're kept. And then have a seat." I pointed to one of the stools. "In the spirit of this new friendship, I need information."

"What do I get out of it?" Casio shoved the stool back before sitting.

"I'll let Fab make up her own mind and not hound her to never say yes and sell that beautiful car out there on the black market." I motioned for Fab and Didier to sit. "There are plenty of buyers that wouldn't be bothered by not getting a title."

"This ought to be good." Casio slammed his beer bottle on the island top.

"You mar my countertop and you replace the whole thing." I glared. "You're working in the area." I waved him off. "Don't deny it. I've seen you in Tarpon maybe once or twice since I've lived here, but now you show up at my house twice in two weeks. I've had several break-ins here and no clue as to why. And a couple of men showed up, claiming to be collectors, short on details but with a friendly warning of sorts. Anything going on in the neighborhood that you'd know about and I wouldn't?"

Casio took a long swig of his beer. "The murder next door snagged the headlines for a while. Local cops are still running down tips. So far, none have produced anything. Kevin's the man to ask. Isn't he related or something?"

"His only goal in life is to arrest me for murder," I said. "I don't think he'd care whether I did it or not. He's been assigned the case; at least this time, he gave up on me as a suspect early on."

"He's fun to party with – always gets the girl."

"He's only got one criteria, and it's not high IQ," I said.

Casio arched his eyebrow.

I held my hands under my chest.

Didier banged his head on the counter.

"Call the tow driver back," Fab instructed Casio. "A Lexus is not a Porsche, and besides, if you check the driveway, you'll see I already have one. And it's been decided we don't need another car." Her nose took a scornful tilt.

"Will you at least talk to him?" Casio asked.

"He can call and make an appointment, like any other client," Fab said.

"You changed your number."

Fab reached in her pocket and shoved her phone across the counter to me. I picked it up and called Casio's cell. "You have it now."

"One more favor." Casio turned his attention to me, smiling. I did a double take. He resembled a cartoon worm.

"You owe me, and no bitching and moaning when it comes time to collect. Got it?" I asked. He nodded. "You also owe Fab and Didier, though he probably wouldn't ask."

"Keep me up to date on the comings and goings next door, no matter how insignificant you think they might be. Any more break-ins here, make me your first call. I don't like being second to that bastard, Stephan."

Fab looked at me quizzically. "Help," I mouthed, and she nodded.

"You done asking for favors?" Didier asked sarcastically. "Next time, knock and wait until someone actually invites you in."

Casio flipped him the finger and walked out, sporting a huge smile.

"That man has more up his dirty sleeve than he's letting on," Didier said in disgust.

Chapter Twenty-Nine

I set the tray of coffee and the pink bakery box on the floor outside Brad's front door. Thanks to Fab, I now had a keycard, so I could park in the underground garage and not have to worry about leaving my SUV on the street. According to the city, the area was under revitalization, but it was still an iffy neighborhood.

To get up to the penthouse, I used the code Fab had given me to ride the elevator to the top. It annoyed me that I hadn't gotten a key for emergencies; Brad kept putting me off with vague excuses. I should take back my house key. He knew I wouldn't just come over and snoop. His secretive crap was annoying me.

I'd knocked several times and got no response. That was when I set the box and coffee on the floor and pulled my lockpick out of my pocket. First, though, I tried the doorknob; it surprised me when it opened. I picked everything up and used my foot to close the door behind me, walking through the large open space, through the dining room, and into the kitchen. The view that stretched out across the Atlantic was worth the price. I immediately noticed that there weren't any feminine touches; everything was leather, chrome, and minimalistic. Not a single dead fish on any wall.

I could hear water running in the direction of Brad's bathroom, so it was a good bet he was showering. Scaring him would amuse me. Unless he shot me. Even more fun if he trotted out half-naked and I could embarrass him with that story for years to come.

I got to work and pulled plates out of the cupboard, opening a couple of drawers before locating the utensils, helping myself to paper towels, bending back the box lid, and setting it on the oblong kitchen island. He hadn't bought stools, so we'd have to stand.

I heard Brad's feet slapping on the floor before he appeared around the corner from the hallway.

Brad jumped. "What the hell?" he asked, tight-lipped. He was shirtless and wearing black suit pants that appeared tailor-made. If he wasn't my brother, I'd give him a second look.

I smiled and waved. "Your favorites." I pointed to the familiar pink box.

He held out his hand. "I want the lockpick."

"No! I don't have time to stop and buy another one. Besides, I didn't use one; you left your door unlocked."

"Fine." He looked me over. "I'll wrestle you to the floor and take it myself." He took a step forward.

I stepped back. "We're not six years old. You even try that, and I promise, you'll limp for a week."

"You'd maim your own brother?" His eyes snapped with irritation, but his lips curved slightly with amusement.

"Oh stop, your coffee is getting cold. How long did you think you could blow me off before I took matters into my own hands? You're lucky I didn't barge in at a more inopportune time."

He snorted. "I don't bring anyone here."

"No comment on what I think about that. I suppose sex-and-run makes for a quicker getaway when it's not at your casa. So ungentlemanly to kick the woman out of bed with a 'get going.'"

"Has anyone ever done that to you?" he growled.

"Down boy. Sweet of you, though. I don't think about past boyfriends; the one I've got is a keeper. When he leaves in the middle of the night, he leaves me in a soft bed with a lip-searing kiss."

"Stop, you'll ruin my appetite." He picked a large cinnamon roll and dumped it on a plate. "You're getting to be like Mother." He tore off a large piece. "Sweets aren't good for you," he said and shoved it in his mouth.

"You worried about a setback in toning your abs?"

"Looking damn good, aren't I?" He flexed his

muscles. "I assume you're here to annoy me about something. You need to hurry it up. I've got a meeting, and you know I hate to be late."

"I checked your schedule and know you have plenty of time. So why don't we go sit in the living room, and I'll get to my interrogation?"

"I'm going to need another cup of coffee." He strode moved to the opposite counter. He didn't bother with fancy beans or some mix; he popped in a plastic cup and voila, a satisfying drink.

"I'll help myself to a water." It was a great opportunity to snoop in his mammoth refrigerator. Not sure what I expected to find, but I was disappointed; it held water, a few condiments, and an assortment of European beers. On impulse, I opened the freezer side, and not a frozen food in sight. "You have any food at all?"

"Why? I do take out. Even Mother sends me home with food." He laughed. "You're staring. That used to start fights as kids."

"You've got the whole dominant look going for you. Like you stepped out of one of Fab's naughty books that I borrow on a regular basis."

"Don't share those with anyone."

"By 'anyone,' I know you mean Mother, but she started borrowing the books first. Our father was a happy man for a reason. The only time he ever got really mad was if one of us made her cry."

"I only did that once – drag racing."

I gasped. "How did I never hear about that one?"

"You're lucky. I had to sit through Mother sobbing about how me and my posse could've been killed, although I believe she used a ruder term for my friends. When Dad got home, he scorched my ear drums and sentenced me to hard labor." He grabbed a bottle of water for me and his coffee, pushed back the sliding glass door, and led me out to the patio, where we settled into chairs to enjoy the view. "I'll ask this nicely: what do you want?"

"Big fail on the nice part." I made a face. "I came to get my big brother back. We've grown apart, and it's your fault. Stops now."

He drifted off for a moment. "Getting kidnapped requires a lot of adjustment. There were times I wondered if I'd get out alive. Even went to a therapist afterwards; she was full of it, and I told her so, wanting to go back to childhood and blame our parents for my being tied up and used thirty years later."

"You know I'm good at other people's problems. It's a specialty of mine."

"That's too embarrassing." He ruffled my hair. "I made new friends through my business interests; they all work out like madmen. I wasn't all that eager to sweat my ass off; it took me by surprise when it adjusted my attitude in addition to giving me new muscles." He grinned. "Signed up for self-defense classes. The teacher realized

I'd had an 'incident' and helped me to open up and get things off my chest. It helped that he'd been in a similar situation. He took me under his wing, kicking my butt in every class, allowing me to vent while also teaching me better survival skills."

"Fab and I used to go to Krav Maga classes; we need to get back to it. The added incentive for learning to kick butt is if Fab goes crazy on me, I can take her down."

"I could sell tickets, take bets, and make some side cash." He laughed.

"Mother would want in on that action. All the money would be on Fab."

"Fab would never throw a match, so you'd really have to KO her."

I winced. Knocking her out would never happen. "What's up with the Pamela chick? She's self-absorbed and snotty and can't be that good in bed."

"Madison Westin," he mimicked Mother. "She's a friend and no strings."

"The woman is serious about you." I poked my finger at him. "Be careful. She's got some of those whack-job tendencies that usually attract you to the opposite sex. Julie was the exception."

"Julie and I have had the 'let's be friends' conversation. She's coming back for a month to hang out with Liam before shooting the new film. I know she worries, even though Liam has eight pair of eyes on everything he does. I did enjoy that Mother made you the bad guy in the whole prison-chick drama. Mother reminds him constantly that if he doesn't behave reasonably well, Julie will yank his ass off to California. Her exact words."

"LaLoose, she call back?" I asked. Brad shook his head. "Any more girls that need to be run off, Fab's available."

"I had 'the talk' with him. Boy, that was damn uncomfortable."

"Did you share any of your kinky bents?"

Brad nearly spit his coffee back out. "Of course not."

"Gotcha."

He scowled.

"Sorry I missed it. Did you happen to make a recording?" When he shook his head, I told him, "I ran a check on Richards."

He groaned. "Was that really necessary?"

"You'll have to decide." I went on tell him that Phil had reported that he had a clean record for the past five years, but before that, he didn't exist.

"There's probably a good reason. He's damn good in real estate, would hate to cut the partnership short."

"You need to get some information before you and Didier sign on the dotted line."

"Anything else going on? I'm kicking you out soon."

"Not really." I pouted. "It would be nice to do

this more often, without my having to push myself on you. But don't think I won't."

He pulled me out of my chair and into a big hug. "If you're feeling ignored again, give me a good punch. You're great sister material. I like that you're kick-ass yourself; just wish you didn't use it so often. I never want to lose the close connection that we have."

"I love you and would do anything for you. You can call twenty-four/seven; I'm here for you. Creole won't mind, so don't use that as an excuse. Besides, you and Didier are his closest friends."

"Thanks for reminding me; it's my turn to organize the next bike ride. We're taking the bikes to South Miami and riding up the coast along the beach. We want to be ready to ride at sunrise."

"Careful of the traffic."

"Got that worked out. Since we're leaving early, we'll start by going north—no one gets up at dawn in a party town—and coming home, we'll take it slower. There's a hole-in-the-wall bar I want to take them to. Entertainment, ice-cold beer, and healthy food choices, if you can believe that. Ex-bodybuilder owns it." He pushed me back into the chair.

"Favor?" I asked. Brad looked surprised, and I continued. "Didier is going to pitch another job idea for Fab, and I'd like you to seriously consider it." I gave him a brief rundown on the security idea.

"I like the idea."

"This was fun." I stood and hugged him. "Next family dinner is at my house. Get me a nice piece of fresh fish, and you can cook it up on that fancy grill that's been ignored lately."

When the old Webber kettle rusted a hole through the bottom, Brad had volunteered to find a replacement. I'd never imagined he'd have a king-of-the-line one delivered that could cook food for a crowd… if you knew how to turn it on. That assured the guys got cooking detail.

Chapter Thirty

After stopping by Jake's and watching Junker empty his truck of new finds, excited to see a couple of items that I would score for my garden, I arrived back home in the afternoon and dropped my bag in the entry, sending my flip-flops sailing one at a time into the boot tray.

"About time you got back!" Fab shouted from the kitchen. "Food's on the way."

I rubbed my ear. "I'm not hard of hearing. Whatever it is you want, you can ask in a quieter voice."

Didier flicked his gaze between the two of us. I knew he had a mental bet on one of us, but which one?

"What are you doing home, Pretty Boy?" I asked, using the moniker the guys gave him when he was the new kid.

"I'm not allowed to entertain Casio alone," Fab said.

"Casio? Again? I don't think she'd shoot him, if that's what you're worried about." I pointed to the blender. "If that's tequila in there, I'll have a double." I licked my lips. "By food, I hope you mean enchiladas."

"Phil's delivering. I placed the order right after you left." Fab grabbed up a chip, feeding it to Didier.

"Stop with the chip foreplay. The children are headed this way." I pointed to Jazz and Snow. The mention of food always roused them from a nap.

Didier winked at Fab.

"Are we feeding him too?" I pointed to Casio, who was coming up the driveway. "Why is he here? You never got to that part."

Didier had the door open before Casio could pull out his lockpick. Why bother to knock, especially when he knew it annoyed everyone inside? The two men exchanged a restrained greeting. Didier went out to meet Phil in the driveway, taking her shopping bags and following her back inside.

"Good thing I brought extra." Phil nodded to Casio. "Madison won't be happy – no leftovers."

"This family relishes their leftovers." Didier laughed.

Casio salivated, watching the food being spread out on the counter. "Some days, a guy gets lucky, showing up at the right time." He fist-pumped. "I'll take a beer."

Fab pulled Phil off to one side and whispered something that I'd find out about later. I glared at my partner, and she flicked her gaze to Casio and shrugged, no big deal.

Phil dropped a manila envelope in front of me.

"Paperwork." I stood and nodded, crossing to the tall cabinet in the living room and tossing it inside.

Fab put a plate in front of Casio. "If you're not planning to be helpful, you better eat fast because you're out of here."

I settled back on a stool, taking a long sip of my margarita, making sure to include salt. "This is your meeting." I bowed slightly to Fab. "Spill it."

"You need a couple of things from me." Fab slugged Casio in the shoulder.

He winced. Didier didn't bother to hide his smile.

"You want information about the neighborhood, and the question is, why? You also want me to help your brother, which I won't do unless I get what I want first. Keep in mind that although Brick and I have a meeting set up for the morning, that is tentative, as far as I'm concerned." Fab intensified her glare to match Casio's. "My *partner* is going along. If he doesn't like it, he can pretend, like we often do."

"Your neighbor, Scotch, was the son of longtime family friends," Casio growled, seething at the injustice. "He didn't deserve to be blown away in his doorway. No one had a motive that I've uncovered." He managed to calm down slightly. "Local cops believe it was random. In this neighborhood, I don't believe it."

"As a lottery winner, Scotch's picture made

the papers," I said. "Too many of them end up dead, usually at the hands of a relative or some so-called friend."

"Bad idea to let them print your name and picture," Fab said.

"I can hope someone brags." Casio clearly didn't like that idea. "So far, nothing. That leaves either someone who knew him and wanted the money or someone who didn't and wanted the same thing."

"What about Kevin?" Didier asked. "Don't you trade information?"

"The case isn't high priority to our friend Kevin. He offered to trade info, but so far, he's contributed zip."

"How do we figure into one of your scenarios?" I asked. "We didn't know Scotch. I did the friendly neighbor wave thing, exchanged a few words…" I turned to Fab, eyebrows raised.

"After he moved in, I went over once 'looking for the cat' to check out the garage. Nice guy. Never went back."

We shot each other looks across the counter. She often chastised me for using the "missing animal" story, and here she was, out using it behind my back.

Casio looked as though he was about to say, "Think," but thought better of it. "Don't you think it's odd that your house is getting broken into—or attempted break-ins, anyway, by dumbasses—out of nowhere? No burglaries have been reported lately, another plus for the neighborhood, and your property is the only one with dead bodies connected to it. Lucky, I guess. The old timers think you two *lovely girls* have had a little bad luck. Followed by, 'They haven't been arrested.' Don't worry, I haven't let it out that you two get hauled in on a regular business, and it's just that nothing sticks."

"Watch our backs, is that your advice?" I asked.

"Why not tell us all this the other night? Or were you too busy mooching beer?" Fab asked.

"You didn't ask."

Didier unleashed some words in French that had Fab laughing.

"I hope that wasn't about my parentage. I come from good stock." Casio puffed up. "Anything else is probably true."

"What is your working theory anyway? It better not be that one of us did it. I'm sick of hearing that." When he didn't immediately answer, I pointed to the entry. "Get out."

"I have to clean my plate." Casio held up his fork. "Let's face it, you don't have the best reputation with law enforcement."

"You're a useless waste of our time and food." Fab glared.

"None of you were ever on my list. Satisfied?" Casio leered at Fab. "Now that that's cleared up, you'll find that damn car for Brick and he can stop blowing up my phone."

"Did Brick report this to the police? I already know the answer is no, so why not?" I asked.

"You know how the paperwork is." Casio looked me straight in the eye, trying to sell that piece of fiction, then switched his attention to Phil. "I heard rumors of a side business you have going. Heads up, I may use you sometime. If you're any part in solving this case, I can make sure you have plenty of clients when you hang out that lawyer shingle of yours. That's if you're not too picky. All your clients can't be innocent."

I had forgotten Phil was still in the kitchen, she'd been so quiet. She had pulled a stool to the side of the island and listened to the exchange.

Didier crossed his arms and glared at the detective as soon as he took his last bite of food.

Casio downed his beer. "I don't suppose there's dessert?"

"We don't eat dessert," I said dryly.

Chapter Thirty-One

"Would you stop fidgeting and sit in your seat like a grownup?" Fab honked and cut around an old sedan that should have been using the far right lane.

"Calm your shorts," I said, rolling down the window and counting slowly to see how long it took for Fab to start complaining again. "Humph." I loved the part of the drive through the top part of the Keys, all green and lush. It never lasted long enough, and we slowed, hitting the concrete jungle crawling with cars, more going south than towards Miami.

"I don't know what that means, and I don't want to. Now roll up the window. Why do I have to keep reminding you that you're not a dog?"

"Why are you letting this meeting with Brick get to you? Not even the double latte has made a dent in your mood." I picked up her cup and shook it.

"He's such a bastard."

"I get to be Didier today. Tsk." That earned me a smile. "You can always say no. Whatever you decide – I'm in. Have a line in mind that you're not going to cross. I'd suggest that you replicate your old relationship, where you deal only with him; forget any other interference, such as his so-called bodyguard. No miscues that way."

Fab slipped into a silent funk, concentrating on the road, gripping the steering wheel like a woman about to have a fit.

After the third signal where she honked the instant the light turned green, I snapped, "Stop that. Or I'm going to drive."

"That will make me nauseous."

"You? What about me? I'm tired of these long drives. Hopefully, I won't barf."

"You know better than to do *that* inside the car."

I tapped her shoulder, pointing out a police speed trap up ahead. She slowed to the speed limit or a little above and kept her eyes peeled as she maneuvered through traffic.

Famosa Motors was located on a busy corner in an upscale part of South Miami. Brick specialized in pricey autos for sale and lease. He'd gotten away from cash rentals, as they'd turned out to be more trouble than they were worth. The cars typically had to be tracked down and recovered, generally in terrible shape.

The traffic was moderate for an early weekday morning. Fab rocketed across the highway and into the parking lot, pulling up in front of the roll-up doors, which were closed. I scanned the parking lot and, upon completion of a car count, determined that Brick and his bodyguard were the only ones at their desks. The salesman didn't show up for another hour, and even then, malingered around the parking lot, drinking coffee.

"Take a deep breath," I said to Fab. "There's two of us. We can take Brick."

"Bring your tote; that way, you can get our junk food bag refilled. It's been empty for a long time," Fab said, as we got out of the SUV.

"That's because everyone knows that forbidden sweets don't taste as good if you have to pay for them."

Fab looped her arm in mine.

"We're back," I announced as we walked in the side door. "You don't look happy to see us," I said to Everly, noticing her pinched features.

Everly Lynch was Brick's receptionist/bodyguard/not sure and not asking. Her spiky hair was the same virulent shade of fluorescent red it had been the last time we met and her dress was just as skimpy.

Brick stood in the picture window of his second-floor office, bulky frame on display, and beat on the glass. He motioned with his hand, breaking up the silent love fest. His bellow of "hurry it up" floated down the stairs.

Brick waited in the doorway of his office. He hugged Fab and shot her a crooked grin. "Missed you. Happy you're here." He acknowledged me with a nod. "You too."

I settled into one of the massive leather chairs

in front of his desk. Leaning forward, I emptied the candy bowl into my bag. So much for my usual handful. Fab gave me a thumbs up and perched on the ledge of the window overlooking most of the lot and the boulevard below. Brick grunted as he settled himself behind his desk, brushing back his dark hair.

I perused his shelves and noticed he hadn't added any new philanthropic awards, Cuban business dude of the year plaques, or trophies for his exploits in the boxing ring. For a shady fellow who owned a string of pawn shops, bail bonds offices, and recently added check cashing joints, plus his baby, the strip joint in Alligator Alley, he had an impeccable reputation. As long as he didn't generate negative headlines, he'd retain his status. Although there had been more than one South Miami felon who, after a stint in the federal pen, was able to reclaim their social standing.

Brick leaned sideways, reaching into the refrigerator, and then pushed water across the desk.

He beat his fist on the blotter. "I want the damn car back." He let out an exasperated sigh. Jerking open a side drawer, he tossed a file on his desk and took out the top document. "This is the car. Sweet baby." He pushed it into my open hand.

I glanced at it and handed it to Fab. Fancy sports cars were lost on me; whether on the road or parked, I couldn't tell one from the other. Fab was the one with the car savvy, and she let out a low whistle.

"Do you really think a man who can afford a 200K custom auto is going to steal it?" Fab asked.

"It's the thrill of getting away with something. Besides, it's low risk. He knows I don't want word getting out that I was scammed; then I'd be overrun with cockroaches."

"Any other possibilities?" Fab handed me back the photo.

"I suppose." Giving it some thought, he groaned. "Yeah, one of my employees. But where would they get the connections to unload the damn thing? Unless one of them is stupid enough to let it go for a couple thousand."

"We find it, then what? You want me to steal it back?"

"You call me, then stand guard until I arrive, and I'll have it hauled away on a flatbed." He handed me a couple of sticky notes, which I pressed to the back of the photo. "Check out his home. He disrespects you, tie him up and threaten the fuck out of him."

I looked down and squeezed my eyes shut, wanting to rub my temples.

"Nothing illegal," Fab shot back. "First off, you're not sure that it's him anyway. There will be no gunplay. Your client brings fire power, and we're out of there." She gave him a warning look. "I had to get special permission to come here today; if you want me to come back, don't screw it up by withholding anything."

He grinned at her. "Thanks, babe. Bill me whatever. I know you'll be fair."

The audacity of that statement had me contemplating a dramatic faint. The man protested every cent and always threatened to withhold pay, eventually coming through, but only after much grumbling.

"Can I talk to Fab for a minute?" he asked, tilting his head and motioning for me to leave the room.

I nodded, grabbed the photo and my tote, and went out into the corridor, closing the door behind me. I wanted to slide down the bannister, which was forbidden with the excuse of jacked-up insurance premiums, but didn't want to sit at the bottom and risk having to engage in small talk or a glare off with Everly. Instead, I made my way quietly down the stairs and took the long way around back to the SUV.

Chapter Thirty-Two

It didn't take long for Fab to finish her meeting, and she was soon back downstairs and sliding behind the wheel. "Brick made an apology of sorts. I stressed the new working rules. I threw out marriage and babies as a major hint for him to start looking for someone else. He didn't say anything, but it was clear he didn't think I'd excel at either."

"Something you forgot to mention to your best friend?"

Fab shook her head. "Just creating drama. Got that from you."

"For the record, you'd be a great mother. They wouldn't get away with a damn thing, but they'd be the coolest kids in town. After mine, of course."

Fab half-snorted. "The Naples address plugged in?" She eyed the GPS.

"South Beach first, then over to the west coast. South Beach because I called Mr. Westmont's office and tricked out of the receptionist the fact that he's the first one in the office when he's not out of town, and he's not. I'm putting him on notice that he'd better replace that unsigned

261

check he messengered over with cash, as agreed to in the original deal." I pulled the envelope out of my purse and put it on the console.

After ranting over the phone, blaming Fab for his daughter's undisciplined behavior, Westmont threatened not to pay and sent over a check that he'd failed to sign, with a big "0" for the amount and a note that read, "This is what the job is worth."

"He'll never see you." Fab scowled.

"I've planned for that contingency. I promise I'll get my message across."

"Westmont was so adamant about not paying one red cent, how did you get him to send a check, even a useless one? To think I thought you were full of yourself." Fab grinned. "A reminder not to bet against you."

"I haven't collected – yet. Called a mutual friend, explained the situation, and asked for legal advice."

"I thought your lawyer dumped you?"

"Look." I pointed through the windshield. "There's one of Cruz Campion's billboards." It said 'When you want the best lawyer in Florida' over a picture of his smiling mug. "He leaves off the part that he's not a bargain." Early on, I'd made a deal to trade services, which had saved me a lot of money but resulted in some serious aggravation. "Mac kissed and made up for the both of us, same terms as before. Either of us gets arrested, and he shows up and sprinkles his magic 'get out of jail' dust."

"How does that work when someone else does the apologizing?" Fab asked.

"Didn't ask." I'd paid Mac a huge bonus for all the groveling she said she did, said her knees were sore. "Hit pay dirt with Mac. The woman can handle anything. I think she missed his relatives crowding into The Cottages, demanding fights and such."

"I'm letting you know now: if you ever get rid of her, I'd be unsuitable for the job."

I laughed. Put Fab in charge of the tenants, and they'd be afraid to come out of their cottages.

The traffic was in our favor, and we made it across to Ocean Boulevard in record time. Fab pulled up in front of Westmont's office building, pulling into a red zone.

"Don't go far," I admonished. "This won't take long. Don't make me hang out on the sidewalk with my thumb out." Getting out, I barely set my feet on the ground before she took off on a joyride.

As I walked up the steps of the all-glass building with a view of the Atlantic Ocean, I inhaled the sea air, hoping to calm my nerves. Entering the lobby, I looked around and realized I couldn't get to the bank of elevators without checking in at the reception desk manned by an armed guard. His job was to keep people like me from going upstairs.

The guard looked up from his magazine,

asked my destination, scanned his clipboard, and picked up the phone. "You have an appointment?" he asked after speaking to someone on the other end.

"Tell Mr. Westmont that I have a check for him."

The guard's eyebrows rose at that, and he shook his head at me.

"I'm happy to leave it here." I tore the envelope in half, helped myself to his pen, wrote, "This wasn't the deal," and handed it to the guard. "Thank you." I turned toward the exit but not before seeing the man's smirk.

Fab had found a legal place to park at the curb.

"You going my way?" I asked, sliding into the passenger seat.

"What happened?" She pulled away, hanging a u-turn.

"Just as you said. He wouldn't meet with me. Left a message that I expect the cash to be delivered posthaste. Wanted to give him a chance to do it the easy way, before calling in the big guns. I'm sure he has enough to pay the bill in his change jar, so I expect the cash soon."

"Thank Cruz for me. Surprised he'd get involved with collection."

I waited until Fab took a drink of her water to answer. "Actually, it was the chief who came through."

The woman was good—she didn't spit any

liquid out, but she did cough. "I suppose I'm going to jail?"

"You're so dramatic. I would never do that to you, and you know it. Knowing that he and Westmont were friends, I called him for legal advice, and the chief graciously offered his help."

"This is your favorite non-felon," I said, a little surprised that my call had gotten put through without delay.

"I know I'm being set up, but I want to hear what you want. Must be good," the chief said gruffly.

All of the chief's friends called him Harder or Chief. Even Phil, who had one of those friends-with-benefits deals, called him Chief.

"I need some legal advice."

He snorted. "That's what your hotshot lawyer is for."

"You remember that little incident the other day with Chrissy Westmont and her friends?"

"I suggested Westmont bring his daughter in for an overnight in a holding cell, so she'd re-think her behavior before landing in one for real. Westmont didn't appreciate my parenting advice."

Now that was some tough love, I thought. "Now that Westmont's gotten his beloved daughter home, he doesn't want to pay up. I suppose I could threaten to sell the story to a gossip rag, tell anyone who wants to listen, but I'm thinking that falls under blackmail."

"Funny thing is, I figured out what you want all on my own. What's in it for me? I don't want to hear about my good heart, as I don't have one." The chief laughed.

EBORAH BROWN

I didn't remind him that we'd already helped him out once. His goddaughter – another woman getting involved with a crappy boyfriend.

"I'd owe you," I said.

"Does Creole know that you're shaking me down?"

"No, and it would be nice if you didn't mention it. And your description isn't apt, as you just offered your help."

"Send over the bill."

"I just pushed the send button on the fax machine."

"Hold on a second."

I could hear shuffling around but couldn't identify the noises.

"Damn." He let out a low whistle. "Your friend charges enough. Once this invoice is taken care of, that's the last we ever hear about this situation."

"You're a damn good friend, and if Westmont doesn't know that, you should remind him."

"Thank you, I think," Fab said. "I can't believe he'd help."

"According to Creole, who I confessed to after… never mind, Harder already wanted a favor that I can make happen. This makes it easier for him to ask. Creole didn't know the nature of said favor. I told Creole that even if Harder said no, I'd do anything he asked, considering how many times he's helped us." I glared at Fab. "Any favor-doing extends to you also. No excuses."

Chapter Thirty-Three

I punched up the address on the GPS and muted the sound. Fab and the anonymous voice had a tendency to fight. "Samford Kasey lives in Port Royal, a pricey waterfront subdivision in Naples. According to this realtor website—" I tapped my phone. "—the community isn't gated, but his house has a massive set of gates. There's no street parking, so I'm not sure how we'll handle that."

Only half-listening, Fab revved the engine, impatient for the light to turn. She used a little-known shortcut to the highway that ran through the Everglades, shooting across and making it to Naples in record time, veering off on the road that ran along the Gulf Shores.

I pressed my feet against the glove box in an attempt to relive a cramp and stared out the window, wishing I had a reason to yell "stop," so I could go for a walk along the sugary white sand and dip my toes in the water.

"Put your feet down," Fab barked. "This is a nice car."

"I know. It belongs to me. How about I roll down the window and stick my feet out? They'd like some air."

Fab hit the window lock button. "Have you come up with a plan yet?"

"I've got some questions and no answers. According to the realtor site, it's a mansion with a five-car garage. Stashing an auto wouldn't be an issue. But if I were to steal a pricy sports car, the last place I'd hide it is inside my garage. My hunch is Brick does more than 'suspect' this guy is involved; wouldn't be surprised if he sent Everly out here already and she got zip. Probably couldn't climb the fenced-in compound in spiked heels."

"I'll get pictures; that should mollify Brick."

I snorted. "Highly doubt that."

Fab slowed and eyed the mega mansions behind locked gates, security cameras prominent. The houses were set back from the street and shielded by palm trees along the front of the property line. Fab pulled over a few blocks up, in front of an empty lot with a "For Sale" sign posted, leaving the engine running. She released her seatbelt and climbed into the back. "You drive. Drop me off at Kasey's, park at the private club up a few blocks on the right, and wait for my phone call."

"In case you haven't noticed, it's broad daylight, which increases the risk of being seen doing something illegal. Even if you aren't, it's not like you'd go unnoticed."

"I'm not here to steal anything or do anything that would necessitate a police call. Look at me, do I look like a thief? Maybe the shoes; I'm borrowing a pair of your flip-flops." Fab emptied out her purse on the back seat. "I knew these would come in handy." She fastened a diamond bracelet around her wrist and shoved a matching ring that could poke an eye out on her left hand. "Nice, huh? Best bargain ever. Five bucks each. Best paste I've seen in a long time."

"When you get bored with them, I call dibs on the bracelet, but only if the gold hasn't worn off." I crawled into the driver's seat.

"That's the drawback of cheap stuff."

"In case you get caught loitering on private property, do you have a picture of Snow on your phone? Work it—you know, worried, weepy if you can pull that off, 'she just had babies' in a slightly hysterical tone. That might also be hard for you. Do your best." Fab professed to not be an animal lover, but the cats loved her, and she never turned them away, always bribing them with deli treats that she picked out herself.

Fab shot me a dirty look, shoving a couple of large bills in her pocket. "Let me out at the end of the property line. Wait until I get over the fence."

I dropped her off and watched as she checked out the front and cut through the bushes and around the side. A minute later, she came through the trees and waved. It was hard to be inconspicuous cruising the million-dollar neighborhood in a high-profile SUV, and I breathed a sigh of relief when I pulled into the parking lot of the private club. Thankfully, it had no security guard, and I headed to the back, pulling in between two Mercedes.

I attempted to stay calm, tapping my foot against the accelerator. Getting out and walking in circles around the SUV would attract attention. Fingers crossed, if Fab got caught trespassing, that it would be by Mr. Kasey. She could charm any man, the older the better.

I checked my watch for the fifth time with a disgusted snort. It usually didn't bother me that my watches never told the time, since I never set them. I picked up my phone – ten minutes. This waiting business gave me a stomachache, which had begun as soon as we turned off the highway into Naples.

Five more minutes went by, and I made a new hard-and-fast rule – no more jobs without a Plan B. It was taking too long. I powered down the window, listening for an approaching siren. I wasn't sure the cops did that when responding to a burglary call.

Finally, my phone rang, Fab's picture popping up. She disconnected before I could answer. I zipped out of the space, bypassing the circle drive, and shot out the exit. Happy to see Fab walking towards me, I drove past her, hung a wide u-turn, and pulled up next to her. She jumped into the passenger seat.

"You're only driving until we get back to the Interstate." Fab kicked off the flops, throwing them over the seat. She knelt on the seat and grabbed her heels off the back seat.

"What took you so damn long? I was ready to do something possibly stupid."

"No pricey sports car, thank you for asking."

"I'm just happy that you're not handcuffed and headed to the local jail."

"Ran into the groundskeeper, sitting under a banana tree smoking a joint. I ditched my elaborate lie for a little blackmail and cash. Suggested his boss might take it poorly if he found out an employee was a pot smoker. Then tried to sound sympathetic and told him it would be hard to phony up a drug test unless he had time to go to the weed store and get the concoction to drink and even more time to drink ten gallons of water. I figured I'd scored when he paled under his leathery cheeks."

"This is where you mentioned the money? How much? Brick's reimbursing," I said.

"This is why I need you; you keep track of the pesky details. I pulled out a hundred and said, 'I need some info, and then we'll forget we ever met.' He looked so relieved, I felt a bit sorry for him."

"You get anything?" I asked.

"He gave me a tour of the garage, forewarned me he hadn't seen the car I was trying to locate. Didn't bat a lash when I snapped photos. I held up another hundred and asked, 'Do you have any useful information?' planning to give it to him anyway."

"Good idea."

"Turns out, Kelsey owns an airport hangar where he parks his car collection. Thought maybe it was local, but he didn't know for sure. Did tell me Kasey never talked to the 'help'— sent the butler out to relay messages. It's a condition of employment not to 'chat it up' with any of the other employees. He thanked me for not turning him in, told me the job paid good for a man who liked to indulge; he cited nerves."

"That's where rich people make their mistake. A few hellos and his groundskeeper would have taken the money to keep his secret and offered up nothing else." I shook my head at the stupidity of most people, not knowing how far being a little nice went in inspiring loyalty.

I spotted a coffee drive-thru sign up ahead, stopped at the entrance to the order lane, and crawled across the seat while Fab went around. She rolled down the window, and I hollered across the car, "Strawberry Lemonade."

"It's got sugar in it." Fab screwed up her nose.

"Lots of it." I licked my lips. "There's money in the console." I flipped up the lid. While we waited, I retrieved my phone from my pocket and made a call. "Hello," I said overly sweetly and pushed the speaker button. "I got a job for you. No penny pinching; you get to bill full rate."

"What are you two up to now?" Phil asked.

"You're suspicious?" I clasped my chest.

Fab shook her head.

I relayed the details of the Kasey case and asked if she could locate a private airport hangar.

"I can find most anything," she said smugly.

"Need this yesterday. It's for one of Fab's big clients."

"When you have time, I've got a business proposition for you," Phil said.

Fab and I exchanged raised eyebrows. My stomachache came roaring back; this might be the "I'm leaving Jake's" talk. Knowing it was coming and hearing the words were two very different things.

"Do I get a hint?" I asked.

Phil laughed. "No, I think I'll spring it on you in person."

I groaned. "I'll stop by Jake's tomorrow. It'll take us a while to get back, even with traffic on our side." I clicked off.

"Time to find another bartender," Fab taunted.

I ignored her. "You better call Brick before he starts burning up your phone."

Chapter Thirty-Four

I planned to sneak out of the house and head over to Jake's first thing in the morning, knowing that Phil opened early. Oftentimes, she used the outside deck as office space. As I was reaching for the door handle, Fab came rocketing down the stairs.

"Oh no you don't. I'm going," she said, grabbing her bag off the nearby bench.

"I can repeat the conversation word for word when I get back. You can spend the morning with Didier."

"You always leave something out in the retelling. Besides, Didier's left already."

Fab jerked the keys out of my hand and was behind the wheel of the SUV before I got the front door locked. If I didn't know better, I'd think she put an energy shot in her espresso. She backed out of the driveway, tires squealing.

"Have you forgotten that the corner is a favorite speed trap location?" I hung onto the sissy bar.

Fab ignored me, hunched over the wheel, and pulled out on the highway, flying down the road.

I need a helmet.

I didn't time it but felt certain we made it to Jake's in record time. Since a food delivery truck blocked her usual space in front of the kitchen door, Fab whirled around and parked in front.

Even though we both had keys, Fab flipped out her lockpick and had the door open in record time.

Phil waved from behind the bar.

"No caffeine for her." I pointed to Fab.

"It's natural energy." Fab pirouetted on her toes.

"The meeting is being held out on the deck." Phil set a plate on the tray that held the drinks and headed outside. The private table reserved for special clientele had place settings for three. "You're in a good mode." She eyed Fab with suspicion.

"You can thank Didier," I teased. "I guess you knew I wouldn't be able to shake her and come by myself." I licked my lips at the sight of the pecan roll balls.

"You have to be kidding." Fab picked one up and sneered at it.

I snatched it out of her fingers, taking a bite. "More for me."

Phil banged her spoon on the table. "Calling this meeting to order." There was a note of solemnity in her voice. "Nothing new on Richards. Did a good job burying his past. I'd be careful until you find out more about him," she reported.

"Forget about checking into Richards any further. Told my brother, and he wasn't happy that I had his client checked out without a forewarning. What about Pamela?"

Phil glanced over at her laptop, sitting on one side of the table. "No arrest record. Her neighbors had nothing to say; they didn't even make the effort to make up something pleasant. 'Don't want to get involved' attitude, appeared uncomfortable, and shut the door in my guy's face. He used the excuse of checking the woman out for a high-profile job."

Phil paused, continuing to stare at her screen. "There was one small thing—the last boyfriend dumped her and moved out of state. He married soon after and his wife is pregnant, so I didn't bother him."

"How did you get that info?" Fab asked.

"My guy can talk a good game—schmoozed up one of her friends, 'accidently' ran into her and convinced her to go on a date with a stranger. He got her liquored up, and she spilled her guts, although she knew little, saying Pamela didn't share her personal business."

"That's low," I said in disgust.

"You won't think so with this last tidbit. Two boyfriends ago, his house burned down. Listed as arson. The cops took her in for questioning, didn't hold her, but showed up at her house a couple of times with more questions. I tracked down and interviewed the detective on the case, who'd retired and moved to the boonies. He said that she's the only one still on his list of suspects. He has a couple of cases that went unsolved that he goes through every once in a while, wondering what he missed."

"You took advantage of an old man?" Fab looked impressed.

Phil let loose a snort. "Hardly. He stared and smiled, saying 'I know what you're up to, young lady, and I'm enjoying it.' I ditched my well-rehearsed lie about why I wanted to pick his brain and ponied up the real story. His advice for Brad…" And here Phil read off the screen: "'She's the kind of woman with whom, after a hot night of sex, you wake up missing your boys.' I promised to stay in touch, keep him updated, and gave him my lawyer and Jake's business cards."

"There's no proof." I gulped a couple of times. "Wonder if it's enough to get my brother to listen. He already knows I don't like her." I should've known. Brad's dating record stood at one on the normal side, the rest whack jobs.

"He needs to be careful," Fab said. "Break-ups happen, but arson…"

Phil's phone dinged. She picked it up and read the screen. "My guy has an update on Pamela – says it's good. He'll call when he gets some privacy."

"Next call is to me, please," I told her, and she nodded. "You mentioned your business card…

I'm offended I didn't get your first lawyer card, after your parents, of course. I want a handful. I'll pass them around to people who owe me favors and can pay your fees."

"I'm willing to take a few pay-by-the-week clients to get started."

Fab grunted, shaking her head. "That means free. Hand me some of those cards. Just know there's a high likelihood anyone I refer is guilty. But they can pay."

Phil picked up a black leather briefcase off the floor, snapping the locks up. Reaching in, she handed us each a stack of cards.

Fab's smile turned to a glare, first at the card and then at Phil herself.

"So this is where you tell me the best bartender ever is leaving my employ?" I asked, puzzled by Fab's reaction.

"It's not finalized, but I hope it will be in the next few minutes." Phil crossed her fingers. "Using the deck as my office isn't professional, and I won't be taken seriously. I'm partnering with Old Man Dale. He's hasn't taken on new clients in a long time—he's mostly retired—but has agreed to mentor me. He'll do his usual: smoking cigars, reading the local weekly, and keeping an eye out that I don't step in it in any big way. I turned down a big-name firm, figured it wouldn't take me long to hate it. Tarpon needs a good lawyer; one that isn't crooked."

"Your new offices?" Fab tapped the card on

the table.

"I'd like to rent the lighthouse. I realize you own the building," Phil said to Fab, "but Madison owns the land. So I'm asking both of you."

I thought it was a great idea and told Phil so. I was surprised when Fab didn't join in.

Phil ignored her silence. "If I were your lawyer, I'd suggest that you clean up the ownership issue. The court might question where it came from and how it got here."

It was the one thing we did fifty/fifty – sort of, anyway. Fab allowed me to have it power washed, give it a coat of whitewash, and surround it with potted tropical flowers, though she drew the line at lights. The mishmash of plant containers came from Junker's on the other side of the driveway. "You know you'd have to tolerate people stopping for pictures. It's been quite popular," I reminded Phil.

"I factored that in as good advertising."

"You might want to look at her business card; she's already got the lighthouse's address on it."

"You're confident," I said.

"If the answer is no, I'll get new ones today."

I winced. "Oww. Don't kick me," I said to Fab. "I don't know if that means yes or no."

Phil took her case to Fab. "I'd be close by for your investigative work; you won't have to tear around town looking for me."

"It's not the worst idea I've heard," Fab

conceded.

"So it's settled." I raised my eyebrow at Fab, who scowled at me before nodding. I smiled and changed the subject. "I need to interview a day bartender. All the others are going to school and need night shifts."

"Got that taken care of. I asked Doodad, and he's interested. He said to tell you 'no pressure.' He pointed out that he didn't have my C-cup assets and wouldn't want it to affect business."

"We could buy him a pair of those, but it wouldn't be the same. Not sure he's a fit," I said.

"In his defense, he's a people magnet," Phil said. "Simpatico with the weirdos, since he's one of them. Get him out of the mom jeans, trade them in for a pair of shorts and a tropical shirt, and the women get some eye candy. He's also a guy's guy, when he doesn't go off on an 'I'm smarter than you' rant. Wicked smart, military background, can shoot someone between the eyes if necessary."

I flinched.

Fab flashed a toothy grin.

"I should check with Brad before poaching one of his employees." I had gotten Doodad a job on the condo project when his house blew away in a hurricane, leaving him only a shed to call home.

"Your brother…" Phil smiled. "His new look is f-ing hot."

Speechless, I stared at her.

"What about the chief?" Fab asked. "I thought you were banging him."

I blushed, certain I must be beet red, and swore my cheeks kept getting hotter.

"We mutually decided to be friends." Phil refilled our glasses. "We're geographically undesirable. Once I made the decision to stay in the Cove and not light out for Miami, it was inevitable. I can give him a recommendation in the sex department—a real gentleman. We were incompatible, though; he likes to party and have a good time all the time. I don't mean drinking, but boating, hanging with friends, cookouts on the beach, always something. I enjoy cuddling, walks on the beach, watching a movie once in a while. I introduced him to a friend who knows anyone worth knowing in South Beach and told her to take care of him and not introduce him to any nutjobs."

"You... uh... like Brad..." I broke off, not sure what to say.

"Has he shown any interest?" Fab asked.

"He's ogled my girls a few times but has always been excessively nice, which I know is code for not," Phil said.

"Take old Brad for a test drive—you know, a date," Fab suggested. "Madeline loves to interfere in people's love lives; she'll do it."

I was careful to put my forehead on the table gently; last time I banged it, it hurt for a day. "You sure?" I raised my head.

Phil nodded.

"I can get the two of you together, but you have to mix the chemistry yourselves." I rubbed my hands together. "I'll rip a page from Mother's ambush playbook. With her help, this will be fun. Don't worry, it won't be strange; my brother won't let it be. He's a good guy that way."

"Plan a family dinner," Fab suggested. "Have it in a restaurant to minimize any scenes, unless we all get drunk. Phil can ride with Didier and I, and Brad can take her home."

I couldn't believe Fab was being so helpful.

Phil also looked surprised.

"This might work out," Fab said. "Maybe not true love but friends. You're not certifiable, the family already loves you, and you're damn sexy."

"Couldn't you just set us up in the normal way, both parties knowing ahead of time?" Phil asked.

"You're right." I smiled. "I'll plant the idea next time I see him."

"That was too easy." Phil stared me down.

I kept my smile firmly in place.

Phil's phone rang. She looked at the screen. "I need to take this. It's about Mr. Naples." She answered, "What did you get?"

Fab tapped her index finger on her phone, indicating for her to put it on speaker. Phil frowned in response, then grabbed a pen and wrote on a napkin, pushing it across the table.

Fab nodded.

"Good job. Text me the pictures." Phil disconnected. "That's the address of the hangar." She pointed to the napkin. "My guy checked the place out. It's an old private airport used by locals and a couple of small airlines; all locked up, and he couldn't see inside. There's no one around to question about it."

"Great, another trip to Naples," I grumbled.

"The sooner we get this done the better. Brick's making a nuisance of himself. Had to tell him if he texted me one more time, I'd quit. I did promise that I'd call as soon as I got any info. Forward me a copy of the pics." Fab got up, taking her phone out of her pocket, and went over to the rail.

"The lighthouse is yours. Don't worry about Fab. By this afternoon, she'll agree without any urging from me." It wasn't like she had any plans to use it, now or ever. "Wait until Mother hears that you're interested in number one son."

Phil faded out for a moment. "I think your Mother likes me."

"Of course she does."

Fab got back into her seat. "Told Brick we'd leave early tomorrow. How much is the rent on the lighthouse?"

"How about a trade for services?" I suggested. "It's not like it's costing either of us to have it sitting there. The block was willed to me with the express caveat that I wouldn't succumb and sell out to a condo development. I've said no to developers so many times, they've stopped calling."

"On the jobs for my clients, you get paid," Fab told her. "You tell us how much, Madison keeps track of the bookkeeping, and you'll get cash."

"You surprise me," I said to Fab. "In a good way."

Chapter Thirty-Five

My phone rang. I looked down, and Phil's face flashed on the screen.

"I've got an update for you," Phil said after hellos were exchanged. "Are you sitting down?

"Do I need to be?" I claimed a bar stool, elbows on the counter top.

"I've got an update on Pamela."

By the time she finished, I had a headache threatening.

"Thank you for following up." I disconnected and rubbed my temples.

I punched in Brad's number; after incessant ringing, the call went to voicemail. *Fine!*

My next call went to Didier. He answered on the second ring. "Cherie."

"I'm looking for Brad."

"You just missed him. He left for lunch, mentioned going to The Swamp Shack."

I thanked him and ran upstairs, changing into a knee-length black sundress and low-heeled black sandals. Going back downstairs, I scribbled a note and left it on the kitchen counter. Fab would see it when she woke up from her nap by the pool. I grabbed my purse and raced to the SUV.

Traffic was light. I cut across the highway and down to the docks. The Swamp Shack was Tarpon Cove's newest restaurant, having opened in the updated section of the docks to rave reviews about the food.

My stomach was aflutter as I pulled into the parking lot, finding a spot next to my brother's SUV. I'd decided on the way over that if he wasn't alone, I'd wait for him in the bar. A small voice suggested that I wait until later, but he'd made being elusive an art form as of late.

I walked up the ramp and couldn't be sure who saw who first, me or Brad and Pamela. So much for sitting at the bar; I could hardly do that now that they'd spotted me. I waved and headed straight to their table on the outside patio overlooking the water.

Brad frowned and stood, pulling out a chair. "Are you meeting someone?" His chilly tone let me know how annoyed he was at running into me.

I acknowledged Pamela with a nod. "I'm here to talk to you."

"It must be important." His eyes narrowed.

The waiter asked for my drink order. "Margarita, please."

Brad groaned.

"If you don't mind," Pamela spoke up. "This is a romantic lunch for two, not three."

"Now is the perfect time." I knew it wasn't, but I'd be damned if I'd let myself be brushed off by Pammy. "I've just received a report about you, Pamela." My eyes bored into hers; then I turned my head towards Brad. "I thought it in your best interest to hear the findings ASAP."

"You ran another background check," Brad ground out. "This isn't the place to air dirty laundry."

The waiter delivered my drink. Brad and Pamela must have signaled for refills, as he set down glasses in front of them as well.

"It's the perfect place. Less likelihood of creating a scene. Right, Pammy?" I pasted a phony smile on my face.

"Brad won't say it, but I will: get lost." Her lips pulled tight.

"You're right; he'd never be so rude."

"I want you to finish your drink, and we'll talk about whatever it is *later*." Brad pushed my glass closer.

I took a long drink. "You need to be careful of this woman. Ask her last boyfriend, an NFL football player. She came close to ruining his life and ending his career; he damn near ended up in jail."

I heard Pamela hiss. The facts coming back to haunt her didn't sit well. Phil was too good at her job. I knew everything she told me in the phone call had been triple-checked and was true.

"He made the mistake of breaking up with

her, and within an hour she filed assault charges. He was immediately suspended from the team. The police investigated, but they couldn't find any corroborating evidence, not even a mark on her, and no other woman, not even his ex-wife, had anything bad to say. The district attorney declined to press charges. What did she do then? She sued him, but the judge threw the case out. How often does that happen—almost never? He's still working to get his reputation back."

"That doesn't mean she lied," Brad defended her.

"The ex before the football player, his house burned down shortly after their breakup. To this day, she remains the only suspect."

"I didn't…" Pamela stammered. "You're distorting the facts." She grabbed Brad's hand.

"Poor Pammy," I gushed.

"Enough. Pamela and I will discuss this later," Brad said.

"You're going to give her a pass, aren't you?" It infuriated me when he looked away. "I have one more thing to say, and then I'm leaving."

"Stop. Her," Pamela implored.

"My brother has a huge heart, and it's wasted on you."

"Bitch," she hissed and downed her wine.

"Pamela worked for a veteran's organization, raising money, until about two months ago, when they fired her for embezzlement. She worked there for several years, and until now, they hadn't questioned that ninety percent of the money raised went to expenses. *Her* expenses. She's currently under investigation by the Feds."

"Is it true?" Brad asked without emotion.

Pamela looked down, appearing to compose herself, and said nothing.

"Before you deny it, Brad can read about it online. It's all there in various news reports; even made the sports pages."

Pamela stood and threw the contents of her water glass in my face.

Patrons at a nearby table gasped.

As she turned to leave, I said, "Anything happens to my brother, and I'll hunt you down."

"Was that necessary?" Brad asked, ice in his voice.

"What? Jail, arson, thievery... that's some resume for a girlfriend. Pardon me for looking out for you." I shoved my chair back. "Personally, given what I've seen of her, I say good riddance."

A man looking vaguely familiar appeared at the table, tall enough that if I had to stare for long, I'd get a crick in my neck.

"James Bordello," Brad introduced him, waving him to take a seat.

"Madison, I presume." His grey eyes, dark and dangerous, bored right through me. "You're the one who ran off Richards. I should thank you; your brother and I are going to do some business."

A snotty reply of, "That's nice," sat on the tip of my tongue, but I managed to bite it back. He'd apparently forgotten that we'd already met – fine with me.

"Branching out?" I asked.

"Nothing's been inked," Brad said but didn't bother to look at me.

I stood. "Nice to meet you." I briefly glanced at James.

"Wait." Brad held out his hand. "Not a word about what happened here today – to anyone."

"Swear." I held out my pinkie finger.

Brad ignored the gesture.

"You'd rather I'd let her burn down the condo with you in it?"

"Of course not. Thank you."

"I wish it looked like you meant that."

Chapter Thirty-Six

"I'm sick of this drive already; I want sore-butt pay," I whined, twisting around in the seat. We'd finally made it to Naples, the abundance of traffic slowing Fab's lead foot.

"Don't make me pull over."

"Go ahead." I smirked. "Preferably in front of a coffee joint."

"It's an easy job—snoop around, take some pictures, and we'll be back on the highway, headed home to collect our pay."

"I hope you didn't jinx us. Remember, this is a Brick job. Beware of bullets." I sighed. Brick's jobs were never that easy.

"First, we do a drive-by, case the joint. It's a small municipal airport with a private road for an entrance. Looked at some pictures on the internet, and it doesn't appear guarded. The hangars are privately owned and located on the back side of the property."

"You need to stay in touch," I admonished. "I don't want to have to smash through doors, guns blazing."

"You've been watching too much television."

"Make the next left. It's a long driveway. I

looked at the same pictures. Veer to the right and follow the road to the end. Another right. We're there." I crossed my fingers. "Hopefully."

I got my last glimpse of the sun flickering on the water off the Gulf as Fab followed my directions.

After making the last turn, Fab hit the brakes. "If I'm not mistaken, the hangar we're looking for is surrounded by cars. Law enforcement, all of them."

"Forget casing the joint." I tugged on her arm. "Turn around, now, and hopefully, we won't attract any attention."

"Don't you want to know what's going on?" Fab asked, wide-eyed.

"I flat-ass don't care. Now turn around."

"Yeesh. Calm down." Fab ignored me and continued slowly around the circle. "I'll head to the exit; keep your eyes peeled for a spot nearby to watch and take a few pictures. No place here." She scanned the property. "We can't use any of the other hangars; they're locked up and no one's around."

I breathed a silent sigh of relief. "Judging by the two large flatbeds, Mr. Kasey isn't having a good day if he's inside. Wonder what he did to invite such a large turnout?"

"We can't be sure Kasey is involved."

"I can. There's a 'C' on the side of the building, and it says here—" I pointed to the note Phil had written on the napkin. "Building C."

"I need a hangar of my own. Closer to home."

"In Tarpon, it's called an old building, and there are plenty of those around. What would you do, sit around inside, admiring the dirt and spiders? Everyone in town would be convinced you were running something illegal."

"I might have made a small error in judgment," Fab said, eyes glued to the rearview mirror.

"I don't want to know." I tried not to yell, but the words came out louder than I wanted.

"Take a deep breath." Fab slowed, waiting for the security fence to open so we could make our getaway. "There's a black sedan that pulled out of the parking lot and is headed this way."

"Turn here." I pointed. "The road winds in the opposite direction, but it's a faster way to the Interstate. I can't take another trip across the Everglades."

Fab drove with one eye on the road and the other on her side mirror. The car behind us was rapidly approaching. Two local police cars coming in the opposite direction made u-turns and flipped their lights on.

"That didn't take long," Fab said. She sounded impressed.

"I just said a little prayer that this is somehow a big mistake and we're not going to be arrested for something we know nothing about." I unlatched the glove box and pulled out the insurance card, sticking it under my thigh.

I shoved my feet back into the tan flat sandal slip-ons that I'd brought along to go with the white scoop-neck spaghetti-strapped dress I'd worn. Fab was wearing a backless black sundress.

Fab pulled onto the grassy side strip, rolled down the window, and left the engine running. It was too hot to be without air conditioning. She kept her eyes glued to the rearview mirror. "Wonder what's taking so long. One officer got out of each car, and they're huddled together."

I took a deep breath, exhaling slowly. After a few seconds, I said, "I'm calling Creole." It went to voicemail. I tapped out a text: *Pulled over by locals outside Naples airport.* "He knows we drove over here today and was fine with it, since we're only here to gather information, with the added plus that Brick volunteered to do the dirty work."

"Got the same pep talk from Didier. I wonder who called who?" Fab tapped her fingers impatiently. "I wish I could see better. The dark tint on these windows is sometimes a hindrance, but usually only at night, when you have to roll down the window to back up with a bit of assurance that you won't run into anything." Fab reached for her purse, which was wedged between the side of the seat and the door. "I'm handing over my License to Carry, following the law for once."

Creole texted back, *Call me when you're back on*

the highway.

"Finally," Fab said, clearly exasperated. "Two of them are headed this way; one cut over to your side."

"License and insurance." The officer stuck his head in the window, taking a look around the interior. "Shut off the engine."

Thanks to Fab, the exterior and interior were always spotless. Even if we had anything to hide, it wouldn't be out in the open.

My anxiety ratcheted up a notch when the other officer knocked on my window. I powered it down.

"ID," he demanded grumpily.

I reached between my legs and produced my driver's and carry licenses from my purse, handing them to the officer and then placing my hands on the dashboard. I noticed that Fab put hers at ten and two on the steering wheel. I heard her say, "We currently have them on our persons. How would you like us to proceed?" I repeated that to my officer.

"Where is it?" Fab's officer asked.

Fab responded, "Inner thigh."

"Me too," I said to mine. "I mean, inner thigh."

"Both of you out," the one on Fab's side barked. "Hands in plain sight."

Both officers had their guns out.

I clutched the side of the door and stepped down.

"One hand in the air. With the other, remove your gun and place it on the ground."

I lifted my dress and followed his instructions, making sure that he could see what I was doing and there'd be no misunderstandings. He directed me farther down the grass strip and had me stand away from my SUV and a foot from the front of the first police cruiser. It surprised me when the other cop directed Fab to stand not far from me.

"Can I ask why we got stopped?" I asked. "I didn't think we were speeding."

"Don't go anywhere," one officer instructed and followed his partner back to the car. The third one continued to lean against the front of his car.

"I should've taken your advice and turned around."

I clutched my chest. "Could you repeat that? Several times would make me happy."

Whatever the officers were doing, it was taking a damn long time. I shifted from one foot to the other and stretched a couple of times. I bent over and inspected the grass for bugs, coming face to face with a grasshopper and jumping back.

"You want me to step on it?"

"I do not. Me being a sissy is not a reason to kill it."

"Finally," Fab whispered.

The third cop sauntered up and, with no

introduction, jumped into his first question. "What were you two doing in a restricted area without the necessary clearance?" He directed his question to Fab, including me with a flick of his eyes.

"I'm a licensed PI and was here to locate a missing car. Drove in, out, no stopping." She waved in my direction. "She came along for the ride."

"You a PI?" he asked me.

I shook my head. "Working on getting my license." Since Brick and I were always on the outs, I had given up on that goal, but he didn't need to know that.

"What kind of car? And what if you found it?" he asked.

"Custom red Ferrari. I have a picture on my phone," Fab answered. "I had instructions to call my client, and he'd make arrangements for a pickup."

"Client's name?"

"Brick Famosa. You may have heard of him— he writes bail bonds up and down the state and is a private investigator himself. His brother, Casio Famosa, is a decorated Miami police detective."

Casio won't appreciate his name being dropped, I thought.

Oh hell. I re-thought the name-dropping business. "If we need a personal reference, you can contact Chief Harder in Miami; he knows us both." I wasn't going out on a limb when I said he'd vouch for us. I saw more favor-doing in my future if this officer took me up on the offer.

Fab coughed, which I knew was probably a shocked laugh at my audacity.

"What do you know about Mr. Kasey's business?" the officer asked, staring between the two of us, closer than before.

"Not a thing." Fab explained about the custom order and how it went down. "I got a tip he was a car collector and owned a hangar down here, came by to check it out."

"Stay put." He walked back to his friends, who were both sitting in the car. They immediately got out when he reached them.

"I'm impressed. You didn't tell one falsehood," I said.

"It was painful, but I got through it. It took one second to decide jail was the last place I wanted to end up tonight." Fab kept her eyes on the police cars. "Here's a to-do for you. Make sure Phil can arrange bail twenty-four hours a day. Brick's our first call, but he can't always be depended on."

"I'm probably going to have to find us a new attorney. Mac made up with Cruz, but I'm not sure I can rely on him responding promptly, given that I haven't spoken to him myself," I said, a worried frown creasing my forehead. "It's not my fault that when his granny visited, she acted like a horny teenager. Fingers crossed Cruz is over it by now. It's not like she got arrested; she just bumped knobby knees with Crum, which is dangerous all on its own. I'll deal with Phil, and you find out from Crum if he uses condoms and if not, suggest it."

Fab stuck her fingers in her ears and yelled, "Please let us go. She's driving me crazy."

Two of the officers turned, one smiled, and they went back to their conversation.

We stood like statues in the steamy Florida weather. Fab did anyway. I took up a game of hopscotch, mostly in place. I hoped excess sweat wouldn't ruin my dress.

After an interminably long time, two of the officers walked back, the third, already in his car, pulled a u-turn and went back in the direction of the airport. One officer handed us back our identification and handguns.

"Do you know why there wasn't a stolen car report filed on the car you're looking for?" Fab's officer asked.

"You'd have to ask Brick," Fab said.

He turned his attention to me. "Why don't you tell me what you know?"

"I looked the address up on Google; that's the extent of my contribution."

"You understand we need to check everyone out," the officer said. "Thank you for your cooperation." Without waiting for an answer, they went back to their cars.

Fab waited until they were both back in their

cars before exploding. "What the hell?"

"I vote we go home, jump in the pool, and get our drunk on."

Chapter Thirty-Seven

I was stretched out on the daybed, thoroughly sauced. My first clue was when I'd planted my feet on the wall and saw my toes dancing around.

Didier smiled indulgently. He'd come home early and came out on the patio, stern faced, presumably to quiet down our off-key singing. He ordered us out of the pool, and in reply, we splashed him with water. He bribed us with another drink if we'd come in the house. Now, he and Fab lounged on the couch across from me, and she had her feet in his lap.

Fab downed the last of her martini and slammed the glass down on the table.

"You break it, you buy another set. I won't have mismatched glasses." I stuck out my tongue.

She stuck hers out.

"Ladies..." Didier laughed.

The front door blew open, even though it was a relatively calm night. "Look who's here," Creole yelled.

"Don't slam the door," Fab yelled back.

Bang.

Creole swept into the living room, bowed, and winked at me.

I held up my glass. "If you get me a refill, I'll kiss you twice."

Creole stood at the end of the daybed. He arched his eyebrow at Didier. "They both drunk?"

"They've had a bad day." Didier patted Fab's knees. She giggled. "Brick Famosa. Need I say more?"

"It could have been worse." Creole bent down and kissed me. "I'll get the refills." He pointed to Didier's beer bottle, and got a nod in return. "Message from the chief." He looked down at me. "FBI called about your *reference*. He said to tell you, 'that makes two.'"

I blew out, "I knew it."

Fab's foot nudged Didier's hand. He kissed her toes and started giving her a foot rub.

I smiled at the sound of the blender. Creole rustled around in the kitchen. He came back, tray in hand, and served the drinks.

"Bricker took it well when I called and ran down how the stop with the police went." Fab slurred a few of her words. "He's sending over payment—I didn't have to prod him—and I mentioned we had to hire a freelancer. Damn happy we didn't get arrested."

Didier bit her big toe.

Fab groaned.

Creole stood over me. I held out my leg.

"Want to bite my feet? Looks fun." I giggled.

He leaned down, kissed me, and pulled me to a sitting position. After sitting down behind me, he plumped the pillows and lay back, hauling me back against his chest.

"You two would still be in custody if you'd been caught on the property when the feds rolled up." Creole took a long swig of his beer. "They'd been watching Kasey for a while. They just got their case together, and a judge issued an arrest warrant. Kasey will probably never get out of prison—twenty years is a long stretch for an older man, and that would be on the light side."

"Twenty." Fab whistled. "This ought to be good."

"Kasey was running a ponzi scheme, getting people to invest their cash in two companies that didn't exist. Add to that money laundering for one of the biggest South American drug dealers. He was about to take a flight to Brazil with a hundred million in cash. I don't believe he planned to come back, leaving the wife in the lurch. He cleaned out their accounts, left the house mortgaged to the hilt. Nice guy."

"The cars?" I asked.

"Kasey sold them to a collector. Anything he owned, he sold, turned into cash. Had a duffle bag stuffed with bundles of hundreds from the sales."

"Brick any part of this?" Didier asked.

"Appears he was also conned. Good luck

getting the car back." Creole brushed his hands together.

"Do you know if the fed guy call Brick?" Fab asked.

"They did one better and showed up at his office in person. I hear they were all over him like white cat hair on a black suit." Creole reached out and petted Snow, who'd jumped up and snuggled her head in his hand. "Brick remained cool under pressure, answered their questions. I called a friend at the Bureau from back in the day; he was in on the visit, thought for the most part, Brick came across as truthful but smarmy."

"You'd be proud of Fab," I told Didier. "She answered every question directly and truthfully."

Didier kissed her ankles and said something quietly in French that left Fab blushing.

"What about Kasey's victims?" I asked. "Do they recoup anything?"

"It'll be years," Creole said. "The wheels of justice often lag when huge sums of money are involved."

Didier slid Fab's legs off to the side and stood, gathering glasses and bottles and heading to the kitchen.

"Let's go for a run in the morning," Creole said to his back.

"Not too early, please," I groaned.

"You won't even know I'm gone."

I arched my head back. "Oh yes I will." And

blew him a kiss.

"Stop." Fab made a gagging noise. "Don't ruin the good news that we're not under investigation."

"You shouldn't drink. You're surly and introverted. Me, on the other hand, I'm outgoing." When I saw two pairs of raised eyebrows, I amended, "Okay, obnoxious. But a happy drunk."

"And charming, cherie," Didier said, sitting down next to Fab. "Sometimes."

"In the morning, knock, and I'll be ready in five." Creole rolled me off him. Standing, he lifted me in his arms, carrying me to the stairs.

"Fab and I will cook breakfast and have it ready when you get back," I said.

"Sure we will," Fab groaned.

Chapter Thirty-Eight

"Big thank you." Fab said out of nowhere, slinking into the kitchen. She shoved an envelope across the island. "This was delivered by a major delivery company. Even had to sign. Westmont would've never paid without your strong-arming him. I'll try not to complain if I have to put out for the chief."

I opened the envelope and flicked through the freshly minted money, flashing a smile. I knew without a doubt that she would've been stiffed without the chief connection. Another reason I disliked these private clients of hers.

"I'm happy it's over with. You deserved to get paid. You earned every cent."

"What are you up to?" Fab flicked the top of my pen.

"Just leaving you a note."

"Don't bother. I'm coming."

"I'm going to meet with Spoon. It might go better if I'm alone. I can pick you up on the way back," I suggested.

"I am family." Fab's hands shot to her to hips in a silent dare. "Wouldn't Stepdaddy like to see both of us?"

"That stepdaddy moniker is only amusing sometimes. You make it sound downright creepy." I returned her stare. "Can you behave yourself?"

"Of course," she sniffed.

Fab grabbed the car keys out of my hand, nudged me out of the way, and flew out the door.

I followed, wincing when she slammed the driver's side door. "First stop, the Bakery Café," I said, getting in. "Caffeine and whipped cream are conducive to a good mood."

Fab whirled through the drive-thru, and I gave her Spoon's order and told her, "My regular." I'd gotten Spoon's favorite from Mother when inquiring where to find him, or ambush him, as Mother put it.

Fab handed me the drink holder and shot across the highway to the other side and down several side streets, taking the back way. She parked in the only visitor parking space in front of JS Auto Body. The repair place didn't appear to be open for business, but then, it never did. The ten-foot barbed wire fence was meant to be a deterrent to trespassing, and was always closed and locked. Spoon's guys worked on high-end cars for exorbitant prices and by invitation only. He no longer took new clients, catering only to his well-established client base.

Spoon had the security door unlocked and was standing in the doorway before we got out.

"Both of you." He stared us down. "I believe this is a first." He took the cardboard tray from my hands. "A bribe? Which one is mine?" He waved his hand toward the leather chairs in front of his desk.

You'd never guess from the outside that this repair business was different from any other, but you'd get your first clue walking into Spoon's office. The large space was spotlessly clean, with no trace of an oil smell. It had painted concrete flooring and was decorated in silver and black, all masculine. A small kitchenette lined the back wall, and a side door opened to a large full bath. The times I'd visited, I hadn't seen anyone use the pool table or either of the arcade games. From the sounds emanating through the walls from the bays on the other side, it was a busy day.

"In the spirit of upfront disclosure—" Spoon popped the lid off his coffee, sniffing before taking a drink. "—your mother forewarned me."

That sniffing thing was something he had in common with Fab.

Spoon flashed an even smile. "Madeline dispensed some advice. She suggested that I listen to what you want and not just agree upfront."

Fab withdrew her Walther from the back of her waistband and blew on it. "Dusty."

My head whipped in her direction. "Your promise lasted thirty seconds," I hissed. "What are you doing?"

"I'm also interested in the answer," Spoon said, a hard glint to his eyes.

Fab barely acknowledged me. "I wouldn't shoot our stepdaddy," she drawled. "Not unless he said no to you or made you cry… something like that."

Fab and Spoon exchanged deranged smiles. Who won was a toss-up from my vantage point.

"Put that away," I mouthed, then said aloud, "I know how much you enjoy snooping; why don't you entertain yourself elsewhere?" I turned to Spoon and pleaded silently.

He nodded. Opening his side drawer, he laid a .44 Magnum Smith & Wesson on his desktop. "I'm not saying I'd shoot you either. While you're snooping, do not touch anything and stay out of the way."

Before Spoon changed his mind, Fab stood and slipped out the door.

"You took that well," I said.

"If she'd been a biological daughter of Madeline's, not sure I'd have married into the family."

"Fab does like you."

He snorted. "Yeah, I like her too. Don't keep me in suspense, skip to the point."

"I need a favor."

No response at first, his face a blank. Then Spoon leaned back in his chair, arms crossed. "The point."

"Hear me out. This involves Chief Harder, and

I'm well aware he's not your favorite person. I needed a favor from him to do a favor for Fab, who is like a real sister to me, and in return, he needs his DeLorean worked on."

"Do you know why the slimy bastard isn't my 'favorite'?"

I shook my head. I'd had no clue they even knew one another until I told Creole the chief's favor. His response was, "Good luck with that."

"Your friend, Hard-ass, was instrumental in getting my best friend at the time a plea deal to save his own ass. He testified that I was involved in a drug deal gone bad—the leader ended up dead." A tic of angry muscle jumped along his jaw. "There wasn't a scintilla of evidence against me, but plenty showing my friend was in the operation up to his neck – all ignored. Harder wasn't going to lose sleep over the wrong man going to jail."

"You were acquitted?" I asked. He nodded. "Thank goodness."

Spoon downed his coffee, tossing the cup in the trash.

"Your friend, what happened to him?" I asked.

"Disappeared. One day, enough pieces of his body were spit out by an alligator to make an identification. The coroner couldn't rule it an accident or otherwise. My hunch is the latter. As far as I know, the case got little attention.

No one gave a damn. He wasn't a man to

inspire sympathy."

The silence hung between us.

"I'm sorry. I shouldn't have asked, but I didn't know."

Spoon let out an exasperated sigh. "It's old news. I need to get over it. He's still a bastard, asking you for such a favor. I'll do it, but I'm doing it for your sake, not that bastard's."

"You're the best. I'm willing to facilitate the whole process; you'll never have to speak to him."

"This isn't some freebie," he ground out.

"We didn't discuss money."

"Harder pays or forget it. I'm not relenting on that. No respectable man lets a woman pay his auto repair bill."

"I'll get the address for pickup. I can be there, and the driver can deal with me. Same on the return."

"Not necessary. I'll handle it."

"You sure?"

Spoon nodded. "What was the favor?"

I told him about the college girl limo ride, the trouble on the way home, and laid it on a little thick about how the chief had saved us from arrest.

"Your mother isn't going to be happy that she knew about none of this. She's already told me she wants a verbatim replay of our conversation today. At one point, I expected her to demand that I record it."

I laughed. "You can tell her. I'm happy she can badger you that way."

He frowned, but the sides of his mouth quirked up. "What other trouble have you gotten into?"

I ran down the details of the latest Brick case.

"Read about that online. Thought it was stupid that the man stuck around so long. That was his biggest mistake after getting involved in the scheme in the first place." Spoon made a note on his desk calendar. "I'll have Harder's car picked up tomorrow. Don't make a habit of this, get my meaning?"

I groaned and told him about Harder's part in the Naples fiasco and how he'd vouched for us. According to Creole, it was what kept us out of jail. "He holds another IOU."

"Let's hope he doesn't have a second car." Spoon shook his head.

"This doesn't have to be a one-way street, you know. You need something, ask. Answer is yes."

"Just keep your mother happy, and whatever you do, don't get arrested. You ever think about another line of fun and games? One with no guns involved."

"Got any ideas?"

"I come up with something, I'll call."

"I'm about to make Mother really happy. I've got a date ambush for her to set up. Brad's going to be her victim this time. I'm roping in Liam as a co-conspirator. She gets a twofer: a family dinner and the chance to meddle in her son's love life. Raise your right hand."

"No. I won't say anything; this can be *your* surprise." Spoon unleashed a growly laugh.

I told Spoon about Phil's crush.

"He's stupid if he passes on getting to know that morsel better."

"An added plus: there's no mental instability in her background," I said.

"Anything else? Your 'sister' has been gone a while, and it makes my skin itch. I need to check on her." Spoon stood up.

"I'll text her."

"Forget that. I'm sneaking up on her."

"I'd better stay behind and not ruin your plan. Later, you can tell me who won at that game."

Chapter Thirty-Nine

Fab backed out of the auto body shop, honking and waving to Spoon, who'd walked us out to the SUV and waited for us to drive away.

"I take you to Spoon's, and you can't play nice for a millisecond, pulling your gun…" I half-snorted.

"It's not like I pulled the trigger," Fab defended herself. She twisted through the side streets and back to the main highway, braking for a signal.

I powered down the window and stuck my head out. "Pull over," I said over my shoulder. "That's Miss January. I need to find out what's going on."

"Who let her out?" Fab pulled to the curb, the car behind us honking.

"She's a drunk, not a ten year old." I opened the door and jumped out.

Miss January was sharing the trolley bench with a woman I'd never seen before. Ignoring her, I zeroed in on Miss January, going to stand next to her.

"Hi, honey." Miss January exhaled shakily, her rummy eyes focusing with difficulty.

"I stopped to give you a ride." I put out my hand, catching hers up in mine and tugging gently.

Miss January stood shakily, then sat back down with a bounce. "Come on, Alverta." She signaled to the other woman.

I turned my attention to the buxom woman, who was staring at me, an unlit stogie hanging from her lips. She wore a gaudy lime dress that hung like a tent over her ample form, still showing too much cleavage for a woman her age. With more gusto than necessary, she hawked spit on the concrete between her feet.

"Jany, you forget we have errands?" Alverta turned to me. "I'll get her home okay."

"My hair." Miss January clutched the side of her head, and at least a quarter of her hair fell off. "Damn glue, didn't work. Makes my scalp burn and itch."

Fab walked up. "What's taking so long? Where's her hair?"

I pointed to Miss January's lap. Her head had a few bald spots, her hair cut jaggedly, a little longer than beard stubble. A thin layer of something was stuck on the top of it, and with the flick of my nail, I confirmed that it was hard, wisps of longer hair sticking to it.

"What happened?" I asked, struggling to keep the anger out of my voice.

"Got in a fight at Custer's last night." Miss January ran her hand across her head, wincing.

"Duked it out in the alley. Mello pushed me face down, then dragged me by the hair. When I first realized it was missing, I thought she pulled it out, but then I saw the knife in her hand; maybe it was that." She swiped at a tear on her cheek. "Custer broke us up, came out yelling we were old hags and he'd called the sheriff. Alverta, bless her heart, got me out of there." She stood and stumbled, clutching the pole. "Waiting on the trolley. Need to get the glue off before going home. Don't have anything there."

"You didn't go home last night?" I glared at Alverta. "Where—"

"Who are *you* anyway?" Alverta demanded, standing up belligerently. "You're a nosy broad." She bumped my hip, sending me stumbling back, and looped her arm through Miss January's. "Trolley's coming."

Fab delivered a quick chop to the woman's arm, and she released her hold on Miss January.

"Miss January's coming with us." Fab put her arm across the woman's shoulders and turned to Alverta. "You hit my friend again, and I'll kick your behind up to your tonsils."

I chuckled.

"What? I heard Crum say it." Fab led the way back to the car.

I opened the back door, helped Miss January inside, slid in next to her, and fished my phone out of my pocket. "Do you know what kind of glue was used?"

"Superglue," she sing-songed.

I turned away, rolling my eyes, and called Shirl; she'd know if a doctor visit was required.

When she answered, I informed her of the problem. After Shirl got a good laugh out of it, she told me it was her day off and she'd be waiting when we got to the property.

After I hung up, I asked Miss January, "Where did you sleep last night?"

"Went to a nearby park, slept on one of the benches. Someone was nice and left their newspaper behind. Alverta and I split it up and used it to stay warm. We each got our own bench." Miss January's head lolled to the side.

Thank goodness last night was another mild night in Florida.

"Listen carefully," I admonished. "I'm going to make you repeat it. You need a ride, call me or Mac anytime. There will be no more sleeping under the stars. Now repeat it."

Miss January patted my cheek. "You're such a nice girl." She repeated most of what I told her.

Fab zipped into the driveway and honked at Mac and Shirl, who held her doctor's bag. When they stepped out of the way, she passed them up and came to a stop in front of Miss January's cottage. Fab got out, opening the back door and helping Miss January out. "She's all yours." She handed her off to Shirl.

"Is it going to hurt?" I wrinkled my nose.

Shirl shook her head. "Alcohol and lotion

should take care of it." She whispered to Miss January and led her up the stairs to her cottage, settling her in her favorite chair outside on the landing.

"Pool or office?" Mac threw her arm out in a flourish, first in one direction, then the other, setting the bells sewn on her t-shirt jingling. Her dingy brown full skirt almost matched her ankle-top slippers with yellow floppy ears.

"Pool," Fab answered for me. "You have refreshments ready?"

"The refrigerator by the pool is stocked," Mac said.

"Pool? Drinks? It must be all bad news." I led the way across the driveway.

Fab entered the gate code, and we trooped in, gathering around the shallow end and putting our feet in the water.

"Before you start," I said to Mac. "I know you're not Miss January's caretaker, but she's so easy to talk out of her foolish notions. She slept on a bench last night."

"Miss January and that new friend of hers snuck off the property last night. I didn't see them leave," Mac defended herself. "I had no idea where to look, or I'd have jerked her butt back here."

"The rest of your news, blurt it out," Fab ordered.

"Joseph's new lady friend had a heart attack, and he's been on a drunk ever since."

"My RSVP for the funeral – NO!" Fab said. Noting my incredulous expression, she added, "In case you were going to ask."

"She's not dead, and they weren't doing it when it happened." Mac scissored her fingers. "He's only drunk because he's overwhelmed by getting back on the woman hunt again. Confided that if she died in his bed, his wanker might not recover."

"Can't wait to whisper 'wanker' to Didier in a romantic moment, just to see his expression." Fab laughed.

"You better not tell your boyfriend that it was my idea." I glared at Fab, then switched to Mac. "You've got 'more news' written on your brow, which is arched awfully high."

"She drew them on," Fab volunteered.

I looked down, afraid to meet Mac's eyes for fear I'd burst out laughing.

Mac thrust her chest out, and her hand shot to the water. I grabbed her arm. "Don't you dare get me wet."

Fab inched away.

"Crum's started a walking service." Mac sighed. "I don't expect it to last long." She had a "why me?" look on her face.

"Dog walking?" I asked, confused. "Didn't know he had any animal rapport. Although his cat seems happy."

"That's a little too normal for him," Fab said. "What's the catch?"

"He's walking old ladies."

Fab and I looked at one another and burst out laughing. When we recovered, I said "That's a good one."

"Truth." Mac held up her right hand. "Two takers so far. First one approached him, and for a crisp twenty, he paraded her around the neighborhood. All went well until Crum found out the woman in question had taken some side bets as to her ability to pull it off and made quite a bit of money. Crum had smoke coming out his ears, complaining that had he known, he would've demanded a cut."

Fab laughed again.

"Just walking?" I asked.

"Never saw the woman around here before their outing; now I've seen her twice, leaving with her wig rumpled. She's bragging about town that they're in a relationship. I suspect it's strictly sex."

"You said there were two," Fab reminded her.

"The second woman was a copycat scammer. Problem was Crum hit her up for a cut of the jackpot. She exploded and stomped off, but not before swinging her purse and trying to clock him in the head. He managed to jump back but fell on his backside."

"It's not illegal," Fab said.

"That's all you have to say?" I said. "You need to remind Crum that The Cottages has an air of respectability to maintain."

They both laughed at me.

The gate rattled. Doodad stood on the other side, a good six foot five, with the widest damn shoulders, and clean-shaven; last time I saw him, he'd had a full beard.

"This a good time?" he asked.

I called out the code. He stepped back and held it open for Shirl, who'd walked up behind him.

"Step into my office." I waved to Doodad to have a seat by the pool. I introduced everyone. "Beat it, girls."

"You are the rudest," Fab huffed.

"I know," I said and winked at Doodad.

Fab organized a silent mutiny and waved for Mac and Shirl to sit with her on the other half of the steps.

Charles Wingate III, aka Doodad, was a retired sea captain and another person useful in coordinating information in exchange for money, and keeping the lowlifes away from Fab and I. I'd used my influence to get him a job with Brad and Didier.

"I left a message for my brother that I wanted to poach an employee and haven't heard back," I started. "It would have to be okay with him."

"Brad's good. I talked to him before coming over. Since the project's almost complete, they're downsizing the crew, first come, first go, and that would be me. Works out good."

"Phil highly recommended you. Any

experience?" I wouldn't hold a lack against him; I knew nothing about dive bars when I bought out one of my aunt's old friend's. In my plus column, Jake's was still standing and busier than ever.

"Last weekend, I hung around, watching Phil. The majority of your customers order beer; that's easy. I got a drink book, and I'm studying up on the popular drinks, such as margaritas and martinis." He flashed a smile.

"Good suck up. I know you own a rifle; can you use it?" Judging by the glare, the answer was yes. "There's a Mossberg under the bar, and I'd like to think you'd adopt a 'scare rather than shoot' stance. If you're a sissy and can't handle an occasional bar fight, this isn't the job for you."

He crossed his arms across his chest and stared me down. I returned his stare. "I'll have to keep my eye on you. I've been in a few fights, so I suppose I can break them up without getting my pretty face rearranged."

"Just so you know, I don't expect you to risk getting hurt in any way," I said. "Phil's got a few tips for restoring order. If you blow a hole in the roof, let me know so I can send out the roofer."

"I'm pretty good with people," Doodad said. "Heard no breasts could be an issue, but I can shake my bar towel and charm your female drinkers."

"You have to provide your own uniform. Tropical shorts and shirt. Clean is a must. No ugly shoes that will bother my friend over there."

I pointed to Fab. "You're also not allowed to shoot her, annoying as she can be."

"Phil gave me the rundown on all the players and your weirdo friends." He chuckled.

"You've got some nerve, calling someone weird. You used to parade about town masquerading as a Civil War general."

"Good money on the weekends. Just so you know, I wasn't spouting crap. History is my thing." Doodad looked proud of himself. "And my picture has been used in a class project or two."

I couldn't help myself; I laughed. When I recovered, I said, "You have the perfect amount of eccentricity to fit right in. You're hired."

"That's a pretty word for weirdo."

"I'll have to get back to you on when you start."

"Next shift. Phil's eager to get out to the lighthouse. Surprised me it was real; I'd have bet on a kit," Doodad said. "Phil's going to stick around for my first shift, make sure I don't screw up too bad."

"Careful," I whispered. "It belongs to…" I shook my head in Fab's direction. "But it's on my property, which makes it mine."

"Get a girl knock-down going, and I could make some good money on the side."

"Yes, you're going to fit in just fine," I said.

"Does jingle bell girl over there always stare?" Doodad whispered.

"That's code for she's hot for you. I'm not against employee fraternization, as long as you act like adults. If it's just a screw, be upfront and don't call it love."

"Thanks for the advice, Mom."

"Wait until you meet Mother Westin; you'll know where I get it from. She runs the gambling interest at Jake's and the back room like her own private domain, which it basically is, because even though it was designed for fun, no one else has ever been interested. FYI: her husband is Jimmy Spoon."

Doodad raised his eyebrows. "Good to know." He stood and shook out his legs. "Nice to meet you." He acknowledged the group.

Mac wiggled out from between Fab and Shirl and walked him to the gate, saying something about him needing her business card.

"If I didn't have my Stephan, I'd go for that morsel." Shirl licked her lips.

Fab rolled her eyes and lifted her feet out of the water.

Stephan and Shirl had been together for a while, and whatever Shirl didn't know when they first got together, I suspected she knew everything now. Truth time probably came shortly after Help caught her ransacking his briefcase.

"Can we go now?" Fab whined.

"There is one thing." Shirl looked around. "Ran into Joseph at the gas station, about to get arrested for using the air hose on Svetlana. The owner came out and yelled, 'Free air is for tires, not perverts.' Anyway, I think she has a hole and needs to be repaired."

"Probably from the stress of him cheating on her," I said.

"If you don't get her fixed, he'll end up getting arrested."

"This isn't Svet's first medical emergency. Mac knows what to do," I said. "Were you able to get the glue off Miss January's scalp?"

"Most of it. I'll work on it again tomorrow." Shirl smiled sadly. "She'll have an ugly hairstyle for a long time."

Fab shook the gate.

"You break it, you buy a new, better one." I stood, stepping out of the pool.

Chapter Forty

On the way home, we stopped at Bruno's, a shotgun-style pizzeria. They served up individual pizzas for those who couldn't agree on toppings. We took our food out to the deck and took the stairs to the seawall, sitting on a pile of rocks with a bird's-eye view of the waves crashing below our feet.

Fab held up her plastic-stemmed glass—we'd ordered the house wine. "To... something," she toasted.

I laughed. "That's a crappy toast."

I devoured my grilled shrimp pizza, and Fab did the same with her assorted fancy cheese concoction.

"We've got to go," Fab said, after her phone rang. She stood and took the trash from my hands, dumping it in a nearby bin.

She fished her phone out of the pocket of her jeans when it rang again, a tone that I didn't recognize, and motioned for me to get a move on. I ran to catch up to her as she headed to the SUV.

"That was the security company; the alarm has gone off at the house." Fab got behind the wheel, hitting the door locks. "The police were called. I forgot to tell them to call me first with any emergencies. Maybe we can get there ahead of the cops."

"My name better be on the damn contact list," I huffed. "While we're at it, why is it that I don't know anything about this new system, such as how it works and who's doing the monitoring? Please reassure me that it's a reputable company and not one of your skeevy business associates."

She patted my shoulder. I shrugged her hand off.

"I got a little ahead of myself," Fab said. "The inside wiring will be finished today. It's the fence alarm that went off. If we get there fast enough, maybe we can keep the intruder out of the house."

We didn't have far to go. Fab drove with intensity but stuck to the speed limit.

"I planned to call a meeting," Fab said as she drove. "I oversaw the details, kept everything simple so we wouldn't be setting the alarm off all the time. I want to impress Didier, show him what I can do."

"Kevin," I groaned, pointing to the squad car that had just turned the corner from the opposite direction.

"No lights or sirens. Guess we're not a priority." Fab pulled into the driveway across the street, leaving room for Kevin to park wherever he wanted.

"I think those are saved for a chase or something lifesaving."

Fab hopped out of the car and headed in Kevin's direction before I even put my feet on the ground. Looking at the house, all seemed as we left it. No broken windows, about which I was happy.

I heard Fab tell Kevin, "I can take it from here," before he set foot on my property. I turned, big smile on my face. Motion from the corner of my eye had me turning, and I saw Casio lumbering up the street. I refrained from yelling, "Hurry, everyone inside."

As Fab and Kevin walked the front perimeter, she talked the entire time. Finding nothing exciting, they headed into the house.

"What are you doing here?" I asked Casio.

"That's a piss-poor greeting for a friend." Casio bared his teeth.

I waited for a growl, for him to paw the ground and charge.

"Another break-in." He nodded at the house. Without dragging his eyes away, he said, "Need a favor. Get friendly with the chick next door. I tried a little come on—" He swirled his hips. "—but we're just not simpatico."

"I'll be the buzzkill: you have a wife and kids."

"Flirting, not screwing," he said with a shake of his head. "Back to the friend request. You can do friendly, can't you?"

"I don't make friends for the purpose of eliciting information. You're better off pitching your *request* to Fab."

Casio roared with laughter. "If I wanted her tied up and interrogated, I'd do it myself. But I'd have a hard time selling that approach to the chief." He grimaced. "I think Ruby Dailey knows more about her boyfriend's death, and it is tied to your break-ins. Got a heads-up that she had a male caller asking for her by name, and she pointed him to your house. And look – here we are – another break-in. I was thinking—" He tapped his temple with a grin. "—another woman could comfort her in her time of grief."

I shook my head, making a face. *Friends, ha! Ruby was about to get two of them.*

Casio stuck his hand out. "That info cost me a twenty."

I wiped away a non-existent tear and left him standing on the sidewalk.

"I don't know why Brick doesn't like you," Casio said from behind me as I opened the door. "You're much more fun than scary girl." He followed me into the living room.

"It belongs to Didier," Fab told Kevin as they came through the patio doors. She had an ugly shoe in her hand, reminiscent of a jail freebie only dingy grey. No chance it ever belonged to the sexy Frenchman.

"Hey, bro." Casio waved to Kevin.

Kevin looked at him like he'd grown an extra

329

head. "Yeah... uh... Casio?" He swept the big man from head to toe, taking in his grimy clothing and filthy feet shoved into taped-together flip-flops.

I turned and whispered to Casio, "I can tell you two are close."

"The alarm must've scared the intruder off. Or, given that the system is new, it might have malfunctioned." Kevin flashed a dopey smile. "I'll take some water."

Casio raised his hand. "Me too, and how about a sandwich?"

Mother would be thoroughly appalled at what I wanted to say, besides get the heck out of here. An F-word or two popped into my mind. Instead, I waved my hand. "The kitchen is that way. We're out of Wonder Bread, but I'm sure you can find something." I added with a touch of snark, "Clean up after yourself."

Fab moved to my side. "I'd have thrown them out."

"Dare you."

"Why is it when I've got a good idea, instead of following up, you resort to childishness?"

I pouted and edged around her, following the guys to the kitchen and slipped onto a stool. "What's the latest on the murder?" I asked Kevin.

"You know I can't discuss that, with you or anyone." He pulled out a soda and bottle of water, popping the tab on the can.

"Throw me a tidbit, in the spirit of this new best friendship we've got going." I watched as he downed the soda. "So many new friends lately," I mused.

Fab sat down next to me, making an unintelligible noise.

"I'm not blowing you off, but really, I've got nothing new." Kevin downed his water, capped it, and looked around for the trash.

Fab pointed. He tossed his trash and helped himself to more water.

"Get me another beer," Casio said, in between stuffing his mouth with the leftover chicken enchilada he'd found in a to-go container.

"Listen up, boys." Neither looked impressed. "No one comes to your door and blows you away unless you screwed them or they got the wrong address. How many cases do you get of the latter?" I asked. Kevin shrugged. "I find it hard to believe that someone walked down the street, chose a house, and bam!" I said a little loudly, blowing on my index finger.

Casio and Kevin rolled their eyes.

"Greed makes people do stupid stuff, but I heard…" Fab paused and continued, "somewhere… that there's no will. Scotch wasn't married, so I suppose it would go to his parents."

"Dickie told me that Scotch's family appeared genuinely distraught over the loss of their son," I imparted. "If anyone would know, it would be him. Said it was a drama-free, respectable funeral."

"Who's Dickie?" Casio wiped his mouth on his sleeve.

"Funeral director. If you're going to shuffle around our city, you need to get to know the shakers." I stood and ripped off a paper towel, handing it to him.

Casio snorted. "That skinny little gravedigger?"

"You're a jerk. The funeral home yields good information… sometimes anyway. Another plus, there's always leftover funeral food."

"Thanks for the water." Kevin added, "Mind if I take another one with me?"

"Help yourself," Fab said sarcastically.

"We should play some golf sometime," Casio said to Kevin.

"Not my game. If you're up for volleyball, we're at the waterside courts on weekends."

Judging by Casio's turned-up nose, I'd bet the answer was "not interested."

Kevin waved.

"One down, one to go," Fab said when the door closed behind him.

I confronted Fab. "That shoe never belonged to Didier."

"Someone was definitely in the backyard," Fab said. "I found it at the base of the fence I'd guess our intruder used for escape. I snatched it up before Kevin could get his paws on it."

"Hiding evidence from law enforcement is a

bad idea." Casio scowled at the two of us.

"I'm in favor of hiding the cars and lying in wait," I offered. "Make it easy for the wannabe intruder and leave the door unlocked."

"Sounds good to me," Fab said.

"Another bad idea." Casio banged his fist on the counter. "Call me and I'll be a lookout from a different vantage point. Just know that doing a stake-out might not be a onetime deal. They're are often time-intensive and almost always require more than one-time surveillance."

Hearing an engine, I got up and crossed to the sink, looking out the garden window. "We've got more company." A white pickup blocked the driveway.

Fab looked over my shoulder. "That's my guy."

"I'd like a business card," I said to Fab's retreating back. "The security company is finishing the system," I answered Casio's inquisitive stare.

To my surprise, Casio picked up his trash and cleaned the counter with his used paper towel.

I flinched. "Not to be rude, but you can go now. I'm out of nice, and I desperately need a nap."

"When you talk to the chick next door, let me know." He jerked his head. "Thanks for feeding me." I nodded, and he left via the backyard.

I hauled Jazz into my arms and headed upstairs. Snow had taken to sleeping on my bed when people invaded the house.

Chapter Forty-One

Before leaving the next afternoon, Fab gave me a one-on-one on how to operate the new alarm keypad. I'd already texted Creole. He was happy that it had been installed and forewarned me that he had a few questions for Fab.

She started with a long-winded speech about the intricacies of the installation, and after my eyes rolled back in my head, I told her, "Skip to which buttons to push." She was quite proud of her and her accomplice's work. He didn't have a business card. Shock! All emergency calls were directed to our rarely used business number. When asked, she assured me the man didn't have a prison record, but she acted shifty, and in retrospect, I should've included the word "jail." I wouldn't make a distinction, but she would.

On the way to Mother's for dinner, I detoured to pick Liam up at school. I'd already texted him, so he knew I was on the way. Fab grumbled about not going, but since neither of us wanted Didier to find out what I was up to ahead of time, she mumbled something about cooking and I left.

Turning onto the Overseas Highway — the

high school was located south of town—I wondered, "Cooking what?" My guess was she'd buy something and Didier would fire up the grill.

Liam had forewarned me to bypass the pick-up line in front of the school. His instructions were forgotten when I turned the corner and spotted him and a couple of friends a half-block up.

After I pulled up to the curb across the street, he crossed in front of the SUV, knocking on the hood. He threw his backpack over the seat and hopped into the passenger seat.

"Your friends need a ride?" I asked.

"They're all good." Liam fastened his seat belt. "You never pick me up; you must want something."

"So suspicious." I smiled at him. "I'd do cool stuff with you more often, but you know how Mother is at hogging your time."

"She thinks if she lets me out of her sight, I might stub my toe. We had a talk, and she's lightening up, as long as I don't start sneaking around. You did that, didn't you? Now I don't get to," he mock-accused.

"I was the perfect child. Brad, on the other hand…" I laughed.

Liam shook his head, a big grin on his face.

"You're right about me having an ulterior motive for fetching you home." I pulled out on the highway away from the cars lined up to get into the school. "How would you feel if I fixed Brad up on a date? Without your approval, I'll drop the idea. Just so you know, I'm good with the answer either way."

"Mom and he are throwing out the 'friends' word, code for it's over. She loves Los Angeles, and Brad, well, he's not leaving here. Not that I blame him. Is this a prank date or for real?"

"Real."

"Happy he got rid of that Pamela cretin." Liam raised his eyebrow. "Is the new one anyone I know?"

"Phil."

He whistled. "I like her a lot."

"I got the idea when she told me he was 'hot.' She's smart, clever, and a looker, as my grandfather would have said."

"If I were legal, I'd ask her out. Does she know how bossy Brad can be? Seriously bossy."

"I'm swearing you to secrecy until this plan unfolds. If Brad gets wind, he'll bail." I relayed what Mother and I had already discussed.

"Grandmother must be excited about this; she fancies herself a modern day cupid." He shook his head. "Does Spoon know?" I nodded. "He wouldn't care as long as it makes her happy."

"Grandmother? She finally made a decision." Mother had tried every variation of grandmother she could come up with, including in Greek, Hawaiian, and a few other languages.

"I can pretty much call her anything except

Granny or Madeline."

I winced at "Granny," knowing Mother would flip. Brad and I had used it in the past on our own grandmother, but only to annoy her.

I turned into Mother's complex behind a Lexus, waited while the driver entered the security code, and followed in behind. Guest parking was empty, and I took the space closest to the door.

"Use your lockpick." Liam made a keying motion. "I want to see how it's done."

I groaned. "You can watch, but I'm not teaching you." At the lobby door, I showed him in slow motion. "Make up some good reason why you need to perfect the skill and sell Mother on it; she might teach you. She knows how; she was Fab's star pupil."

"Kevin told me you two were best friends now. I tried not to laugh, thinking he'd lost his mind." Liam pushed the elevator button, and the doors opened immediately.

"That's a stretch."

"I told him to be nicer. He wanted to know why, and I told him everyone else likes you and so should he. It might shine up his image, rather than being known as the cop that gave the old lady a ticket for talking to her bicycle."

I laughed. "Hadn't heard that story."

"True story. Bringing it up annoyed him. He reminded me it happened when he was new on the force, and it was a misunderstanding."

We got out on the top floor in front of Mother's door. "No lockpick needed; I got a key." He smirked.

"I'll text you the code for the security system Fab just had installed at the house."

"Fab already did." He unlocked the door. "Mrs. Spoon," he yelled, "I'm home."

"Loud," I squealed. "The neighbors."

"I heard you tell Fab to make her presence known, in case they were doing something she didn't want to know anything about. There are things I don't want to know about either."

"She's on the patio," Spoon rumbled from the kitchen. He walked out with an apron tied around his waist.

"You need to learn to cook." I lightly elbowed Liam. "You might hook up with a girl with no culinary skills, the same as the rest of the men in the family."

"He's got breakfast down." Spoon scooped me up into a hug. "I came home early so I wouldn't miss the scheming."

Liam dropped his backpack in the corner and disappeared down the hall.

Mother came through the sliding pocket doors from the patio and checked me over from head to toe. Apparently my pink cotton tiered skirt and long-sleeve white top met with her approval. I'd kicked off my sandals inside the door.

"Honey, let's have wine out on the patio." Mother took hold of my hand, half-dragging me to the door.

"Stop right there," Spoon boomed. "You're to stay where I can hear every word."

Mother pouted. "I told you I'd share."

Spoon shook his head. "Heard that before, and it's not always true. Besides, I'm ready for you two." He wiggled his fingers between the stems of the three wine glasses and grabbed up the bottle, then swept his arm out for us to proceed.

"It's beautiful out here," I said, slipping into a chair and resting my feet on the footrest. The view of the water was spectacular, and quiet, as there was no beach but instead a grassy knoll that ran above where the blue-green water splashed against the rocks.

Spoon sat next to Mother, kicking up his feet. "To not getting in any trouble," he toasted. When we had taken a drink, he said, "What's new?" His attention was fixed on me.

"Mother, you keep joking that you're going to fix Brad up, and you don't follow through. Time to act. I've got the perfect girl."

Spoon shook his head. "How many times did your mother do that to you and you hated it?"

"Exactly. Which is why it's Brad's turn."

"What about Pamela?" Mother turned up her nose. "What does Brad see in her? It isn't that she's not perfectly lovely…" She paused, scrunching her nose again. "She's bitchy."

Spoon laughed. "Noticed that right off."

"Caput. Finito. If Brad tells you they broke up,

pretend like it's the first time you heard it," I said.

Mother's gaze zeroed in on me, and I looked away. "You know something that I don't." She continued to stare.

"Let's just say I pointed out that she wasn't a good fit and he listened," I weaseled. "I've got a much better choice. Time for him to move on."

Mother's face was quite expressive, and it was clear she had already starting making plans. "Who do you have in mind?" she asked, skepticism in her voice.

"Phil."

Mother's eyebrows shot up. "The bartender?" She went back to her mental scheming. "Phil passed the bar; she's a lawyer now. It would be nice to have one in the family."

"Since it's unanimous that we all like Phil, forget the dating, skip to the wedding," Liam said from the doorway.

I squeezed my eyes shut. "Mother," I groaned, "you've corrupted your grandson."

Mother beamed at him.

"Does Phil know about your plotting?" Spoon asked. "Or are you planning to trick both of them?"

"Oh yeah, Phil knows," Liam answered. "She's hot for him." He dropped into a chair.

"Phil gets my thumbs-up. But what if she gets her heart broken?" Spoon asked brusquely.

"We can't control everything," I said with a

sigh. "We get them together; chemistry does the rest. They both know how to do friendship. Another added plus: neither of them is in immediate need of mental healthcare."

"I heard a little crazy makes the woman more fun," Liam said, a hint of amusement in his eyes.

All eyes turned to him.

"Who told you that?" I demanded.

"I got the dude-to-dude talk from Crum. It was rather enlightening." Liam's lips quirked; he was clearly enjoying the turn of the conversation.

Mother and I shared the same look of horror. Spoon roared with laughter, shaking his head.

"You." I pointed to Liam. "Go back and demand the details on how his so-called relationships, more like sexcapades, end. One left on a stretcher, mumbling to herself. There have been others since he barreled into my life. Who knows about before. He's a horny old whore. He's takes exception to that description, but it fits."

Mother groaned.

"I've met a couple of them in passing," Liam said. "When I lived at The Cottages, I closed his bathroom window a few times to keep the screams from bringing the cops. He assured me that he was the King of Passion and the women left happy. I never heard the word 'help,' or I'd have called Kevin."

"If you want to know about…" I paused. "…stuff, there are better people right in our own family to ask questions of."

"Stuff?" Liam teased. "You mean sex."

"No more advice from the professor." Mother sniffed. "About anything. The man wanders around in his underwear, for heaven's sake." She motioned for Spoon to fill up her glass.

I wasn't much of a wine drinker, so I was good with one glass.

"I've got some ideas for this dinner for the newest lovebirds." Mother flashed me a conspiratorial smile. "Family dinner at a restaurant; Phil and Brad arrive separately, and I seat them next to one another. That way, if Brad figures out what I'm up to, he won't make a scene. The two of them will know after one dinner if there's a spark that they want to follow up on."

"If you get any resistance, tell him we're all confirmed to attend. As soon as you get the date, let me know; I'll need to tell Creole."

Chapter Forty-Two

There was a loud bang from the front of the house. "Hell-ooo," Fab called out, announcing her return from lunch with Didier.

I peeked around the corner of the chaise and saw her standing in the patio doorway. I raised my hand over the top of the cushion and waved.

"Be back," she said, and her voice faded out.

I snapped my book closed and lay back against the pillows. I'd been for a long midday swim and now sat under the umbrella, drip-drying.

Fab flew back outside in record time, and I heard the tinkling of ice hitting the inside of a glass. Earlier, I had brought out a tray—a large pitcher of flavored water, ice cubes, and a chilled bowl of sliced oranges. She grabbed up my glass, refilled it, and stretched out on the chaise next to me.

"Where did you go for lunch?" I asked.

"We stayed at the office. Didier planned a picnic, and we spread out on a blanket and ate on the floor."

"I'm surprised you'd sit on the floor."

"It was so romantic. He even placed a rose on

my plate."

"Happy to hear all is well in lovey-land." I clinked my glass against hers. "I hate to burst the romantic bubble, but I'm about to tell you something I contemplated not telling you."

"You're keeping secrets?" Fab accused.

"Not for long." I patted her hand, which she jerked away. "You're not to go off half-cocked without warning me ahead of time so I can talk you out of it." I thrust out my little finger. "Pinkie swear."

"How about instead I beat the hell out of you?"

"Don't think I won't land a few punches. And what would you tell Didier?"

Her finger encircled mine and squeezed until I winced. "What already?"

"Casio told me the chick next door, is telling people who are in search of her that she lives at this house." I ran down the details of our short conversation.

"I'll go talk to her."

"Calm down." I tugged on her arm to keep her seated. "I say we both confront her. Why direct people over here? Why not say she moved, or better yet, not answer the door? I'm guessing, like Casio, she knows more about her boyfriend's murder than she's told the police. Maybe she knows who murdered him. But if she's involved somehow, why not leave town?"

"I've wondered why she's still living there.

One thing I have noticed is that Scotch's family hasn't been around that I've seen – only Ruby. If I were a family member, I'd have tossed her to the curb." Fab refilled her glass and topped mine off.

"Drawing on my extensive experience with poachers and deadbeats, she probably won't go easy; it'll take the threat of court action." I frowned, knowing how complicated evictions could get when the courts got involved. "Maybe I should contact Scotch's family—I could get the number from Dickie—and find out what they know about her. And if she is causing problems, give them a few tips on how to get rid of her."

"I saw a car over there when I came home." Fab looked down at her four-pieces-of-string bathing suit. "We should change."

"Calling on the neighbor in a bathing suit is so Floridian. Friendly. No place for a gun, but if necessary, you can trot out those butt-kicking skills you're always bragging about."

"You got a plan worked up?" Fab eyed me suspiciously.

"I'm working on the intro. You'll need to pay attention, and when I pause, you take over the questioning. In the end, we make it clear that sending people over here would not be good for her health. Toss in a smile. A friendly threat. Don't kick her butt unless she starts it. If it looks like I won't get hurt, I'll break it up."

Fab crossed her arms and scowled at me.

"Or you can sit here, and I'll take care of it myself." I almost laughed, knowing that she'd not only come with me but lead the way.

Fab stood and tied a cover-up around her waist, slipped into her sandals, and headed to the side path. I pulled a sheer floral top over my head, covering myself to just above the knees, and slid into flip-flops.

We walked out to the street, looking around cautiously as we headed to the driveway next door. No one suspicious about; in fact, there was no one around at all. Fab motioned for me to stay back while she checked out the house and the one car parked in front of the garage. After a minute, she waved for me to follow her to the door.

She raised her fist to pound, and I knocked it away. "Don't scare her before she opens the door. Do you need me to do it?"

Fab knocked.

"What do you want?" came a voice from behind the door.

"We're your neighbors." I waved erratically at the peephole. "I dragged my roomie over to make introductions."

It took a minute, but the woman finally opened the door. It was hard to guess her age, and her hardened glare made me want to step back. This was no pushover. She checked us over in one sweep, and whatever her conclusions, they didn't show on her face.

"Hi, we're your neighbors. I'm Gertrude, and this is Fiona." I pointed to Fab, who clearly didn't approve of my name selection for her. Apparently, she'd forgotten we'd used those names in the past. "We're here to welcome you to the neighborhood. Sorry about the... boyfriend, wasn't it? Murder's unsettling, don't you think? Any suspects?"

"I'm rather busy right now."

Fab pushed past her into the entry and stopped in the living room.

"Fiona," I called. "She likes you already." It didn't escape me that the woman didn't offer up her name.

I took advantage of her indecision—her attention fixed on Fab's retreating back, she opened the door wider, and I scooted in. Some might consider that an invitation.

"Stop," she yelled.

I turned and pasted on a friendly smile. "I didn't catch your name."

"Ruby," she sputtered.

Her idea of busy was watching a soap opera, which she had on pause on the widescreen television, a bowl of popcorn on a table next to a recliner. The living room was dark and dingy, with threadbare drapes covering the windows and back door. The place reeked of mildew.

"Smells in here." Fab wrinkled her nose.

"Doesn't bother me," Ruby snipped. "Now, if you don't mind…"

"Oh, but I do." Fab turned her full attention on the woman. "I'd like to know why you're babbling all over town that you don't actually live here but next door at our house. Did you happen to mention which one of us was you? Well... to state the obvious... neither of us looks like you."

"I don't know what you're talking about."

"Cut it," Fab growled and stepped forward. "Several people were only too willing to sell the juicy tidbits to the police. You calling *all* of them liars?"

Ruby stepped back and angled herself behind a chair.

"I'm asking nicely." Fab's lips pulled into a hard line. "I could—" She cracked her knuckles. "—beat the hell out of you and then ask again."

"It was only one time," Ruby whined. "A bruiser of a guy showed up looking for Scotch's girlfriend. Like you, he pushed his way in. I didn't get a good vibe. Thankfully, I had a couple of boxes sitting against that wall." She pointed back to the entry. "I made up on the spot that I was new to the neighborhood and that the previous tenant had moved next door. I figured there'd be no harm, as your driveway is always full of cars and the sheriff is always there. Figured you were up to something illegal and the man would be scared off."

"This bruiser fellow accepted your explanation?" I asked.

"I sold it," she said.

I wanted to smack the smirk off her face.

"What did this man look like?" Fab demanded.

"Tall, muscly… brown hair, not that cute."

That description could fit a number of men.

"What did this man want with you and your boyfriend?" Fab asked.

"He insinuated Scotch owed him money. He was here to collect from Scotch or me. I don't have any money."

"Did he say how much was owed?" I asked, knowing the answer would be vague since she wasn't much of a liar or a quick thinker.

Ruby shook her head, eyes downcast. "He didn't say exactly."

"Listen up, *Ruby.*" Fab mimicked Creole's growly dog tone, which he saved for when he was really annoyed. "Keep your mouth shut about me and my friend here. Not a peep. Is that plain enough for you?"

Ruby nodded again.

"I want to hear you say that it's perfectly clear."

She repeated the words, unable to hide her anger.

"One more thing. If I have to come back here, it will be your last stupid mistake," Fab threatened. "Anything you don't understand?"

"No," Ruby mumbled.

Fab stepped to my side and paused, her

signature "let's get out of here" look firmly in place, then continued to the door.

"Nice to meet you, Ruby," I said, and with one last glance around, ran down the driveway to catch up to Fab.

"I don't believe a word she said," Fab sneered.

"That makes two of us."

Chapter Forty-Three

Mother had chosen the Crab Shack, a local restaurant and family favorite, for the family dinner. She'd tried to coordinate all of us going together in the same car, but Fab politely declined; she wanted time to break the news of the scheme to Didier. She hinted that she might blame everything on Mother, and even that she'd been sworn to secrecy, knowing that Didier would never say a word to Mother, no matter what he thought. For once, she could honestly say that, besides knowledge of it, she had nothing to do with the plan.

Creole pulled into a parking space next to Spoon's Mercedes. He went around, opening the passenger door and pulling me into his arms. He fisted his fingers in my hair, bringing his lips to mine. "Here are your rules for tonight. Promise you'll follow them."

"Rules? What are they?" I scrunched my nose, curious about what was coming next.

He held up one finger and then a second one. "No getting drunk. No food fights."

I sniffed. "We don't throw food in public."

Creole laughed. "I love this family." He pulled

me to the end of the seat, wrapping my legs around his middle. Lifting me out, he kicked the door shut and set me on my feet.

The Crab Shack sat off the main highway, looking out over the blue waters of the Atlantic Ocean. The restaurant had a low-key atmosphere, decorated with fake palm trees and fish mounted on walls that were strung with ropes of lights. As we walked through the doors into the lobby, Spoon waved from across the room.

True to form, Mother had requested a window table and would've arrived early to make sure it happened. It was on the other side of the tiki bar area. With the beginnings of dusk, lights flickered on the water visible through the floor-to-ceiling windows.

There was only one person missing from the table of nine – the guest of honor. I raised my eyebrow at Mother and she nodded, letting me know she had everything under control.

Creole and I sat at the opposite end of the table from Mother and Spoon. The server appeared at our side and took our drink order.

Brad hurried up to the table and kissed Mother on the cheek. "Sorry I'm late." He scanned the table and took the only empty seat, which was next to Phil.

Once the server returned with our drinks, Spoon made a toast. "To family."

"You look beautiful tonight," Mother said to

Phil. "Doesn't she?" She made eye contact with Brad, who appeared embarrassed.

I shook my head at Mother, tempted to drag her to the lady's room and insist she let nature take its course.

"Did you order appetizers?" Fab asked, cutting off whatever Mother was about to say. She elbowed Didier and whispered something; he signaled for menus.

"Bradley," a curly haired blonde with bright-red lips cooed, appearing at the table and sticking her head over Didier's shoulder. "Hon, I've missed you."

All eyes turned to Brad; no one said a word. He looked uncomfortable and at a loss for words.

The woman slunk around the table in a pair of skinny jeans and red patent leather stilettos. She stopped behind his chair, leaned down, and rubbed her cheek against his. "Aren't you going to introduce me?"

"Yes, Bradley, that would be nice, since no one at this table has met her before." I sent an apologetic look at Phil.

The blonde laughed. She was the only one at the table without a deer-in-the-headlights look. The woman exuded coolness, and my admiration at her being able to pull that off went up a notch.

"I'm sure the help can squeeze another chair in so I can sit next to you. Or on your lap," she whispered, loud enough for everyone to hear. She raised her arm to signal a waiter, and Brad pushed it back down.

He shoved his chair back, gripping her elbow. "Excuse us," he said and pushed her into the bar, stopping briefly to say something to the woman, and headed to the exit.

"Is Brad leaving?" Mother asked, shocked. "I'm sorry," she said to Phil. "We should scrap the original plans and... I don't know. So sorry."

"Madeline..." Phil smiled. "I always have a great time when you include me. We should let this night play out on its own."

"Pff," Mother said and downed the rest of her drink, staring towards the front of the restaurant.

"Who was that woman?" Fab demanded.

"Anyone?" I asked.

"Her name is Reality," Phil said. "She's come into Jake's a couple of times. Not sure if Reality is her birth name or one she adopted."

"Reality's a handful," Liam said. All eyes turned to him. "According to *Bradley*," he added. "They went out a couple of times; never got off the ground."

"I suggest that when Brad gets back to the table, we pretend that scene never took place. He will appreciate it," Spoon suggested.

No one said a word, and an uncomfortable silence fell over the table.

"Here he comes," Creole said quietly. "Alone."

Everyone started talking at once.

Brad slid back into his chair, saying something

to Phil that had her smiling.

Spoon signaled for the server to come take our order.

"Are you sure I can't get drunk?" I asked Creole.

"I have plans for you later, and I don't want you falling asleep."

"Maybe we could leave now and no one would notice…" I ran my finger along his leg.

"Behave yourself. Don't make me—" Creole dragged his finger down my cheek. "—drag you under the table." He smiled, a sexy one, a calculating gleam in his eyes.

"I'll try."

At the end of the table, Spoon smiled at Mother with a lopsided grin that she returned with a quick kiss.

* * *

Mother clinked her glass with her fork. "Hope you left room for dessert – it's a family tradition."

I sighed at my empty plate – no leftovers.

Looking at the dessert menu, I suggested, "We should order extra for breakfast," and winked at Didier.

Didier frowned at me, humor in his eyes. "And miss out on my green concoction? That you aptly named."

I made a gagging noise.

All eyes turned to me. "It's not like I *tried* to poison him," I said, trying not to laugh.

Mother turned away, but not before I saw her lips curl up; she'd been subjected to a taste of that nauseating drink, having insisted on trying the recipe.

In the middle of dessert, Brad asked Phil in a voice that everyone could hear, "You my date?"

Once again, you could hear a pin drop, despite the fact that the restaurant was noisy and filled with the voices of people having a good time.

"Kind of." Phil smiled up at him.

"Did you know about this in advance, or are you as surprised as me?" Brad asked, looking around the table.

"I knew," she confessed. "I let it slip that I thought you were cute, and that took on a life of its own. If this works out between us, I'd like to wait to have children," she said, a teasing tone in her voice.

Brad scowled at Mother.

I raised my hand. "Blame me."

"That's a shock," Brad said, not showing emotion one way or the other. He leaned over and whispered in Phil's ear.

Fab and I exchanged a grimace, both of us knowing how tight-lipped she could be. Chances were we wouldn't be able to shake the details out of her.

Chapter Forty-Four

"Is Brad speaking to you?" Fab asked grumpily, climbing behind the wheel of the SUV.

"He called this morning and laughed off the setup." I turned away, looking out the window.

I didn't tell her that he'd brought up the Pamela debacle, thanking me for interfering but saying it was to be a one-time-only event and extracting a promise from me to stop snooping. In the future, he'd decide whether he wanted a background check run on a potential girlfriend or business associate.

"I met her at the coffee shop and suggested we take a break since she has a lot going on and needs to focus on her case with the Feds and hopefully stay out of prison. She changed into a different woman in a second, instantly full of rage. In that moment, I believed the other things you said about her; she scared the hell out of me. All I could think about was getting away from her."

"Watch your back for a while."

"Thank you for looking out for me."

"Anytime and I hope you know that."

Fab was content to terrorize the other drivers with incessant honking. "Stop sulking," I said. "It's not like I beat you over the head to make you come to Jake's with me."

Phil had called, excited. She'd gotten a last-minute call, her first client – a shoplifter – had been referred to her, and she needed to meet with him before his court appearance. I didn't ask whether the thief could afford her fees. I agreed that Doodad could start work immediately. Minutes later, she called back to confirm and apologized for not being able to be there for his first day. She said Doodad felt confident he could handle it.

"I didn't know that Didier was going to be home early; his meeting got cancelled," Fab brooded. She had gotten a text that he was on his way just as she got into the car and had been grumpy ever since.

"I'm not going to remind you that I told you this would be boring."

"You just did." She sniffed.

"Call Didier and tell him to pick you up. As the owner of Jake's, I'm not letting Mr. Doodad fend for himself. I'm staying for a while, and if all goes well, then I'll cut my visit short."

Traffic on the main highway was light for a weekday; the tourist crowd hadn't hit the roads yet. Fab pulled into Jake's; the lunch crowd filling up the parking spaces, she curved around to the back and idled in front of the kitchen door. "I'll meet you inside."

I got out and checked out the other businesses. Junker's displayed a "closed" sign on the short walkway that led up to the door, which didn't surprise me. The missus did a brisk business with out-of-state antique dealers, usually in the early morning, and then went home. At the lighthouse, Phil had hung up her shingle, her name in bold on it. Her car was nowhere in sight.

As I entered the kitchen, I waved at Cook's son, who was behind the grill. Cook was another lucky find; within minutes of being hired, he'd taken over the kitchen and had run it ever since like his own mini-empire, employing only family members. The son always had music blaring; the father preferred to watch telenovelas.

The seats at the bar were full. I'd have to haul up a stool from my hole-in-the-wall office that only got used for storage. The jukebox blasted, drowning out an argument in progress at the pool table, and there were two people playing at the dartboard. Grabbing a stool, I dragged it down the hall and placed it at the end of the bar, sitting in front of the garnishes.

Doodad finished washing glasses, letting them drip dry. "Hey boss, what can I get you?"

"Bottled water," I said. "How's your first day going, Mr. Doo?"

He leveled a stare. "You're not funny."

"The appropriate response is to laugh."

Two men at the end of the bar banged their beer bottles for refills. Doodad took one look, retrieved their brand, and took it to them.

He returned, standing in front of me. "Heard

you were going to stop by, make sure I'm not screwing up too badly."

"Who better than me if you have questions?"

"So far so good. Got your number on speed dial, just in case."

An older woman who I recognized as a regular came to a halt at the other end of the bar. She hollered out her drink order, waving cash, which she then shoved in her cleavage.

The hand of the man to the right of me disappeared up the back of the sundress worn by the woman standing next to him, putting a flash of panties on display. It stayed up there as he jerked her close, whispering something that had her giggling.

Doodad was in his element, joking with the customers and filling orders with efficiency. A couple came in the door and yelled out his name, waving. He clearly had everything under control. I'd finish my water and leave. That would make Fab happy.

The man next to me stepped up his invasive hands, and I was about to suggest they get a room when he suddenly tripped backwards. Another man, who'd come up behind him unnoticed, whirled him around and fisted his shirt, sticking a gun against his forehead and pulling the trigger.

A half-scream erupted from my mouth before I realized he hadn't chambered a bullet. The gun only clicked. *That* time. The next time he pulled the trigger, his target wouldn't be so lucky.

"You piece of filth, putting your hands on my wife," the man screamed.

Doodad swung the Mossberg rifle, striking the man's arm, and the bullet went wild, lodging in the ceiling. Two male customers jumped into the fray, manhandling the guy from behind and securing his arms. The shooter fought and kicked to no avail, screaming about the wife-poacher's ancestors.

"You," Doodad bellowed from behind the bar. "Shut. It."

I slowly let out the breath I'd been holding.

Fab came running down the hall, skidding to a stop. "What did I miss?"

The woman in the middle of the drama rolled out from under the man, who'd pushed her to the floor, covering her with his body. "Honey." She hopped to her feet and threw herself at her husband, burying her face in his chest.

I wanted to smack the woman. I'd had a good view and knew that she'd been a willing participant and done nothing to fend off the other man's advances. That raised the question of whether they knew one another. If not, why would he be willing to put his life on the line for her?

One of the patrons picked up the firearm off the floor, laying it on the bar. Doodad quickly stashed it under the counter.

Sirens could be heard in the distance; someone

had called the cops.

The man who'd almost died crawled to his feet, his face colorless. I expected him to puke and took a step back.

"I just had my last drink… forever." He nodded to Doodad and cut out the front door.

"The cops are coming," Doodad told the couple. "I wouldn't tell you to run, but if you don't, you're going to jail."

The wife grabbed her husband's hand, and Fab pointed towards the kitchen, lowering her voice as she gave them directions for a clean getaway.

"You're banned," Doodad yelled to their retreating backs.

"Kind of happy I don't have brain schmoo all over me," I said.

Fab appeared disgusted. "I can't believe I missed the action."

Doodad shook his head at Fab and turned to me. "It's my understanding that you don't like to call the cops. I figured since no one died… If I'm wrong, I'll know for next time." He wiped down the Mossberg and placed it back under the bar.

"If asked, I don't know what happened." My eyes were drawn to the front entry, where Kevin and another officer had just walked in. "If I know my customers, Kevin will get fifty versions of what happened; that should keep him busy."

"You and the deputy are on a first-name basis?" Doodad asked, one eyebrow arched.

"Long story. One of these visits, I'll make it a short one for you." I rubbed my temples, about to ask for aspirin when the bottle appeared in front of me.

Kevin spotted me and marched over. "Heard there was a shooting."

"Bullet's in the ceiling." I pointed upward, then introduced him to Doodad.

"We're acquainted," Kevin sneered. "Can't you hire anyone without a criminal record?"

Doodad's fist hit the bar.

"Mr. Wingate is a veteran." I struggled to keep the annoyance out of my voice. "All of my employees undergo a background check, and none have records. Mr. Wingate's littering charge got tossed."

Kevin rolled his eyes. "I'll take your statement first."

"It's a blur," I hedged. "I think I'm going to be sick." I clutched my stomach, putting my head on the bar. My plan was to run out the back door when Kevin turned his back. Dammit, I should have gone when the coast was clear.

Fab cut Kevin off when he turned to her. "I was outside and came in when I heard the gunshot."

Doodad spoke up: "There was an argument; shot went off, and people went running. I had no way to sort out who was who and stop the right person. Could've shot a couple of men in the back, but being my first day and all, didn't seem like it would make a good impression."

Kevin's partner interrupted, and they went off in the direction of the deck. The bar had emptied out by half.

"Get me out of here," I whispered to Fab.

"If Kevin asks, I'll tell him you went to the bathroom," Doodad said.

"Phil's right. You're a great choice for the job." I gave Doodad a thumbs up.

Fab grabbed my arm and dragged me down the hall and out the back, past Cook's son, who sat on a stool, craning his neck and smiling.

Chapter Forty-Five

Another quiet day for a change. The police hadn't been to The Cottages or Jake's in the last couple of days. I'd informed Creole and Didier that morning that I'd be buying the ingredients for dinner and one or both were doing the grilling. Then I went to the farmer's market and filled a tote with vegetables; what I didn't use for skewers, Didier could drink. On the way home, I stopped at the seafood store and, following the owner's recommendations, chose shrimp and crab.

Fab turned up her nose at my invitation to ride along when I made it clear I'd be driving. If I didn't get behind the wheel once in a while, I might forget how to drive. She stayed behind to read by the pool. I rolled down both passenger windows and let the wind whip through my hair, sucking in the sea air with renewed appreciation.

Turning the corner to my house, I drove slowly and checked out each house, but the street was deserted and quiet. I turned into the driveway and got out, opening the back and piling canvas shopping bags over my shoulder. I grabbed my phone and kicked the door shut, wobbling slightly.

I managed to get inside the entry without my bags falling into the crook of my arm. With an added "umph," I heaved them all onto the island, setting my keys and phone on one of the stools.

"Hey, sister."

I squealed, and my eyes shot to the barrel of the Smith and Wesson pointing at the middle of my forehead. I recognized the man as one of the two who showed up a while back, trying to collect a debt I didn't owe. At the time, either he or his friend left with a hole in their butt.

"Who..." I stuttered, wondering who he was, then figured introductions weren't important. "Where's Fab?"

"Your friend —" He waved the muzzle of his gun towards the living room. " — is tied up right now." His beady eyes glinted at me.

I followed his hand and saw Fab sitting on the floor, her back to the patio, trussed up with a rag in her mouth. The pony-tailed blond sidekick had his gun leveled at her head.

"We can work out something mutually agreeable." I reached with my other hand, the motion hidden by the countertop and bags, and hit one on my speed dial. "Please don't shoot me," I said loudly, saying a silent prayer that Creole heard.

"What you got in here?" The man upended one of the bags on the counter; the other two followed. "You one of them vegetabletarians?" He shuddered.

I did my best not to roll my eyes. "I'm Madison; this is my house. Like I said before, we can work out a deal. You need money? I can get it and you can leave us both alone." Damn! My Glock was in my purse. Fab would kill me, assuming we got out of this alive. There was always the junk drawer, but it was just out of reach and not a good idea, since the movement would easily draw attention. Somehow, I needed to stay in the kitchen.

"I'm Larry, that's Barry." He indicated the other man with his free hand. "Rhymes. Clever, huh?" I nodded. "Barry's got dibs on killing your friend. He had to go to some quack doctor to get that bullet dug out of his ass. No anesthesia. The screaming…" He winced.

"My ass still itches from the incision," Barry whined.

"That's too bad," I mumbled inanely. "I'm sure we can agree on a number that will compensate Barry for his pain." I glanced over at Fab. "Take the rag out of her mouth; I know she wants to apologize." I shot her a penetrating stare. "Everything was so hectic that day. The gun misfired, and she's mentioned several times how sorry she is and that she wondered how you were doing."

Barry smacked her in the side the head with his slab-like hand, patting and combing her hair with his grimy fingers. "Make it pretty." He jerked out the bandana and dumped it in her lap.

Fab spit a couple of times, spitting whatever was stuck in her mouth across the room. "Sorry, dude." She smiled seductively. Her eyes, narrowed and hard, bored into him, communicating, *I'd kill you if I wasn't tied up.*

"The two of us get out of this unscathed, meaning you don't touch either one of us, and you can name your price," I offered.

"You don't got enough money." Larry chewed on his dirty thumbnail. "We're getting the bucks to off you, minus a percentage since we acquired this account from our boss. But we've made a sweeter deal, a little extra for dumping your bodies where they'll never be found." He looked pleased at his last statement. "I'm thinking a quick trip to the dump and let them incinerate your bodies."

"Who'd pay to have us killed?" Fab asked.

I admired her cool under some very bad odds.

Barry poked her again, this time with a finger to the side of her head, running it down her cheek. "I didn't give you permission to speak." He peered down, his lips curving in a smirk.

Fab shuddered and wrinkled her nose a couple of times, attempting to lean sideways, but she had little room to move around. Barry's shorts and shirt were filthy, covered in stains, and appeared not to have been washed in a long time, if ever.

Larry had apparently forgotten that I wasn't secured, although his gun rarely wavered from my head. I was careful not to remind him by making any sudden moves. I mentally kicked myself for not having a gun on my person, but even if I had, Larry had had the element of surprise. I'd have been dead before I could get a shot off, and Fab would have been next.

"Wasn't that part of the problem the last time you showed up, a client who didn't pay?" I asked. "Are you certain they'll pay this time? We're a sure bet. Ride with me to the bank, and you can be on the road to a new life in less than an hour."

"We got the goods on our Little Miss now; she screws us this time, and we'll make sure she fries." Barry made a sizzling sound.

"Shut up," Larry barked. "I say we shoot 'em here and drag 'em out to that fine set of wheels."

"You promised that I'd get alone time with my woman here. You're so purty." Barry ran his fingers along Fab's lips. "I forgive ya for shootin' me. But I've got to get me a taste, get close-like." He grinned down, showing yellowed teeth.

It appeared that maybe I'd meet a fast death, but Fab would suffer first, and the thought made me sick.

"Big mistake when I shot you in the butt," Fab ground out. She and I exchanged looks, both of us thinking, *should've shot him dead*. "You start shooting in this neighborhood," she added, stopping just short of sneering, "and the cops will show up before you hit the corner."

The best thing I could do was keep them talking about murdering us and not fixated on doing it. "Can you at least tell us why this person wants us dead and why you're willing to do the dirty work, risking a long, slow death? It doesn't matter whether you manage to get away or end up in jail; your fate is sealed."

Larry half-laughed, although I could tell my words bothered him. "We're leaving town with a pocketful of cash. Who's going to tie us to you two? You know the odds of finding a killer with no connection to the deceased?"

"I've heard slim. There's a big difference in this case." I motioned between Fab and me. "You ever hear of Jimmy Spoon? He's my stepdaddy; you hurt us, and he'll put the word out, track you, and find you. You'll wish for a quick death, which you won't get." I could tell from their looks of surprise and fear that they had heard of Spoon and had not known about the connection. They looked like they were having second thoughts. And I hadn't even mentioned Creole and his undercover friends. Larry and Barry might make it to a cell, but not without looking like a dog had worked the two of them over to within a half-inch of their worthless lives.

Barry let out a long moan.

"Boys, boys, you're not letting these two scum bitches charm you, are you?"

Chapter Forty-Six

Ruby stood in the patio doorway, a handgun at her side, finger on the trigger. "Gertrude should be tied up. Better yet, kill her now."

Larry repeated, "Gertrude?"

I interrupted to ask, "What are you doing here?" I didn't know if it would help or hurt us that Fab and I had lied about our names but decided that keeping her ignorant was best for now.

"She murdered Scotch," Fab said, matter-of-fact.

"You did?" I asked in confusion. "Why?" I glanced over at Fab, *how did you know?* written on my face.

She flashed her signature smirk, along with a silent reminder that we weren't dead yet.

"Money." Larry snorted. "Goody two shoes here lost her mind and got her hands dirty. Didn't you, sweets?"

"You shut the fuck up." Ruby raised her gun to the middle of Larry's chest.

"Woah, sister." Larry held a hand up. "We're going to get the job done."

"I'm in this deep. Don't think that you and

your friend aren't expendable." Ruby's eyes drilled into him, her jaw clenched and cheeks burning red.

The best thing I could do was keep everyone talking, fighting, until Creole could send someone or come himself. I needed to untie Fab too, but if I got close enough, I'd probably be tied up myself, and that wouldn't be helpful. If I was going to die, I'd choose inside my house and not dragged off to the dump.

Larry's eyes narrowed, fixed on Ruby. "You're sayin' we do the dirty work, you kill us?"

She didn't make eye contact. "Don't get your shorts in a bunch."

I snuck a quick peek at Fab, and she shook her head slightly, sending a "don't give up" message. These two men would do Ruby's dirty work, and it wouldn't surprise me if she rode along to the dump and they ended up left behind.

"This is all about Scotch's lottery winnings," Fab sneered. "You're so smart, tell us: how do you get your hands on the money now?"

Barry spoke up. "How you gonna pay us if you don't got the money?"

The two men were now burning a hole through her, which she chose to ignore. Larry straightened, his attention turning to his boss, giving a reprieve to Fab and me… momentarily anyway. Barry was also distracted, gun swaying in his hand.

Larry was the first to catch on to Ruby's plans to scapegoat him and his friend. His face flushed with anger. Barry mumbled something to Fab, who twisted her head away; he hadn't caught on yet that he wouldn't live long enough to spend the money, which he wasn't going to get anyway.

Then he turned his attention to Ruby. "We don't murder for free," he reminded her.

"Risk our asses ending up in line for the needle for nothing? I don't think so," Larry ranted. "You said you two was married and you'd be getting the funds real soon."

"Married?" Fab snorted. "You better ask for proof."

Ruby turned to Fab, hands on her hips, a smug smile in place. "My lawyer has the license and the rest of my paperwork. I assure you, it's all legit."

"Don't think you *have* any paperwork. I'm beginning to think nothing you told us was truth." Larry crossed his arms, continuing to glare. "That's why the dead guy broke up with you; didn't like you trying to trick him into leashing himself to you while drunk. Guess you didn't feed him enough alcohol."

"The preacher refused to marry you when Scotch said, 'Hell no.'" Barry mimicked, slurring the words. "But then Scotch sobered up and married you anyway. Or so you said."

"It was an accident. I never planned to kill

him," Ruby said softly.

"Please, share," I said. "It's not like dead people can talk."

While all eyes were on Ruby, Fab fidgeted, struggling to get her hands loose, but to no avail.

"When you first contacted our boss, he checked you out and got wind you didn't have a damn dime. Boy, was he pissed," Larry said. "You convinced us your finances had changed, that you got it all figured out. Were you lyin' to us?"

Another question Ruby ignored. Her gun hand swung from side to side, depending on the direction she was looking. "Scotch not only wouldn't marry me; he could barely stand to look at me." She turned to Barry, the muzzle of her gun aimed between his eyes.

He flinched and covered his head with his hands, as if that would help.

"The night he died, I tried to get my name on his bank account—even brought the paperwork with me to make it easy for him. He called me greedy, and we got into a fight. He told me he never wanted to see me again, that I was lucky he didn't call the cops. I lost it. I knew where he kept his gun; ran out to the garage, retrieved it out of the tool cabinet, hustled around to the front, rang the bell, and when he answered, I plugged him." Her voice was soft, as though she might have felt a twinge of regret.

My question was: was her remorse for

shooting him or losing all that cash? I suspected the latter.

"The gun was never recovered," Fab stated.

"Thanks to a television show I saw once, I knew I had to get rid of it and leave no trace back to me. That's where you two came in, or the pretty one anyway." She turned to Fab, gun now pointed in her face. "I concocted a story about Scotch banging you. The cops didn't seem to buy it, but it got rid of the bill collectors. And why not? I didn't know you."

"How did your television show end?" I asked.

"That woman ended up in prison. But not me. I got this planned, and I'm much smarter."

I clenched my fists, trying not to react to her gun waving back and forth, her finger on the trigger.

"If you'd only minded your own business," Ruby said. "I wouldn't be here, and you wouldn't be about to die. I wasn't sure how much you knew, so I decided you were a loose end that needed tied up." She laughed. "Tied up, get it?"

"Put your gun down," Larry barked. "You're scaring the crap out of me with your wild movements; you have me thinking I need to defend myself." His voice was heated.

The three stopped paying attention to Fab and me as their angry disagreement heated up.

"Good thing I had a plan to clean up loose ends myself." Ruby had grown impatient, her gun twitching. "I'll get rid of the damn witnesses myself and know it got done right."

I realized that ever since the woman announced herself, her facial expressions had periodically changed, but the tone of her voice had remained flat, as though disconnected from what was unfolding. I'd given up on a rescue; there had been plenty of time for someone to show up. I just erased that option and shoved aside my panic, trying to think of a way for Fab and me to get out in one piece.

Fab peered around Barry's leg, which was momentarily blocking her view, and flashed me a sad smile. "Love you," she mouthed.

"Me too."

My only option was to maneuver close to Larry and take a shot at trying to immobilize him, mimicking one of Fab's moves: a kick to the groin. If I could disable him for even a few moments, I could run out, but that would leave Fab at their mercy, and Barry would kill her. Or if not him, then Ruby. I could go for Larry's gun, but I didn't like my chances of surviving that maneuver either.

Be patient.

A blur passed by the garden window.

"What was that?" Barry pointed.

The other two turned to look. Ruby turned and ran, disappearing out the French doors.

The front door flew open, hitting the wall with a bang, and Creole roared though and flew across the kitchen, putting his body between me and Larry, grasping the hand that held the gun and taking him down to the floor.

I watched in horror as the two men flew through the air and landed with a thud. I swore I heard the crack of Creole's skull as it connected with the tile. The gun went off, and they both lay still.

In a split second, Barry wrenched Fab onto her feet, using her as a shield, the barrel of his pistol to her head.

Casio stood in the entryway, his Glock aimed at Barry. "Drop it," he boomed.

"One wrong move from anybody, and she's dead, brains splattered all over this room. And you all are next," Barry screeched hysterically.

They were all too close, and Fab was being used as a human shield. Casio was damn fast with a gun, but not so fast that a psycho with a twitchy trigger finger couldn't kill Fab before he could get a shot off.

"Get out," Barry demanded in a high-pitched voice.

"Calm down, pal." Without another moment's hesitation, Casio shot Barry between the eyes. He fell backward, crumbling to the floor.

Chapter Forty-Seven

The police, led by Kevin, burst through the door, spilling into the living room and kitchen, weapons drawn. Didier came in through the patio and whispered something to Kevin, who whistled for one of his deputies to follow as he turned and ran out the back.

I crawled across the floor until I reached Creole, pushing Larry off him, checking for a bullet hole. Expelling a loud sigh when I didn't find any blood, I cradled his head in my lap. *Creole saved my life.* Oh my god, he could have been killed saving my life!

"Love you," Creole said, his voice weak and muddled. "Am I going to die?" He closed his eyes.

"You're not dying," I said, sternly. "I forbid it, and to make sure, I'm not going anywhere."

The EMTs hauled in a stretcher, and I moved out of the way to make room for them to shift Creole onto it and strap him in.

"His vitals are stable," the female EMT informed me. "We're going to load him up now. Do you want to ride with him to the hospital?"

"Yes," I said, nervously watching as his eyes blinked open. He smiled faintly.

Casio held out a hand, helping me off the floor. "Don't worry about him; he's got a hard head."

"Fab?" I asked.

"No worries about her either; she's got her boyfriend hanging on every moan." He grabbed his stomach, fake-retching.

The EMTs loaded Creole in the back of the ambulance, and Casio helped me inside, where I sat across from Creole.

"Don't worry, I'll handle everything here," Casio told me.

"There's plenty of food," I said.

He gave me a big smile. "That's why you're my favorite."

The doors slammed shut.

* * *

"Your tests came back fine," I announced to Creole. He'd been checked over and moved to a private room. "But Dr. A hasn't decided whether he'll be keeping you overnight."

"Where's that damn doctor?" Creole demanded. "I'm going home if I have to sign myself out."

"I'll restrain you." I narrowed my eyes.

"Don't come on to me while I'm lying in a hospital bed," he said in an amused tone.

I bit my lip to keep from smiling. "I'm not leaving your side."

"Did that f… bastard hurt you?" Creole shifted on the pillow. "My head hurts."

"I'm fine, thanks to you." I smiled slightly, running my finger across his lips. "You cracked your head on the tile; I'm only surprised you didn't chip the tile."

"It's hard to keep a Baptiste down; we're from strong stock." He grinned. "Some have said we're just plain stupid and wouldn't know if we were hurt, that we don't even know that we're not normal. But never to our faces."

"I didn't think I was ever going to see you again." I took a deep breath to hold back my emotions, keep the tears at bay. "I love you." I twisted my fingers in his hair, lightly touching his face.

"I heard your voice on the phone and knew you were in trouble. It took me a minute to figure out what was going on. Thank goodness I was with Stephen; he made the phone calls rallying the troops, the cops, anyone and everyone he thought would be helpful. He drove while I continued to listen until I lost the connection. I barked directions the rest of the way; Stephen was about ready to kick my ass out of the truck. Told me to shut up." He frowned.

I laughed, my eyes filling with tears. "It was the only thing I knew to do. If you hadn't shown up, we'd be dead."

"What the hell happened?" Creole ran his thumbs across the corners of my eyes.

I filled him in on the details—everything that happened and what I'd observed.

"All for money," he snapped in disgust. "That she was never going to get her greedy hands on anyway. In too many cases, it doesn't pay to win the lottery; the winner ends up dead at the hands of greedy relatives or acquaintances."

My stomach roiled at the thought of what could've happened.

I saw the anxious look on his face and knew he was worried about me. I took a calming breath, holding my emotions at bay until Creole was home; then I'd unleash them.

"Climb in." He flipped back the sheet, scooting over to make room for me in the small bed.

"I like your gown." I winked and lay down by his side. "You behave yourself," I said as he wrapped his arms around my middle.

He tightened his hold. "Do you want to talk about it?"

I shook my head. "Just hold me."

The door opened after an unobtrusive knock. Didier and Fab poked their heads into the darkened room, one light in the corner illuminating the small space. Creole waved them forward.

I sat up and climbed off the bed, going to Fab, my arms outstretched. She met me, and we hugged. "You okay?" I said against her ear.

She nodded on my shoulder. "That was a close one."

Didier moved around us and went to Creole's bedside.

He held up one finger. "How many?"

"Seven," Creole deadpanned.

"Good to see you're back to one hundred percent." He leaned down and gave him a one-armed hug. "Thanks for everything. Seems pitifully little, but today could've been a lot worse." He paused, choking up on his last words.

Fab and I grabbed chairs; Didier took them and manhandled them to the bedside.

"I don't know how you managed not to show fear," Fab said to me.

"I focused on staying calm and not doing anything to set the trio off," I said.

"How did they get the drop on you?"

Didier put his arm across her shoulders, tightening his hold.

"My fault. I didn't have my Walther in reach, thinking… well, maybe I didn't need to, not in my own backyard. Should have remembered we've had unwanted guests recently." Fab leaned her head against Didier.

"What happened to the security system?" I asked.

"One of them cut the power." Didier said. "The company sent a guard when they got a warning signal, but they arrived just after law enforcement."

"I was reading and dozed off," Fab continued. "When I woke up, Barry was leering over the fence at me from the top of a ladder, and his friend had a Smith and Wesson trained on me. Barry jumped to the ground, produced a gun of his own, circled the chaise, and hit me on the head. I didn't pass out cold, but damn, it hurt like the devil." She gently rubbed the side of her head. "It took me a few to shake off the dizziness, and by then, I was tied up. Made the mistake of cursing his family, and he shoved a rag in my mouth." She made a disgusted face.

"Fab filled me in on what happened after you arrived," Didier said.

"My only thought was to keep them talking, fighting, anything until help showed up." I looked at Fab—we both had tears in our eyes. We hugged again.

"I don't know how much time passed between when I called Creole and when everyone burst through the door—seemed like a year. I'd about given up." I brushed Fab's hair over her shoulder. "Two hugs in one day. Don't think I'll let you forget that." I smiled at her, happy to be joking. "Did you see any of that coming?" I asked her.

"Didn't like Ruby but had no clue."

"Where is Ruby?" I asked. "Last I saw her, her backside was headed out the door."

"First thing Fab did was tip me off that Ruby was involved. I, in turn, told Kevin," Didier informed us. "He had her in cuffs before she got inside her front door, arresting her on an attempted kidnapping charge. Once the district attorney gets the whole story, a slew of other charges will follow, including murder. She'll never get out of jail. Kevin's funny; his only comment was, 'I never liked her.'"

"Kevin's growing on me," I said. "Don't you dare tell him."

"We should get going." Didier stood, pushing the chairs back under the window. "Let you get some rest."

"I'm leaving as soon as that idiot doctor gets back here and signs the paperwork," Creole insisted.

Fab and Didier waved and slipped out of the room.

"Dr. A hears that, I'm sure he'll hustle to get you released." I raised my eyebrows.

"Kiss me," he demanded.

Leaning over, making certain I didn't touch anything except his lips, I fit my mouth to his and took advantage. Sighing softly, I lay back down beside him.

Chapter Forty-Eight

Creole was discharged the following morning. Fab dropped off my SUV, and I drove us to the beach house. I'd forewarned Fab and asked her to field any calls, letting people know we'd surface in a day or two.

"Do not move," I ordered after parking in his driveway. I cut the engine and ran around to the passenger side. Through the windshield, I saw his lips moving and laughed, not understanding a word. He stuck out his tongue.

Creole opened the door and stepped out before I could get there.

"I wanted to help you." I pouted.

"I'm fine. I'm not an invalid, just like I told the damn doctor."

"That same doctor told you to take it easy." I put my arm around his middle. "Lean on me. Maybe not too hard, or we'll both fall over."

He unlocked the door, and we passed through the kitchen and into the living room. I pointed to the couch, wiggled out of his reach, and walked to the sliding doors, pushing them completely open to let the warm beach air inside.

I retrieved two bottled waters and walked

back into his open arms. He pulled me down into his lap and held me with a firm, gentle hand and a quick kiss. I kicked off my sandals, sending them flying.

Creole kissed me again, a whisper really. "You want to share how you're feeling?

I buried my face in his chest, shaking my head. I just wanted to forget.

"I don't want to ever let you out my sight again. I can't rid myself of the image of you standing in the kitchen, two lunatics waving guns around. I think you're the bravest woman, keeping them distracted until help arrived." He put a finger under my chin, forcing my eyes back to his. "I'm the luckiest bastard in the world to be holding you in my arms right now."

"I was so scared," I whispered. "Afraid for Fab, for me, that I'd never get to see you again. Distraction seemed the right course of action. Ruby bought me time, letting it slip she planned to kill those two stupes." Tears filled my eyes. "I'm glad you shot him. Happy they're both dead, and that they can't come back and try a third time." I turned into his chest, tears coursing down my cheeks. "So afraid."

Creole's arms tightened around my shuddering body, holding me until my tears ceased. "I'm so happy he didn't hurt you." *Or worse* were words that hung in the air.

"You're my hero."

"You alive was all I wanted. I'm glad those

two are dead. I refuse to think about life without you." He continued to hold me, rubbing calming strokes over my back. "We're going to stay here until I'm reassured that you're going to be okay."

"What about your job?"

"I'm milking my sick leave. To come back, I've got to have a doctor's note. I worked it out with the doc that when I'm ready, he'll swing by the house and write me a medical excuse."

"After the abuse you heaped on him?"

"Dr. A pretty much told me to do impossible acts with myself. I told him I'd tell you and it would probably make you cry. He pretty much wanted to slug me— instead called me a bastard." He smiled, amused with himself.

"You know he's a great doctor. Well respected."

"I know, and he knows I know."

I leaned in and kissed him.

"Walk with me," Creole's husky voice demanded.

He lifted me off his lap. Sitting me next to him, he stood, his outstretched hand waiting for me to grab it.

Live in the moment.

Looking into his troubled eyes, I knew wanted to go for a walk because he knew it was my favorite thing to do. Larry and Barry were dead. Ruby was in jail. The threat was over. The two of us could go walk down to the beach without a worry for ourselves.

I thought only with my heart and took his hand.

It didn't take long to change into our bathing suits. I grabbed a sheer wrap, tying it around my waist.

We walked out on the deck and hand in hand down the stairs that led to the beach. Our toes sank into the white sand. Creole tugged on my hand, and we went running into the waves, kicking water, the waves lapping our feet.

"Sandcastle time." Creole dragged me down on the sand.

I wrinkled my nose. "I don't know how."

"You're with the master."

"Another hidden talent." I looked at him skeptically, watching as he dug furiously in the sand.

I copied his movements, helping him to build what he assured me was a sandcastle. Not having made very many, I thought it resembled a pile of sand, nothing remarkable, but I loved it. I wanted to laugh but didn't want to hurt his feelings. I stared, not sure what it looked like – a large square with a shell for a door.

"You dissing my artwork?" When I didn't answer, he tackled me and tickled me.

"Stop, stop," I screamed, laughing, panting, almost out of breath. "I swear it's beautiful."

"I love your laugh." He kissed me gently, drawing out my response. Some of his caresses were meant to brand, and some were just strokes of his lips against mine, as though trying to reassure himself that I was beside him.

He lifted me in his arms, setting me on my feet, and we ran back to the house, wet and caked with sand. We stood outside the sliding door, shedding our bathing suits to keep from getting sand all over the house.

He grabbed my hand, leading me into the bathroom to shower.

* * *

Lying next to him on the bed, I rolled onto my side. The soothing sounds of the ocean echoed throughout the house.

I knew how short life could be. I'd already had more than a couple brushes with death and knew that anything that had to be said should be said, and in the moment, not saved for another time that might not come.

I looked into warm blue eyes filled with promise. "I love you," I whispered, happy to tell him to his face.

I had everything I wanted right in front of me, and I'd be damned if I was going to die early. Intellectually, I knew that this hadn't happened because of some stupid job Fab and I had signed up for, but still, I had to stop taking unnecessary risks. The next neighbor that got offed, I'd mind my own business.

Love could be easy and uncomplicated, and I

wanted a normal life, walks on the beach, friends over for dinner, and a house full of laughter. I wanted to stop feeling like I needed a firearm everywhere I went, including my own patio.

My eyes roamed over the handsome face that I loved so much.

"We should talk about babies." He winked.

"We should?"

"Absolutely."

I touched my fingertip to his lips.

"There will never be another woman for me but you."

PARADISE SERIES NOVELS

Crazy in Paradise
Deception in Paradise
Trouble in Paradise
Murder in Paradise
Greed in Paradise
Revenge in Paradise
Kidnapped in Paradise
Swindled in Paradise
Executed in Paradise
Hurricane in Paradise
Lottery in Paradise
Ambushed in Paradise
Christmas in Paradise
Blownup in Paradise
Psycho in Paradise
Overdose in Paradise
Initiation in Paradise
Jealous in Paradise
Wronged in Paradise
Vanished in Paradise
Naive in Paradise

Deborah's books are available on Amazon
http://www.amazon.com/Deborah-
Brown/e/B0059MAIKQ

About the Author

Deborah Brown is an Amazon bestselling author of the Paradise series. She lives on the Gulf of Mexico, with her ungrateful animals, where Mother Nature takes out her bad attitude in the form of hurricanes.

Sign up for my newsletter and get the latest on new book releases. Contests and special promotion information. And special offers that are only available to subscribers.
www.deborahbrownbooks.com

Follow on FaceBook:
facebook.com/DeborahBrownAuthor

You can contact her at Wildcurls@hotmail.com

Deborah's books are available on Amazon:
www.amazon.com/Deborah-Brown/e/B0059MAIKQ

Made in the USA
Las Vegas, NV
26 June 2024

91523375R00223